Laura

W9-AWB-929

Setting the Scene

Godfrey the cat stood on tiptoe and hissed at the dark-haired woman, a long and menacing hiss. When she ignored him, he tried growling instead.

"Hush, kitty," she said. She stood in Vincent Farwell's library in front of Vincent Farwell's desk. Staring at Vincent Farwell's body.

Uncle Vincent lay slumped across the desk, his head very efficiently bashed in. Blood discolored the desk blotter as well as the two parts of the broken alabaster Hermes. One piece of the statuette lay on the desk near Uncle Vincent's head; the other had fallen to the floor. A few inches from the fingertips of Uncle Vincent's outstretched hand was an automatic pistol.

The fire had long since died out; the ashes in the fireplace gave off no hint of warmth. When she was absolutely certain that Uncle Vincent was dead, she moved around to the side of his desk.

Godfrey leaped to the top of the cabinet and crouched there, watching her every move. She hesitated; then, shuddering, she picked up Uncle Vincent's right hand. She managed to get the dead man's stiffening fingers around the automatic pistol and used his forefinger to press the trigger.

Bantam Books offers the finest in classic and modern American murder mysteries. Ask your bookseller for the books you have missed.

Stuart Palmer

THE PENGUIN POOL MURDER
THE PUZZLE OF THE HAPPY
   HOOLIGAN
THE PUZZLE OF THE RED STALLION
THE PUZZLE OF THE SILVER PERSIAN

Craig Rice

THE FOURTH POSTMAN
HAVING WONDERFUL CRIME
MY KINGDOM FOR A HEARSE
THE LUCKY STIFF

Rex Stout

BAD FOR BUSINESS
BROKEN VASE
DEATH OF A DUDE
DEATH TIMES THREE
DOUBLE FOR DEATH
FER-DE-LANCE
THE FINAL DEDUCTION
GAMBIT
THE RUBBER BAND
SOME BURIED CAESAR
TOO MANY CLIENTS

Max Allan Collins

THE DARK CITY

William Kienzle

THE ROSARY MURDERS

Joseph Louis

MADELAINE

M. J. Adamson

NOT UNTIL A HOT FEBRUARY
A FEBRUARY FACE
REMEMBER MARCH

Conrad Haynes

BISHOP'S GAMBIT, DECLINED

Barbara Paul

FIRST GRAVEDIGGER
THE FOURTH WALL
KILL FEE
THE RENEWABLE VIRGIN
BUT HE WAS ALREADY DEAD
   WHEN I GOT THERE

P. M. Carlson

MURDER UNRENOVATED

Ross Macdonald

THE GOODBYE LOOK
SLEEPING BEAUTY
THE NAME IS ARCHER
THE DROWNING POOL

Margaret Maron

THE RIGHT JACK

William Murray

WHEN THE FAT MAN SINGS

Robert Goldsborough

MURDER IN E MINOR
DEATH ON DEADLINE

Sue Grafton

"A" IS FOR ALIBI
"B" IS FOR BURGLAR
"C" IS FOR CORPSE

R. D. Brown

HAZZARD
THE VILLA HEAD

A.E. Maxwell

JUST ANOTHER DAY IN PARADISE
THE FROG AND THE SCORPION

Rob Kantner

BACK-DOOR MAN
THE HARDER THEY HIT

Joseph Telushkin

THE UNORTHODOX MURDER OF
   RABBI WAHL

Richard Hilary

SNAKE IN THE GRASSES
PIECES OF CREAM

Carolyn G. Hart

DEATH ON DEMAND

Lia Matera

WHERE LAWYERS FEAR TO TREAD

Robert Crais

THE MONKEY'S RAINCOAT

BARBARA PAUL

BUT HE WAS ALREADY DEAD WHEN I GOT THERE

BANTAM BOOKS
TORONTO • NEW YORK • LONDON • SYDNEY • AUCKLAND

This low-priced Bantam Book
has been completely reset in a type face
designed for easy reading, and was printed
from new plates. It contains the complete
text of the original hard-cover edition.
NOT ONE WORD HAS BEEN OMITTED.

BUT HE WAS ALREADY DEAD WHEN I GOT THERE
A Bantam Book / published by arrangement with
Charles Scribner's Sons

PRINTING HISTORY
Scribner's edition published August 1986
Bantam edition / January 1988

ISBN 0-553-27075-3

Published simultaneously in the United States and Canada

PRINTED IN THE UNITED STATES OF AMERICA
O   0 9 8 7 6 5 4 3 2 1

BUT HE
WAS ALREADY
DEAD
WHEN I GOT
THERE

1

"I could kill him!" Dorrie Murdoch said furiously to her husband. "I could just kill him!"

"Now, Dorrie," Simon Murdoch replied in the mildest of tones. "One of these days you're going to forget and say that to his face."

"Someone should have told him off long ago," Dorrie muttered. "Sitting there on his moneybags like King Crocus lording it over the rest of us!"

"King who?"

"Crocus? The guy that was so rich?"

"I think that's Croesus."

"Whatever. Besides, I *hate* rushing through dinner. 'Eight o'clock sharp—don't be late!' " Dorrie's tone of voice made it clear how barbaric she considered such an early hour to be. "Why do we have to go there at all? He has to make such a production of everything. Here, zip me up."

Simon zipped her up. "Did you ever know Uncle Vincent to pass up a chance to grandstand? He likes ceremony, Dorrie. It reinforces his God image."

She sighed. "He does love being the source from whom all blessings flow, doesn't he? Uncle Vincent giveth and Uncle Vincent taketh away."

"Well, so long as he sticks to giveth-ing, you can put up with his irritating little ways, can't you?" Simon was adjusting his tie before the mirror; the Murdochs had only one mirror in their bedroom, but it covered three of the room's four walls. Simon turned his head a trifle sideways and looked at his image out of the corner of his eye, approving of what he saw. "There's no point in getting angry, darling. Uncle Vincent thrives on playing lord of the manor—and as long as Ellandy's takes his money, you're just going to have to put up with it."

1

"That's easy for you to say," she sniffed. "You're not involved in it, Simon—anyone can stand outside and pass judgment. Besides, we took his money only once. You're not going to wear that tie, are you? It's just that I hate being a, well, a *supplicant*."

Simon's easy smile disappeared momentarily. "I don't think I'm passing judgment, dear. And I'm not really outside—anything that involves you affects me. Anyway, you won't be a supplicant much longer, darling—you're almost out of the woods." He looked in the mirror again. "What's wrong with this tie?"

"Ah—nothing, darling. If you like it."

Simon started taking off his tie. "But you don't. Therefore, I shall change it." He smiled winningly.

"Oh, Simon, don't change it because—"

"Dorrie, my love, I wouldn't dream of wearing a tie you didn't like." He walked into his closet and came out carrying two other ties. "Which?"

"That one, I think. Simon, you're sweet."

The Murdochs embraced, being careful not to muss each other's hair. "You're not still angry, are you?" Simon drawled, putting on the tie Dorrie had selected.

"No, you always manage to defuse me in time," Dorrie laughed lightly. "I shouldn't let the old man get to me like that. If only he would do something nice for its own sake once in a while —without making everyone kowtow to him for it."

Simon raised one eyebrow. "Uncle Vincent? You jest. *Not* being nice—'tis the core of his existence and what gives his life meaning. You don't expect him to start acting gracious at his age, do you?"

"I know better than that." She sighed. "Fasten me, darling, will you?"

Simon deftly manipulated the clasp at the back of her neck and then looked at what was hanging from the chain. "Is that the new piece?"

"Do you like it?" She patted the lavaliere possessively and then moved her hand so Simon could get a clear view. "The craftsmen just finished it this afternoon."

"It's lovely, Dorrie." It was a Maltese cross, with the arms so extended and curved as almost to meet in a circle at the tips. Made of gold and encrusted with rubies, the cross stood out nicely against the dark blue crushed silk of Dorrie's dress. "It's one of the best you've done yet."

"Why, thank you, darling—how nice." She lifted her cheek to be kissed.

Simon obliged. "I hope it looks as nice on its owner."

"You *are* sweet. Simon, when Ellandy's is free and clear, we ought to give a party. To celebrate."

"Of course. What a good idea. Shall we invite Uncle Vincent?"

Dorrie made a face at him. "You know, if it weren't for Ellandy Jewels, I don't think I'd even be speaking to that nasty old man."

Something in her tone made Simon pause. "Darling, if it bothers you that much—just tell him to go to hell. We don't have to go tonight."

"Unfortunately," Dorrie said wryly, "I'm in no position to issue my personal declaration of independence at the moment. If it weren't for Uncle Vincent there wouldn't be any Ellandy's."

"Yes, there would. You could have gotten a loan somewhere else. Or you could have retrenched. Malcolm says Ellandy's was not exactly teetering on the brink of bankruptcy."

"Malcolm doesn't know everything that goes on at Ellandy's," Dorrie snapped.

Simon tut-tutted, a half-smile playing around his lips. "Sibling problems?"

"No, nothing like that. I love my brother dearly and I know he has my best interests at heart—but Malcolm doesn't know everything. It was Uncle Vincent's money that kept Ellandy's afloat and that old man's never going to let us forget it. So when Uncle Vincent says be there at eight, I'll be there at eight."

"Still, darling," Simon said firmly, "if dancing attendance on Uncle Vincent makes you feel like a toady, then perhaps it would be better to break away."

"Toady—what a charming word. But tonight's not the night to make the break. Not when he's going to cancel the loan."

"*If* he cancels the loan. You don't know that's what he's going to do!"

"What else could it be?"

"He could merely extend it. That would be a good way to keep you all toadying to him a little longer."

Dorrie turned on her brightest smile. "That's twice you've called me a toady, darling."

"Oh, dearest, I didn't mean—"

"I know, I know. But it's such an ugly little word, isn't it? I really could do without it, dear."

Simon placed one hand over his heart and raised the other in the air. "I hereby solemnly promise never to let *that word* pass my lips again during my lifetime. Or after."

Dorrie's eyes widened in mock amazement. "That's some oath, darling—I'm impressed. But I'm sure Uncle Vincent isn't just going to extend Ellandy's loan. He wouldn't need an attorney present for that, and he did include Malcolm in the invitation. If you can call it an invitation."

Simon lifted one eyebrow. "Malcolm will be there too? Hm, that's a surprise . . . I thought he didn't like your brother."

"Uncle Vincent doesn't like anybody."

"But didn't he once accuse Malcolm of trying to talk him to death?"

"Simon, you know he was just being nasty. Why bring that up?"

"But Uncle Vincent's never let Malcolm handle any of his legal business. So why now? Why isn't he using his own attorney?"

"Who knows? Maybe he's had a change of heart."

They both laughed at the absurdity of that. Then the Murdochs pronounced themselves ready and stood back to examine each other. They were a good-looking couple, and they made the most of it. Their outfits were always complementary and never more than four months old. Both fair-haired, they made sure they were always the exact same shade of blond; one never changed without the other. That month they were Honey Ash Number Seventeen.

"Darling, you have a snag," Simon said with the barest hint of a smile. "Left leg."

Dorrie glanced down in irritation at her leg. "Where? I don't see it."

"Around in back. Just a little one, but it'll turn into a run."

"I still don't see it."

"Take my word for it. You'd better change."

Dorrie made a sound of mild disgust. "These are brand-new pantyhose. How annoying. I'll only be a moment, love." She opened a bureau drawer.

"I'll stay and watch," Simon leered wolfishly, and he was rewarded with a tinkly laugh from his spouse.

The Murdochs were very much in love.

Malcolm Conner glanced at his watch and saw he wasn't going to have time to eat. He'd been in court all afternoon, and the letters he'd had to dictate before he could leave his office had taken an unconscionable length of time. He envied Dorrie; he'd never acquired his sister's knack of dashing off an error-free piece of correspondence without having to ponder every phrase, every piece of punctuation.

The car in front of him was moving erratically—drunk driver? Malcolm concentrated on the traffic until the car ahead turned off into a side street. Then he pressed down on the accelerator; Uncle Vincent didn't take kindly to latecomers—as Nicole would be sure to remind him. How he *hated* to rush.

No parking place in the street presented itself, so Malcolm drove down the ramp into the garage beneath the building. When he at last unlocked the apartment door, Nicole Lattimer greeted him with a wet kiss and a dry martini. "You won't have time to eat," she said. "Unless you want Uncle Vincent snarling at you."

"I know," Malcolm said, and tasted the martini. "You'd think he'd make it a dinner invitation if he's going to insist on such early hours. I'll just shower and change."

Nicole waited until he'd come out of the shower and asked, "What do you suppose this is all about? Dorrie thinks Uncle Vincent is going to cancel Ellandy's loan."

"That's one possibility," Malcolm said in his courtroom voice. "Another is that he might merely extend it. A third possibility is that our meeting tonight has nothing to do with Ellandy Jewels at all."

"In other words, you have no idea. I think Dorrie is wrong —when have you ever known Vincent Farwell to give anything away?"

"He gave Gretchen and Lionel a house when they married, remember." Malcolm started getting dressed. "Uncle Vincent is no miser, Nicole. He is merely cautious."

"Mm. I think he gave them that house to make sure they wouldn't live with him." Nicole smoothed her hands over her dark hair. She was wearing it pulled back tightly from her face, emphasizing her already prominent cheek bones. Nicole went in for the starkly dramatic look, a deliberate contrast to Dorrie Murdoch's cultivated femininity. When Nicole was dressed in black, as she was tonight, she resembled nothing so much as a Russian ballet mistress. Malcolm liked the look. "Exactly what did Gretchen say when she invited us?" Nicole asked.

" 'Summoned' is more like it," Malcolm replied. "All she said was that her uncle had a surprise for us and you and I were to be at his house at eight sharp. When I asked her to be more specific, Gretchen just waved her hands vaguely and said 'You'll see' and 'It's a surprise' and a few other uninformative things like that. I got the impression—perhaps erroneous—that she doesn't know the purpose of the meeting herself. Have you noticed how Gretchen has a tendency to tell all she knows? I'm convinced that if she did know, she wouldn't be able to resist the temptation to drop a hint or two. However, it could be that I misread her and—"

"So Gretchen doesn't know either," said Nicole, cutting through the verbiage. "It must have something to do with Ellandy's. You've already requested an extension of the loan, haven't you?"

"Over a week ago. So far, Uncle Vincent has not seen fit to respond. But he wouldn't summon us all there just to announce he's going to extend. That's a simple legal matter I could take care of in fifteen minutes." Malcolm sat down and put on his shoes. He still nourished a faint hope that Vincent Farwell would turn over his legal affairs to him, but Uncle Vincent wouldn't require all the Ellandy people in his house merely to announce that.

"I can't understand why I was included in the summons," Nicole was saying. "I don't make the decisions at Ellandy's."

"Not yet," Malcolm said encouragingly, "but Dorrie will make you a partner, you'll see."

"Oh, Dorrie's not the problem—it's Lionel who's dragging his feet."

"Lionel loves your designs. I've heard him say so on a number of occasions. Without being asked, I might add. He wouldn't volunteer such an endorsement unless it were sincerely meant, I'm sure of it. I don't see that he has any reason—"

"Lionel's worried about the money. *All* Lionel worries about is money."

"But if Dorrie is right and Uncle Vincent does cancel the loan . . . ?"

"Then my chances improve," Nicole admitted happily. She sat in front of her dressing table and attached two heavy emerald pendant earrings to her rather large lobes; her only other article of adornment was a multicolored scarf tied around her waist. Malcolm loved watching her do things with her hands; every movement was deliberate and precise—no waste motion at all. "Dorrie is going to wear the Maltese cross tonight," Nicole said in a voice that made clear her disapproval. "I wish she wouldn't do that. It's unprofessional."

Malcolm was wise enough to steer clear of that particular bone of contention. His sister always liked to wear every piece of jewelry she'd designed *once* before turning it over to the customer who'd commissioned it. It was a point of pride with her and a source of irritation to Nicole, who wouldn't dream of wearing any of her own designs that she'd created specifically for someone else. Nicole Lattimer wore no jewelry except that which she designed for herself, such as the emerald pendant earrings now firmly in place.

"Are you ready?" she asked.

Malcolm hesitated. "Before we go—did you find time to read the agreement?" He'd drawn up a prenuptial agreement heavily slanted to her benefit in the hope that it might prove the bit of persuasion Nicole needed.

Their eyes locked in Nicole's dressing table mirror; then she turned and faced him directly. "There's no clause saying I keep my own name."

Malcolm looked mildly surprised. "I thought you'd decided 'Conner' wasn't such a bad name."

"What I said was that 'Nicole Conner' has a nice alliterative ring to it. I didn't say I was going to use the name."

Malcolm thought back, and his innate fair-mindedness forced him to admit that that was exactly what she'd said. "You're right. And I can understand your wanting to keep your own name, Nicole—I truly can. Although it's not really yours, you know. To be precise, it's your father's name. A woman has the use of two men's names during her lifetime—her father's and her husband's. It's grossly unfair, of course, a woman never having a name of her own . . ."

"Don't rub it in," Nicole said dryly.

Malcolm didn't hear, intrigued by his new line of thought. "It's one of the vestiges of a patriarchal society I wonder if we'll ever completely rid ourselves of. The only solution I can see is for both husband and wife to change their last names when they marry—thus enabling any issue of the marriage to inherit equally from both parents. Or, alternately, the husband and wife could both keep their own surnames and choose a different one for the child. But think of the problems in records-keeping that would create! Tax reports, credit ratings—"

"Oh, Malcolm, what *are* you rambling on about?" Nicole interrupted. "All I meant was that 'Nicole Lattimer' is the name I've had all my life and I'm used to it and I want to keep it. That's all."

Malcolm blinked at her. "You don't have to explain yourself, Nicole. I'll add the clause tomorrow."

"*Thank you,*" she said heavily.

"Does that mean you find the agreement satisfactory?"

"It's a very good agreement. I see nothing wrong with it."

"Then . . . ?"

Nicole took a deep breath and said what was on her mind. "Malcolm, we've been living together for almost a year, and you've never pressured me about marriage until just recently. Not until Uncle Vincent started making his snide little remarks about our living in sin."

"He's never said that!"

"He's implied it. Every time he sees us together, he says, 'You two get married yet?' And then he snickers. Malcolm, I'd hate to think your new-found eagerness for matrimony springs from some sort of desire to make points with Vincent Farwell."

Malcolm was shocked. "Nicole! How could you think such a thing! That doesn't speak very well for me, does it? Do you really think I'm so shallow that I'd marry just to impress a man whose business I want? Why, it's not even practical! Uncle Vincent wouldn't change attorneys simply because you and I got married. True, he likes having his own way, even in matters that don't really concern him—look at the way he's always telling Lionel and Gretchen how to live. Our marrying might soften his attitude toward us, but it's not enough to persuade him to discharge an attorney who's served him for twenty-five years. Or more—I'm sure it's been more than twenty-five years. I'm not so foolish as to think he'd break a connection like that over a personal matter such as our marriage. No, it would take a lot more than that, and I'm surprised you'd think it would be enough or even that I would seriously consider such a possibility. You must surely understand that I—"

"We're going to be late," Nicole said patiently.

"I hate eating dinner this early," Lionel Knox growled.

"Then don't eat lunch so late," Gretchen Knox said indifferently. "You'd better hurry or you won't have time to change."

"I'm not going to change."

"At least your shirt. You look *wilted*, Lionel."

"I *am* wilted, damn it."

"Then wouldn't a shower and a change make you feel better?"

God, how he hated it when she was right. Lionel Knox admitted that he was indulging in childish stratagems to postpone an undesirable encounter. *If I don't get dressed, then maybe I won't have to go, etc.* Lionel didn't like Vincent Farwell; he didn't like dealing with the man and he certainly didn't like being in debt to him. Most of all he didn't like knowing that the only thing that had saved Ellandy Jewels from almost certain failure was the fact that his wife had a rich uncle.

"You're right," he said more calmly, and pushed back from the table.

Gretchen smiled sweetly at him as he left. It was a good thing she was so sensitive to his moods; Lionel *could* be difficult to live with. She called the maid to clear the table, and then went upstairs to brush her teeth and finish getting ready.

Lionel was out of the shower and dressed in under fifteen minutes. He hadn't shaved. Gretchen wistfully wished he'd take as much care with his appearance as Dorrie's husband did—especially now that he was beginning to get a little thick around the middle. Lionel didn't exercise; that was his problem. Simon Murdoch was as slim as an athlete, and everything he did seemed so effortless. Lionel sweated.

Gretchen looped a long string of pearls around her neck and admired the effect. Lionel was less enthusiastic. "The only time you wear those," he said, "is when you know you're going to see Nicole Lattimer."

"Is it? I hadn't noticed."

"You know she doesn't like pearls."

"That's her problem."

Lionel caught his wife's hand and sat her down beside him on the bed. "Gretchen, listen. Make an effort to be nice to Nicole tonight—please."

"Whatever for?"

"For one thing, she's been carrying more than her share of the workload lately. Dorrie takes a lot of time off, to go to the hairdresser or the gym or whatever else is needed to maintain the body beautiful. And since we're not in a financial position to offer Nicole a partnership just now—well, I'm afraid we might lose her."

"And that's *your* problem. If Nicole is all that wonderful, maybe you should have gone into partnership with her instead of Dorrie."

"No, Dorrie's a good partner—she's just been goofing off a little lately, that's all. Please, Gretchen? Is it all that hard to be nice for just one evening?"

Gretchen pouted. "You make me sound like a monster. I tell you what. I'll be nice to Nicole if you'll be nice to Uncle Vincent."

Lionel was astonished. "I'm always nice to Uncle Vincent."

"You're *never* nice to Uncle Vincent. You never show him any respect at all."

"Possibly because I don't feel any respect at all. But I'm always polite to him, which is more than you can say about the way you treat Nicole. Can you honestly say you're polite to Nicole?"

Gretchen's eyes were wide and innocent. "I'm every bit as polite to her as she is to me. But after tonight you'll be able to offer her a partnership—and then I won't have to be nice to her at all!" Gretchen's whole face lit up at the thought.

"Oh, great," Lionel groaned. "I wish I had your faith in dear old Uncle Vincent. Tonight isn't going to make any difference—Uncle Vincent isn't going to solve our problems for us. He doesn't like us any more than we like him."

"I hope you're not including me in that 'we'. *I* like him."

"Come off it, Gretchen—you couldn't wait to get away from him. That's why you married me, wasn't it? To get away from Uncle Vincent?"

Gretchen batted her eyelashes. "My knight in shining armor."

"Now stop that!"

"On a white horse."

"I don't like horses. They scare me."

"Fighting the dragon."

"There—you called Uncle Vincent a dragon. Ha!"

"Ha yourself. *I'm* not afraid of Uncle Vincent."

"You saying I am?"

"Oh, I wouldn't say that. But I can't help but wonder why you start fidgeting like a little boy waiting for school to let out every time we go over there."

"He makes me itch, that's why. Every time I see that man, I start to itch. Uncle Vincent's too petty to frighten anyone, Gretchen. The effect he has on people is more like an advanced case of poison ivy."

"Charming. So scratch."

"And as far as that goes, did you know your voice goes up an octave whenever you talk to him?"

Annoyed, Gretchen went back to her dressing table and added a pair of pearl earrings to her ensemble. "You're imagining things."

"Like hell I am. Your voice changes, your personality changes, even your way of moving changes when you're with Uncle Vincent. You turn into Lou Ann Poovey."

"Lou Ann *who?*"

"Poovey. Poo, vee. Gomer Pyle's girlfriend—remember her? Every time she set out to be charming, she'd hunch one shoulder forward and talk over it, looking up from under her eyelashes. Her voice would get higher and softer until the honey was positively dripping down the TV screen. Well, that's exactly what you do when you're with Uncle Vincent. Except the accent—you don't have a southern accent. Other than that, you've got Lou Ann Poovey down pat."

Gretchen ground her teeth and slipped on a pearl bracelet. "Honestly, Lionel, sometimes you can be so insensitive I could scream! Where do you get off, making fun of me because I try to be nice to Uncle Vincent? What else should I do?"

"You could work on your southern accent," Lionel said dryly.

"You know what your problem is? You're jealous of Uncle Vincent. He's the success you only want to be. *You* want to be in a position to say yes or no and control other people's lives but you aren't and you can't!"

"I'd like to have Uncle Vincent's *money*, yes—but that's the only thing about him I like. Gretchen, I don't want to control anybody's life but my own—and you're not helping."

Gretchen scrunched up her eyes, not quite crying. "That's right, blame me. Every time something goes wrong, you come home and blame me!"

"Oh, I don't either." Lionel ran a hand through his hair. "But every time I try to talk to you anymore, this happens. I get mad and say things I don't mean to say. And you look for things to get mad about. Don't be so damned touchy."

"I'm not touchy. I'm sensitive."

"Uh-huh. Well, this is getting us nowhere and we ought to be leaving anyway. It's a quarter 'til—oh, for Christ's sake, Gretchen! *Six* pearl rings? Don't you think you're overdoing it?"

By the time the Knoxes left for Uncle Vincent's, they were barely speaking to each other.

2

Bjarne Pedersen stepped into the hall closet for a nip out of the bottle hidden on the shelf. Tonight he was going to need all the fortification he could get.

He heard the elevator start; Mr. Vincent was on his way down. When it was just the old man and the housekeeper and himself, things were fine. But with that crowd coming tonight—Miss Gretchen and Mr. Lionel and that bony-faced woman who walked with her toes pointed outward and the long-winded lawyer she lived with and the two lovebirds named Murdoch, well, any one of them was enough to upset Mr. Vincent. But with all six of them at once? Bjarne took another swallow from the bottle.

"Barney!" Mrs. Polk called. "He wants you!"

He wants you, he wants you, Bjarne mimicked to himself. He replaced the bottle on the shelf and slipped a mint into his mouth, then stepped out of the closet and called back, "Thank you, Mrs. Polk," trying to remember whether he'd paid the housekeeper her weekly compliment yet or not.

Mr. Vincent had wheeled himself into the library and was even then maneuvering into position behind his desk. In addition to the stroke that had cost him the use of his legs, Mr. Vincent suffered a variety of aches and pains that kept him in a perpetual state of crankiness. He'd be complaining about something or other before five minutes had passed. "Barney, I'll be wanting a massage after my guests leave," the old man rasped. "Have everything ready, will you?"

"Yes, sir. And a hot bath?" Good for relieving tension.

Vincent Farwell grunted assent and then said, "Why, hello there, Godfrey!" Godfrey Daniel leaped lightly to the top of the desk, making Bjarne wince. It was a lovely Chippendale partner's desk; and while the cat's claws had never scratched the surface yet, it could still happen. Godfrey Daniel stepped onto the blotter, allowing Bjarne to breathe a little easier. The blotter itself was the replaceable kind, available at any stationer's; Mr. Vincent's niece Gretchen had once given him an expensive lizard desk pad for Christmas, but he never used it. He liked a plain paper blotter, and so did Godfrey Daniel.

Mr. Vincent didn't seem worried about scratches on the furniture, though; he allowed the black, orange, and white tortoiseshell cat the run of the house, indulging that animal the way he indulged no human being in his life. Godfrey went into a long post-snooze stretch and allowed himself to be petted.

"Mrs. Polk left the doors open," Mr. Vincent complained. "And I'll want a fire, Barney."

The old house tended to get stuffy easily; Mrs. Polk aired out the rooms every time the weather permitted. Bjarne closed the double doors leading to the walled terrace that separated the house on three sides from its neighbors. The mild spring night contained no hint of rain, but Mr. Vincent never risked exposing his old bones to the cool or the damp if he could avoid it.

Bjarne crossed the room and lit the fire he'd laid an hour earlier. Then he carefully put the fire screen in place; no sparks on the Sultanabad carpet, please! Sphinxlike, Godfrey Daniel watched his every move. Bjarne's hand shook.

His employer didn't notice. He was preoccupied with his newest toy, an alabaster statuette of the god Hermes. Mr. Vincent wasn't so much a collector as he was an indulger, buying a piece now and then that caught his eye, keeping it in the library until it no longer amused him and then banishing it to some other part of the house. The alabaster Hermes would eventually go the same way.

The library was the center of Mr. Vincent's life. Retired from active wheeling and dealing, Vincent Farwell still kept close track of his many investments; the lifetime habit of making money could never be abandoned completely. So the library had become half office, with desk and file cabinet and bookshelves and a typewriter no one used any more, and half sitting-room: sofa, comfortable chairs, fireplace, and several high-priced knick-knacks on the order of the new alabaster Hermes. The single painting on the wall was a Degas dancer

—young, solid, and with both feet planted squarely on the ground.

"Blast," said Mr. Vincent, "I forgot my pills. Run up and get them for me—the yellow ones. Oh, and Barney—I want you to answer the door tonight. Mrs. Polk is going to have her hands full."

"Yes, sir." Bjarne left him fussing with some papers on his desk and took the stairs to the second floor; Mr. Vincent liked the elevator to stay on the same floor where he was.

The vial of Valium tablets was on the table beside the bed Bjarne had been lifting Mr. Vincent into and out of for the past nine years. Valium, a hot bath, and a massage—to loosen the old man up enough that he could sleep. Bjarne considered taking one of the little yellow tablets himself. Mr. Vincent was going to be in one of his moods after the guests left. Mrs. Polk could just retreat to her room; Bjarne was the one who had to cope.

And he would. He swallowed a Valium dry and put another in his pocket for later. It might not be too bad tonight; maybe they wouldn't get the old man overexcited. The one thing that Bjarne Pedersen lived in fear of was the ever-present possibility that Vincent Farwell would suffer another stroke and die.

For what would happen to Bjarne then? Miss Gretchen would inherit this lovely old house and everything in it. Mrs. Polk's job was safe, but would Miss Gretchen have any need for the masseur/valet/chauffeur Bjarne had become? Mr. Vincent had told him that he'd taken care of him in his will. What did that mean—*taken care of*? Enough to pay the rent on one furnished room for the rest of his life?

Bjarne had been a master carpenter in Norway, but servant's work was all he could find when he first came to America. Then Vincent Farwell had discovered he'd entered the country illegally; and although the matter had never been mentioned again after that one time, that little bit of blackmail had been enough to keep Bjarne in his place. If Mr. Vincent ever became dissatisfied with his service, all he had to do was pick up the telephone and call the Immigration and Naturalization Service and Bjarne would be in deep trouble.

But Bjarne had adjusted to the situation. He'd been easily seduced by the furniture in Mr. Vincent's house, for one thing. As a former worker in wood, Bjarne loved the heavy, solid pieces everywhere in the house, even in his own room. It was amazing how quickly one could become accustomed to the life rhythms of the rich. And if the truth were told, Vincent Farwell's forcing him to stay had lifted a burden from Bjarne Pedersen's shoulders; he'd been relieved of responsibility for his own life. Now he had a good reason not to make the effort to better his position. He'd found a safe haven in this loud, abrasive country in which financial success was the only kind that mattered. Bjarne was content.

At the bottom of the stairs he came upon Mrs. Polk placing a vase of flowers on one of the hall tables. "Pretty," he said. "The flowers look nice."

"*He* doesn't even notice," the housekeeper declared in her high-pitched, clear enunciation that always made Bjarne think of Elsa Lanchester.

"I think he does." *Keep her happy.* "He just doesn't say anything."

The corners of Mrs. Polk's mouth turned up a fraction. Bjarne fetched a glass of water from the kitchen and took Vincent Farwell his Valium.

Mr. Vincent dribbled water on his chin, which Bjarne dutifully patted dry with a handkerchief he carried for just that purpose. Then he noticed his employer's face was contorted with pain. "What is it? Shoulder?"

"Yes. Hurry."

An Infralux was kept in every room of the house. Bjarne hurriedly opened a desk drawer—the wrong drawer, the one with the gun in it. He found the right drawer and took out the heat-penetrating instrument he was looking for. He eased Mr. Vincent's left arm out of his suit jacket and opened his shirt, then plugged the instrument in and held the head against the arthritis-troubled shoulder.

"A little lower—there." In a few minutes the infrared heat reached the site of the inflammation and brought the old man some relief. "Ah, that's better," Mr. Vincent sighed and worked his arm up and down.

"Don't move it so fast," Bjarne scolded. "You'll start it hurting again."

"I know, I know!" the old man snapped. "Stop treating me like a child! Put it away and help me into my jacket." Bjarne quickly restored order. "Now go out in the hall and wait," Mr.

Vincent ordered, glancing at the clock on the mantlepiece. "My idiot niece and her grabby husband and their cohorts will be here any moment now. Go on!"

Bjarne could think of a few things he'd rather be doing instead of playing doorman. He was going to miss a Bela Lugosi movie on television tonight, one he'd never seen. He went out to wait by the front door, stopping in the hall closet for reinforcement first.

The Murdochs were the first to arrive. "Hallo, Barney," Dorrie bubbled. "How are you this evening?"

"Just fine, thank you, Miss Dorrie." Bjarne took the light jacket she was wearing and exchanged nods with Simon. "He's in the library." Bjarne opened the library door for them just as the doorbell rang again.

Gretchen Knox didn't bother to say hello. "The library?" At Bjarne's nod she charged off in that direction, obviously out of sorts.

Lionel Knox dropped a friendly hand on Bjarne's shoulder. "What kind of mood's he in tonight, Barney?"

"A snarling mood. His arthritis is acting up."

"Damn." Lionel followed his wife into the library and re-appeared a moment later, apologetically holding out the shawl Gretchen had been wearing. Bjarne took it and closed the door, just catching Mr. Vincent's voice saying, "No, no, don't sit there, Simon—I want Gretchen and Lionel in those chairs."

Inside the library Gretchen Knox went behind the desk and gave her uncle a peck on the cheek. "You're looking well," she told him.

"I look like hell," Uncle Vincent said, "and I feel worse. Move over, Lionel—don't block the fire."

"Isn't it a little warm for a fire?" Simon Murdoch murmured.

"Simon!" Gretchen exclaimed, moving over and taking his arm—neatly edging Dorrie Murdoch out. "I haven't seen you for ages!"

Simon arched an eyebrow at her. "Yes, it's been, oh, two days at least."

"We never seem to have the time to talk," she cooed, playing with the buttons on his jacket. "*Let's* do lunch."

"A splendid idea. The four of us." He gently disengaged himself and sat down on the sofa. Lionel smothered a laugh.

Dorrie discovered Godfrey Daniel sprawled out on Uncle

Vincent's desk. "Oh, hello, kitty!" she purred, stretching out a caressing hand. Dorrie liked to think she had a way with animals, so she was both startled and hurt when the cat hissed at her. Godfrey jumped down from the desk and majestically staked out a new territory for himself by the fireplace.

"How's business?" Lionel asked Simon.

"Pretty good. Big increase in the demand for industrials."

"Maybe you should handle industrials."

"I've been thinking about it." Simon was a diamond merchant; he and Dorrie had met while she was buying stones for Ellandy's.

Uncle Vincent was staring at Dorrie's new Maltese cross. "Yours or Nicole's?" he asked.

"Mine," Dorrie beamed.

"Nice," he admitted grudgingly, thinking that that frivolous woman did have a good eye.

"There, darling, I told you he'd like it," Simon remarked, although he'd said nothing of the kind.

But Dorrie knew her cues. "And you were right, dear, as always." Husband and wife exchanged a pantomime kiss.

Lionel started to snort but turned it into a cough.

"I suppose you all want drinks," Uncle Vincent said and rang for Mrs. Polk. Vincent Farwell didn't believe in wet bars or even liquor cabinets, so everything alcoholic had to be brought in from the kitchen. Mrs. Polk thought she knew what everyone would want, and she turned out to be right. She brought in two bourbons, one scotch, gin and grapefruit juice for Miss Gretchen the way she liked it, and plain mineral water for Mr. Vincent. It took her two trips.

"Exactly two ice cubes," Gretchen said, examining her drink. "You remembered, Polka Dot!"

"Of course I remembered, Miss Gretchen," Mrs. Polk said affectionately. "Don't I always?"

The warmth of Mrs. Polk's welcome relaxed Gretchen a little. She'd lived in this house from the time she was fifteen, when both her parents had died, until her marriage to Lionel Knox a few years ago. She still thought of Uncle Vincent's house as "home" and the house she shared with Lionel as "our place"—a distinction she wasn't even aware she made. But "home" hadn't always been a happy place; Mrs. Polk was the only truly sensitive person there and it was to her that Gretchen had always run whenever Uncle Vincent made her cry. Which was frequently.

When Mrs. Polk had left the study, Gretchen said, "Uncle Vincent, what is this big surprise you've got for us? Ever'body's just *dyin'* to know!"

"Not now, Gretchen. We'll wait until the other two get here."

"But cain't you give us just one li'l hint?" Gretchen persisted winningly.

"I said wait," Uncle Vincent growled.

"Oh, my—aren't you a grouchy ole bear tonight!" Gretchen teased. "Is somethin' the mattuh, Uncle?"

Simon was puzzled. "Gretchen—is that a southern accent you've picked up?"

"Lou Ann Poovey," Lionel explained, which only puzzled Simon more.

Dorrie said, "I agree with Gretchen. Give us a hint, Uncle Vincent."

"Damn it, woman, I said wait!" the old man barked. "Stop badgering me!"

Dorrie's eyes grew saucer-sized, as Simon said soothingly, "Now, now, Uncle Vincent—nobody's badgering you. It's just chitchat."

"I'm in no mood for either chitting or chatting," the old man rasped. "We'll wait for the other two."

At that moment Godfrey Daniel decided, for reasons known only to himself, to leave his spot by the fireplace and launch himself into Simon's lap. Simon's composure deserted him momentarily. "Oof—shoo, kitty." He pushed at the cat. "Nice kitty—get *down*, nice kitty." Godfrey thumped to the floor and then reclaimed his place on Uncle Vincent's desk.

"Simon doesn't like cats," Dorrie explained to the room at large.

Uncle Vincent cackled. "Isn't it funny the way cats invariably pick out the one person in the room who doesn't like them— and then go shed all over him?"

"Hilarious," said Simon, brushing cat hairs from his trousers.

The sound of the doorbell reached their ears. Bjarne showed in Nicole Lattimer and Malcolm Conner, stumbling a little as he did. Nicole led the way, her walk slightly suggestive of a dancer's duck-waddle. Dorrie greeted her brother with a hug, embarrassing him a trifle; she'd never indulged in public displays of affection before she married Simon.

"You're late," Uncle Vincent rasped. The clock on the mantlepiece said five after eight. "Well, Malcolm—you and Nicole get married yet?" Malcolm pretended not to hear.

"Good evening, Nicole," Simon greeted her. "How are things at the Ballet Russe?"

"Funny, Simon," Nicole said. "Well, Gretchen—I see you're all pearled up this evening."

Gretchen stroked the pearls around her neck in what was meant to be a sensuous gesture. "I can't understand why you don't like pearls, Nicole. They're said to be the most feminine of jewels."

"That's one reason," Nicole said.

"Sit down, sit down," Uncle Vincent commanded impatiently. "Over there." Then he noticed his manservant weaving unsteadily in the doorway. "That'll be all, Barney!" he snapped. "I'll ring when I need you." Bjarne made a visible effort to walk away without swaying.

Lionel noticed too. Quietly he stood up and looked through the library door, just in time to see Bjarne disappear into the hall closet.

"Where'd he go?" Uncle Vincent rasped.

"To his room, I suppose," Lionel said, and took his seat again.

Mrs. Polk brought two more scotches for the newcomers and did not ask the others if they wanted refills. When the door had closed behind her, Vincent Farwell got down to business. "I called you here tonight because I have an announcement to make that affects all of you. I'm not renewing Ellandy's loan."

Six expectant faces watched him, waiting for the words *I'm going to cancel it instead.*

"I expect payment in full on the due date," Uncle Vincent rasped. "That's two weeks from tomorrow."

A stunned silence greeted his announcement. Lionel Knox and Dorrie Murdoch exchanged a look that was at first disbelieving and then horrified. "But why?" Lionel demanded of Uncle Vincent. "I've sent you monthly reports—you know we're showing a steady profit. Small, but growing every month.

If we have to pay you back now, we'll be right back where we were before we expanded!"

"Two weeks," Uncle Vincent repeated, "from tomorrow."

"Oh no!" Dorrie wailed. "We'll have to cut back on our orders and—Uncle Vincent, think of the people you'll be putting out of work. Some of the craftsmen, the sales personnel—"

"Me," Nicole said bitterly.

"And Nicole," Lionel agreed. "The reason we borrowed that money was to hire the people we needed to handle the increase in orders we were getting. An additional designer, extra craftsmen, more space, more equipment like the new Piermatic polisher—and now when the expansion is just beginning to pay off, you want to pull the rug out from under us? For god's sake *why*, man?"

"Yes, Uncle Vincent, you do owe them an explanation," Simon murmured, smoothly differentiating between himself and the Ellandy crowd.

"I can't believe you'd do this—not now," Nicole muttered.

Malcolm cleared his throat. "Uncle Vincent, are you sure you're not acting precipitously? Have you fully considered all the ramifications of calling in the loan? Gretchen is bound to suffer, not to mention all the people who've worked so hard to make Ellandy's a success. And why would you want to sabotage a business right on the verge of—"

"Because he's a mean-spirited old man, that's why!" Nicole cried. "He likes to smash things!" No one contradicted her.

Gretchen listened carefully and said nothing. The others were all talking at once.

Uncle Vincent waited until they'd sputtered themselves out. "Are you finished?" he asked. When no one answered, he looked at his niece. "Gretchen, you're my brother's only child and my heir, and I've done the best by you I could. I knew I couldn't keep you from marrying the wrong man forever—and since Lionel was the first respectable-looking one you ever brought home, I decided better him than the others. I co-signed a bank loan for him to start Ellandy's. I gave you a house to live in. I helped out in other ways."

Gretchen finally spoke. "And we love you for it, Uncle Vincent."

The old man snorted. "But that's all over now. When Lionel

came to me with his grandiose plans for expansion, I decided that would be it. I'd lend him a million and a half of my own money—but that was to be the final test. No extensions, no partial payments. If he defaulted on the loan, that would be the end of Ellandy's. Two weeks from tomorrow, every diamond and pearl and emerald in Ellandy's vault will belong to me. Gretchen, I'm just not willing to underwrite Lionel Knox for your benefit any longer."

"It was a *business* deal," Lionel said hotly. "And it's not smart business to call in the loan just because you don't like *me*!"

"There's something to what he says, Uncle Vincent," Malcolm remarked calmly. "Have you figured out how much you'll be losing in interest if you refuse to renew the loan? It's a considerable sum, you know, and—"

"I don't need the money!" Uncle Vincent snapped. "What I need is to get the leeches out of my life!"

"Leeches!" Lionel echoed unbelievingly.

"Lionel's not a leech," Gretchen objected. "You shouldn't say things like that, Uncle Vincent."

"Let me see if I've got this straight," Nicole said sharply, nervously twisting the ends of the scarf wrapped around her waist. "*We* are all going out of business because *you* didn't want Gretchen to marry Lionel? I don't believe it—I don't believe it for one minute. You want Ellandy's for yourself. You're just using Lionel as an excuse."

"I need Ellandy's the way I need a hole in the head," Uncle Vincent rasped. "But think what you like—I couldn't care less."

"*I* think you're mean," Gretchen pouted. "You're not being very sensitive."

Uncle Vincent looked at her in exasperation. "That's right, I forgot—'sensitive' is your word this year, isn't it?"

Simon spoke up. "Aren't you being unnecessarily petty, Uncle Vincent? You're using that loan as a weapon. I think you're enjoying this ugly little scene. You like hurting them."

" 'Them'? Don't pretend to be so detached, Simon Murdoch. You're affected by this too—now that's enough," he ordered as Simon started to object. "Lionel, I've known all along you married Gretchen for her money. And I can prove it." He pulled a manila folder from under the blotter on his desk. "I hired a private investigator."

"Uncle Vincent!" Gretchen exclaimed, while her husband was too shocked to say anything.

"This is his report," the old man went on. "He—"

"Excuse me, Uncle Vincent," Malcolm interrupted, "but which private investigator?"

"Fellow named Bernstein, Paul Bernstein."

"Good man," Malcolm nodded judiciously. "I've used him myself on occasion."

"Oh, for heaven's sake, Malcolm!" Nicole snapped.

"Now that Mr. Bernstein's credentials have been established," Uncle Vincent smiled wryly, "let's hear what he has to say. The first thing he turned up was the fact that one Lionel Knox is something of a magician. He makes money disappear. Ellandy's isn't the first enterprise he's jinxed." He looked at Dorrie. "Did you know that once before Lionel went into business with a woman and bankrupted her?"

"You mean the chain of flower shops?" Dorrie said. "Yes, I knew about that—but that wasn't Lionel's fault."

"It was a *seasonal* thing, for Christ's sake," Lionel growled. "A lot of flower distributors went out of business that year."

"And a lot of others didn't," Uncle Vincent said pointedly. "Do you ever wonder what happened to your former partner, Lionel? Bernstein tracked her down. She's working as a cashier in a discount house."

Lionel looked stricken. "Oh jeez."

Uncle Vincent grinned at Dorrie. "Do you think you would like working as a cashier, my dear?"

Dorrie shuddered. "I should hate it!"

"That will never happen, darling," Simon reassured her. "He's just trying to rattle you."

"Maybe she needs a little rattling," Uncle Vincent persevered. "Do you really know the kind of man you're in partnership with, Dorrie?"

Lionel stood up abruptly. "I don't have to sit here and listen to this!"

"That's right," Uncle Vincent said blandly. "You can leave any time. If you hurry, you might be able to find a third wife before you're too old to play the game."

"*Third* wife?" Malcolm asked.

"Oh yes—Gretchen is number two. Didn't you know?"

Gretchen said, "Uncle Vincent, what is all this? You and I both knew Lionel had been married before."

"Ah, but did you know his first wife put up the cash for his half of the ill-fated venture into the floral business? And then as soon as he ran through her savings, he divorced her." The old man snorted. "Flowers! What kind of business is that for a man to be in?"

"It wasn't *her* savings, it was *our* savings," Lionel said bitterly. "And she divorced *me*."

Uncle Vincent cackled. "A fine recommendation to a second wife! Gretchen, don't you see the pattern?" He picked up the alabaster Hermes and pointed it at Lionel. "He marries one woman for her money and talks another woman into putting *her* money into whatever scheme he wants to try next. He did it before and he's doing it again. Right now he's got you and Dorrie financing him, you through me."

"Oh, shit!" Lionel yelled. "Bullshit!"

Dorrie looked confused. "But . . . but I put very little money into Ellandy's. Lionel came up with the cash we needed."

"That's true," Malcolm nodded. "Dorrie made a token investment, but her real contribution to the partnership was to be her creative talent. Lionel supplied the working capital."

"So *there!*" Gretchen cried, as if she'd just won some debating point.

Uncle Vincent sighed. "Gretchen, my dear, hasn't it dawned on you yet where that working capital came from? Lionel could never have gotten a bank loan to start the business without my co-signature. And the million and a half I let him have— that was *your* money, Gretchen. It would have come to you after my death, instead of going down the Ellandy drain."

Gretchen turned her head and looked at her husband strangely.

"Nothing has gone down the drain," Lionel said tiredly. "You're exaggerating, Uncle Vincent. You're making things out to be worse than they are."

"Am I? I don't think so. I do know you're using Gretchen's money to pay for your little indulgences."

"*Indulgences?* What indulgences?"

"Well, here's one," Uncle Vincent said smugly, and took an

eight-by-ten glossy photo out of the folder. He handed it silently to his niece.

Gretchen let out a cry; as one, the others left their seats and crowded around her to look at the photograph. What they saw was a picture of Lionel Knox and Nicole Lattimer coming out of a motel, obviously on friendly terms. *Very* friendly terms.

"Whoops," said Nicole.

"Here's more," Uncle Vincent smiled, handing over five or six other compromising photographs, fully aware of his niece's discomfort. "Your husband, Gretchen dear, is a cheat. He's cheating you out of your money, and he's cheating on your marriage."

There was no denying the evidence of the photographs. "Gretchen, what can I say?" Lionel said worriedly. "I made a mistake. It was over almost before it started." Gretchen just stared at him, open-mouthed. "It happened well over a year ago," Lionel went on—and suddenly realized what that meant. "Uncle Vincent, just exactly how long have you been having me watched?"

Uncle Vincent smiled enigmatically.

Dorrie held one of the photographs, a concerned look on her face. "Did you know about this?" she asked her brother. Tight-lipped, Malcolm nodded.

Uncle Vincent wheeled his chair back from the desk a little, feeling well satisfied with the evening's work. "Now do you see why I refuse to pour any more money into Lionel's little jewelry business?"

Gretchen erupted from her chair and whirled on her husband. "You son of a bitch! *That's* why you wanted me to be nice to Nicole tonight!"

"Oh, Gretchen," Lionel sighed. "It was over long ago. It meant nothing to either of us."

Nicole was appalled. "You told her to be *nice* to me?"

" 'It meant nothing'," Gretchen mimicked. "Isn't that what philandering husbands always say when they're found out?"

"*You* told *her* . . . to be nice to *me*?" Nicole repeated incredulously.

"Easy," Malcolm cautioned.

"I always thought it was Dorrie!" Gretchen shouted. "I thought you were having a thing with Dorrie!"

Dorrie's eyes grew wide. "With *me*! Oh, no! Gretchen, how

could you?" She drew closer to Simon, who wrapped a protective arm about her shoulders.

"I'm not having a thing with anybody!" Lionel shouted back at his wife. "With Nicole—that wasn't even a real affair. It was just something we both quickly agreed was a mistake."

"That's the truth, Gretchen," Nicole said earnestly. "In fact, we were both a little embarrassed by what had happened. We put an end to it pretty fast."

Gretchen ignored her, still intent on Lionel. "So you got tired of Nicole and turned to Dorrie!"

"No, I didn't turn to Dorrie! Dorrie, tell her!"

But it was Simon who answered. "Gretchen, don't you think I'd know if Dorrie were having an affair? A man would have to be pretty obtuse not to know when something like that was going on."

"Meaning *I* was obtuse because I didn't guess about Lionel and Nicole? Thank you very much! Simon, hasn't it ever occurred to you that all that fawning she does over you would make a pretty good cover?"

"I don't *fawn!*" Dorrie exclaimed indignantly. "You're only saying that because you want Simon for yourself!"

At that point everyone started shouting at everyone else. Uncle Vincent wheeled his chair out from behind the desk, cackling in delight. "Aren't friends wonderful!" The shouting increased.

"*Stop it!*" Malcolm suddenly roared. "Stop it this instant!" Startled, the others responded to the authority in his voice. "Don't you see," he said more quietly, "we're doing exactly what he wants us to do. He's got us all at each other's throats." He walked over and stood before the man in the wheelchair. "Uncle Vincent, you're a malicious old man whose sole remaining pleasure in life is stirring up trouble. You don't care how much you hurt Gretchen or anybody else."

"Leeches!" Uncle Vincent spat out. "You're all after my blood—Lionel isn't the only one who wants something from me. Malcolm, you've wanted to handle my legal affairs for years—don't deny it! The rest of you are dependent upon my loan to keep yourselves going. Dorrie's found herself a warm spot and doesn't want anything to change. Nicole's an ambitious woman who wants a piece of the Ellandy pie. And Simon,

Ellandy's is one of your best customers. If they go out of business, how will you raise the cash to pay for the new condo?"

"Condo?" said Dorrie. "What new condo?"

Simon raised an eyebrow. "Good lord—how did you know about that?"

"Bernstein," Malcolm muttered.

"You had me investigated too?" Simon's half-smile didn't waver. "I must say, Uncle Vincent, you *have* been thorough."

Dorrie asked, "What new condo, Simon?"

Her husband sighed. "I was keeping it as a surprise, darling, but Uncle Vincent has managed to spoil that too. I'll tell you about it later."

"Tell her any time you like," Uncle Vincent snapped, "but tell her somewhere else. I want you all out of my house. Right now. Go on—get out!"

"Gladly," Lionel muttered.

"I'm staying here tonight," Gretchen announced. Lionel didn't try to talk her out of it.

There was a sudden exodus; Gretchen ran up the stairs to her old room and Lionel yelled, "Barney!" When the manservant failed to appear, Lionel opened the hall closet, half expecting to find the man passed out on the floor. Nothing out of the ordinary, however; Lionel took out Dorrie's jacket. "Nicole?"

"I didn't wear a wrap. Let's get the hell out of here." They got the hell out of there.

In the library, Uncle Vincent picked up Godfrey Daniel and caressed him. "Nice kitty," he said. "You don't want my blood, do you, Godfrey?"

Godfrey scratched him.

3

They went into the first bar they came to that wasn't blasting music out at them; they had some serious talking to do.

And some serious drinking. Lionel Knox, Nicole Lattimer, and the Murdochs all startled the waitress by asking for two drinks each; Malcolm Conner ordered a fish sandwich and a beer. "I didn't have dinner," he explained.

When Malcolm had finished half his sandwich and the other four had one drink under their belts and were working on the second, Lionel said, "I sure came out the villain tonight." He laughed shortly. "Whew! I had no idea the old boy hated me that much."

"Oh, I suspect he hates everyone indiscriminately, Lionel," Simon drawled. "You just make a convenient scapegoat."

"I'm sure that's true," Nicole agreed. "That bastard. He wants Ellandy's for himself, no matter how much he denies it. You were just the excuse."

Lionel scowled. "Still, he made me out to be some sort of Bluebeard—marrying women for their money and then talking other women into putting money into my business. Dorrie," he asked worriedly, "you didn't believe that stuff, did you?"

"Of course not," Dorrie reassured him. "You were honest with me about the flower shops, and I did some checking on my own. I don't regret the partnership one little bit, Lionel. Look how much Ellandy's has grown in just the past six months! No one could have known Uncle Vincent would drop a bomb on us."

Nicole lifted her glass. "To our enemies," she said. "May they all have Uncle Vincents in their lives."

Simon signaled for a third round. "I'm still hungry," Malcolm said, and ordered a sausage sandwich and another beer.

"That mean-spirited old man!" Dorrie raged suddenly. "I could kill him! I could just kill him!"

"Now, Dorrie," Simon said mildly. "Don't get angry, darling. We've all got to keep cool heads."

"How unbelievably naïve I was!" she raged on unhearing. "Thinking he would actually give us all that money! My head must have stopped working."

"It wasn't all that unreasonable an assumption," Malcolm pronounced around bites of his sandwich. "It would have been a good way to assure Gretchen's future—by helping Lionel. We didn't know he was having Lionel investigated."

"And me," Simon said dryly. "I wonder what he hoped to find?"

"Yes, that is odd, isn't it?" Nicole said. "I could see why he might have *Dorrie* investigated—the other partner. But Simon?"

"For all we know, he might have had me investigated too," Dorrie said indignantly. "Who does he think he is, going around *investigating* people?"

"So what are we going to do?" Lionel worried. "Any suggestions?"

Malcolm wiped his mouth and said, "The first thing to do is try to talk Uncle Vincent into accepting a partial payment. Oh, I know, he said *payment in full*. But we have two weeks to try to get him to change his mind. I blame myself for your predicament, you know. I should never have allowed you to sign a promissory note calling for one lump sum repayment, plus interest. Uncle Vincent did give you a break on the interest, but that's supposed to be the advantage of family loans, isn't it? Nevertheless, loans for such large amounts usually require a staggered payment schedule and I should have insisted on it. But all that's water under the bridge. The problem lies in devising an appropriate strategy for getting Uncle Vincent to accept a partial payment. Here we must be very careful, for there are all sorts of undercurrents at work that—"

"You are going to get to the point, aren't you?" Simon interrupted. "Sometime before the bar closes?"

"Allow me to finish," Malcolm said without taking offense. "The question is, who is to beard the lion in his den? Not you, Lionel, for obvious reasons. You wouldn't get in the front door. I'm fairly certain we can't count on any help from Gretchen now. I could do it, but I made a mistake tonight and called Uncle Vincent a malicious old man. I don't think he's going to forget that in a hurry. Nicole, you're out for the same reason —you spoke to him rather harshly yourself, you know. I suppose Simon could approach him, as a semi-outsider with a vicarious interest to protect. But since he had you investigated too, Simon, that would indicate he looks upon you with a suspicious eye and might not—"

"Malcolm," Lionel said impatiently. "The point?"

"The point is that Dorrie is about the only one Uncle Vincent didn't come down hard on tonight. She's the logical one to ask him to accept a partial payment."

"Okay," Lionel summarized, "Plan A is that Dorrie tries to talk Uncle Vincent into changing his mind. We can make a sizable partial payment—I've set money aside for that. Now listen to Plan B. We strip our inventory to pay back the loan in full and then go out of business. Dorrie—what do you think?"

"I think it stinks," she said.

Simon asked, "Isn't there any way you can repay the loan and stay open? Even if it means operating on a minimal basis?"

Lionel ran a hand through his hair. "I don't know—I don't think so. We're running pretty close to the line. It'll depend on the exact market value of the stones we have in the vault right now. I'll have to check the inventory. In fact, I think I'll go in and get started. I'm sure as hell not going to get any sleep tonight."

"We need a Plan C," Nicole said.

"Darling," Dorrie said to her husband. "I just remembered —what's this condominium Uncle Vincent said you were buying?"

"Ah yes, the condo," Simon sighed. "My anniversary present to you, prematurely revealed—thanks to Uncle Vincent."

"How sweet! Tell me about it."

"Six units, now under construction, overlooking the shore. I thought we would keep one and sell the others. It's investment property as well as a weekend retreat for us. It's in a *magnificent* location, darling—we'll drive down and take a look this weekend. When it's completed you'll be able to stand on the balcony and watch the breakers."

"Because you know I love the ocean!" Dorrie beamed. "How

thoughtful of you. I can't wait to see it! You are a darling, Simon." The Murdochs exchanged a smiling kiss.

Lionel stirred restlessly. "If you two can stop playing Jonathan and Jennifer Hart long enough to pay attention, we've got some decisions to make here."

"I have a Plan C," Nicole announced. "How do you folks feel about theft?"

"Rob a bank?" Malcolm looked amused. "Be serious, Nicole."

"I'm not talking about banks. That promissory note Lionel and Dorrie had to sign—how many copies are there?"

"Just the two. Ellandy's and Uncle Vincent's."

"Well, Ellandy's copy is no problem." She paused, letting it sink in.

Malcolm was horrified. "*Steal* the promissory note? You're out of your mind!"

"Not practical, Nicole," Simon objected. "Gretchen knows about it, for one thing."

"Her word against ours."

"There might be a third copy you don't know about. With Uncle Vincent's attorney, say."

Lionel said, "If there is, it's unsigned. We signed only two copies."

Simon's characteristic half-smile was in place. "And what *modus operandi* have you decided on, may I ask?"

"I hadn't got that far," Nicole admitted.

Dorrie giggled. "Maybe we could bribe Barney to steal it for us."

Lionel grinned. "If you can catch him when he's sober." At Nicole's surprised look, he said, "He was drunk as a lord tonight. Didn't you notice?"

"No, I didn't."

"Well, he's pretty good at hiding it," Lionel shrugged. "His walk gives him away, sometimes."

"Scratch Plan C," Malcolm said emphatically. "I can't believe you four are seriously considering stealing a legal document from its lawful owner!"

"We're not," Lionel smiled tiredly. "Relax, Malcolm. It was just a nice thought. I'm going to go on in now and start checking the inventory. Uh, I could use some help."

"I'll help," said Nicole. "I don't think I can sleep tonight either."

"Darling, would you mind terribly if I went with them?" Dorrie asked Simon. "The sooner we know exactly where we stand . . ."

"Of course, dear. Do you want to take the car or—"

"I'll drive her home," Lionel said. "I'll drive them both home." He grinned. "That way nobody can leave before I'm ready to quit."

They all needed to use the restrooms before they left. In the ladies' room, Dorrie took advantage of their moment alone to ask Nicole about something that had been bothering her. She patted her Honey Ash Number Seventeen curls into place and overcasually inquired of the other woman whether everything was all right between her and Malcolm.

"Yes, why do you—oh. You're thinking of Uncle Vincent's little revelation tonight? Dorrie, that silly fling with Lionel was over long before I moved in with Malcolm. It has nothing to do with Malcolm and me."

"Oh, thank goodness!" Dorrie cried with obvious relief. "Nicole, I was so worried that . . . well, I'm truly glad it was nothing important. I think it would kill Malcolm if he lost you."

"No danger of that," Nicole smiled. "And I'm sorry you were worried, Dorrie. Uncle Vincent really is a bastard, isn't he? Totally indifferent to how much anguish he causes."

Dorrie was frowning. "I just thought of something. Isn't working with Lionel every day a little, well, awkward for you? I mean, since you once . . ."

"As a matter of fact, we're more comfortable together now than we were before it happened. Because it's over and done with. We no longer have to worry about the *possibility* of its happening, you see?"

"I think so," Dorrie said dubiously. "Well, if you've got it all worked out and Malcolm doesn't mind your seeing Lionel all the time, I guess everything's okay."

"Malcolm is in no position to mind," Nicole said slyly, "since he is guilty of a . . . a similar indiscretion, shall we say? With Gretchen, believe it or not."

"Gretchen!" Dorrie's mouth fell open. "My brother . . . and *Gretchen Knox?*"

Nicole laughed. "A strange combination, isn't it?"

"And I always thought Malcolm had such good taste!" Dorrie flared.

"Ha—I like that way of looking at it. An affair with Gretchen

Knox equals a lapse in taste. But don't get angry, Dorrie. That too was over long before Malcolm and I moved in together."

"Damn it!" Dorrie cried furiously. "First you and Lionel and then Malcolm and Gretchen and now Gretchen is after Simon! Every time she sees him, she's all over him! Damn it all anyway! Everybody's having affairs except *me!*"

"Well, consider yourself lucky," Nicole said soothingly, not certain whether Dorrie meant it or not. "And you know perfectly well that Simon is not having an affair. Especially not with Gretchen—I don't think he even likes her much."

"Since when did that ever get in the way of sex?" Dorrie cried. Suddenly all the anger drained out of her. "Oh, you're right. I don't really suspect Simon—I've no reason to. Not Simon. I was just letting off steam."

Nicole looked at her curiously. "Dorrie, you get mad faster and cool down faster than anyone else I know. I think we've had enough true confessions for one evening. Come on—let's go count diamonds."

They rejoined the men. The two women left with Lionel for Ellandy's while Simon and Malcolm drove away in their own cars, the latter wondering why his sister had been glaring at him so darkly as she left.

Ellandy Jewels took up a great deal of expensive ground floor space in a new building in an old neighborhood. The neighborhood was considered quaint by the upscale segment of the population and was undergoing an extensive renovation process; chic and expensive new shops were sprouting like mushrooms. As an "in" location, it couldn't be better—although long-time neighborhood residents were less than delighted by the invasion. Already graffiti along the lines of "Yuppie Go Home" had begun to appear.

Ellandy's two owners and Nicole Lattimer had checked in with the nightwatchman. Now the vault door in Ellandy Jewels stood open as three nervous people tried to figure out whether they were going out of business or not. Dorrie was studying a printout sheet. "According to the list," she said, "drawer E-3 is supposed to hold a hundred twenty-five stones. I count a hundred twenty-three."

"Let me," said Nicole. Quickly her forefinger flicked each emerald aside as she counted. "One twenty-one."

"Lionel," both women said.

Lionel counted. "I get one twenty-two." The three exchanged a bleak look. "I guess this wasn't such a good idea," Lionel said. "We're so jumpy we keep making mistakes. We've been here over an hour and we haven't really accomplished anything—let's pack it in."

Dorrie nodded but Nicole said, "It's not going to be any easier tomorrow."

"It might. After we get a little sleep."

"Can you sleep? I don't think I can."

"I know how you feel," Dorrie said. "I'm too keyed up just to lie down and close my eyes."

"Let's try again," Nicole urged.

They counted the stones in drawer E-3 one more time, separating the emeralds into groups of ten and double-checking. The final count was one twenty-four. "One short," said Dorrie.

The fate of Ellandy Jewels would not be determined by one missing emerald; but it was the sort of inconsistency that would have to be tracked down through the computer records—a chore none of them was up to at the moment. "Let's go on," said Nicole.

Two drawers later, Dorrie announced, "I think I've got a Plan D." She immediately had the attention of the other two. "Suppose we hired whatsisname, Bernstein, or some other detective. To investigate Uncle Vincent. A man doesn't get that rich without leaving lots of dirty footprints behind him. Suppose our detective was able to turn up something Uncle Vincent would rather not have known—"

Lionel was already laughing. "Blackmail him?"

"Well, yes, I guess that's what I mean—"

"Oh, Dorrie, be realistic!" Lionel said. "Don't you think if Uncle Vincent left any *discoverable* dirt behind him, someone would have had his claws into the Farwell fortune long before this?"

"How do you know someone hasn't?" Dorrie said stubbornly. "Someone could have been blackmailing him for years and we wouldn't know about it."

Lionel shook his head. "That old fox has covered his trail, you can be sure of it. Nobody gets the better of Uncle Vincent."

"Oh, Lionel—don't say that!" Nicole protested. "Actually, it's not a bad idea at all. Shouldn't we at least try it? It seems to me we ought to try everything we can think of—and I mean *everything.*"

Eventually Lionel agreed that it couldn't hurt to hire a private detective. "I don't know what he can find out in only two weeks—but okay, I'll take care of it tomorrow. And Dorrie, you're still going to try to persuade Uncle Vincent to take a partial payment?"

"I'll try," she sighed. "But I don't think it'll do any good."

"Neither do I, but as Nicole says—we ought to try everything." He looked at his watch. "It's after midnight. I don't know about you two, but I've got the heebie-jeebies so bad I can't concentrate. Let's call it a day."

Nicole nodded. "I'm ready to quit now."

They locked the vault and started turning off the lights. Then, as if driven by a single thought, all three of them headed toward the workshop, where Dorrie's and Nicole's designs were translated into finished products. They stood looking for a while at the benches and the tools, the bottles of nitric acid and the small storage bins of jewelry findings. Kilns, centrifuges, vacuum pumps, steam casters. The sawyer's wheels, the brutter's lathe, the expensive new Piermatic Automatic Diamond Polishing Machine. They stood looking, looking and wondering if they were going to lose it all.

Nicole was the first to snap out of it. "Enough of this sentimental journey. We're all acting as if Ellandy's is doomed. Well, it needn't be! We've got a little time—we'll think of something. We mustn't be defeatist now!"

"Yea, team," Lionel said glumly.

They found the nightwatchman, told him they were through, and left.

Simon wanted a shower. It had been a dirty evening.

As he undressed, he ran over in his mind what he still had to do. Cash some securities tomorrow morning; that was the first thing. Next, take care of the diamonds. Then see a lawyer. Malcolm Conner was a competent enough attorney, but he was too closely involved in Ellandy's affairs to maintain an objective point of view.

Not for the first time, Simon wondered whether Dorrie had been wise to go into partnership with Lionel Knox. Simon liked Lionel, but Lionel did seem to get himself into hot water a lot. And this time Dorrie was getting splashed. An independent audit of the Ellandy books might not be a bad idea.

Another thing. He was going to have to do something about Gretchen Knox. The way she kept coming on to him in public—well, it was getting out of hand. Simon was convinced Gretchen wasn't interested in him at all; she just wanted to embarrass Dorrie. There was a lot of Uncle Vincent in his niece.

Ask her privately to cut it out? She'd pretend she didn't know what he was talking about. Humiliate her in front of other people? Crude, but probably the only thing that would work. He'd give it some thought.

He stepped into the shower and let the needles of hot water massage the tension in his neck and shoulders.

Gretchen Knox sat at the small desk in her old room on the second floor of Uncle Vincent's house and tried to draw the Maltese cross Dorrie Murdoch had been wearing that evening. She couldn't do it; it kept coming out lopsided. She crumpled up the paper in disgust; a fitting end to one bummer of an evening. No material there to be stored away as a beautiful memory.

Gretchen had hoped that the familiarity of her old room would offer some comfort, but it hadn't worked. Mrs. Polk had already retired, so there was no friendly shoulder to cry on. Gretchen had bathed and put on one of her old nighties that had never made the trip from Uncle Vincent's house to her own. She went through all the drawers in her room, looking for something to keep her from thinking about Lionel and Nicole.

Lionel and Nicole! Gretchen would never have believed it if it hadn't been for those pictures. If it had been Dorrie, Gretchen could have understood it, in a way. But Nicole? Ugh. Well, that was the final straw; she'd see a divorce lawyer tomorrow. Secretly, she was more than a little pleased that Uncle Vincent had provided her with such a dandy excuse. If she was going to have to choose between Lionel and Uncle Vincent, Gretchen knew which side her bread was buttered on.

She lay down on the bed and started imagining sexy scenes, starring herself, as a means of relaxing. But every time she got a good one going, Lionel's face would intrude. She tried substituting other faces, but nothing really worked. Simon Murdoch, for instance, had outworn his usefulness as a fantasy object weeks ago.

Outside, a dog barked nearby. Then a little later a car door slammed and an engine started up. After a while Gretchen listened to what sounded like the rattle of garbage cans; who puts out garbage in the middle of the night? Almost immediately the blare of a transistor radio jarred her nerves, accompanied as it was by loud voices talking and laughing, voices that gradually faded as the music-lovers passed on by. The dog barked again.

Gretchen slipped out of bed and felt her way across the dark room to the little desk. She switched on the lamp and rummaged through the lap drawer until she found what she was looking for: a pair of earplugs. She turned off the lamp.

Earplugs in place, she lay back down on her bed and tried again. It was times like these that she saw most clearly the *dis*advantages of being so sensitive.

Malcolm Conner couldn't sleep. He thought he'd heard a car a while ago, but Nicole hadn't come in.

He reached for the remote control and turned on the television. He sat up in bed for a long while, staring at the screen but not listening as a football coach talked about his buddyship with God. Malcolm couldn't stop replaying the scene at Uncle Vincent's in his head.

Legally, the old man had them; there were no loopholes in that promissory note. And as a result the two women who meant the most in the world to Malcolm were going to get hurt because of Vincent Farwell's vendetta against Lionel Knox. There had to be some way of stopping him.

Perhaps if Lionel could win Gretchen back and then she could win over Uncle Vincent—Malcolm knew that was foolish even as he thought it. The Knoxes' marriage had been in trouble for a long time. Also, Uncle Vincent made no secret of the fact that he considered his niece a birdbrain whose opinion was not worth consulting on any subject whatsoever.

Malcolm felt a sudden rush of pity for Gretchen Knox. His own brief affair with her had shown him what a basically focusless person she was. She didn't really have anything of her own. She had no talent, as Nicole and Dorrie did. She did no work, meaningful or otherwise. She had no money, except what her uncle or her husband gave her. She had no purpose, no place to go. And before long she wouldn't even have a marriage, unless something miraculous took place.

But Gretchen's problems were secondary; what happened to Ellandy Jewels was the only thing that mattered now. There had to be some way of stopping Uncle Vincent. Malcolm sat without moving, marshaling all his powers of concentration, seriously considering breaking the law for the first time in his life.

4

Godfrey Daniel stood on tiptoe and hissed at the dark-haired woman, a long and menacing hiss. When she ignored him, he tried growling instead.

"Hush, kitty," she said. Nicole Lattimer stood in Vincent Farwell's library in front of Vincent Farwell's desk. Staring at Vincent Farwell's body.

Uncle Vincent lay slumped across the desk, his head very efficiently bashed in. Blood discolored the desk blotter as well as the two parts of the broken alabaster Hermes. One piece of the statuette lay on the desk near Uncle Vincent's head; the other had fallen to the floor. A few inches from the fingertips of Uncle Vincent's outstretched right hand was an automatic pistol.

The fire had long since died out; the ashes in the fireplace gave off no hint of warmth. Nicole shivered. When she was absolutely positively certain that Uncle Vincent was dead, she moved around to his side of the desk. She couldn't find what she was looking for on top of the desk. After a moment's thought, she untied the scarf she was wearing around her waist and used it to open the desk drawers. A hurried search through all nine drawers proved fruitless; a second, more careful search was equally unproductive.

Distressed, Nicole looked around the room—and her eye fell on the file cabinet. Again using her scarf, she opened the top drawer and started going through Uncle Vincent's files. Godfrey Daniel leaped to the top of the cabinet and crouched there, watching the dark-haired woman's every move.

Stock reports, correspondence, bank records. Nicole worked her way through the second drawer and then the third without finding what she'd come for. She sat crouched on the floor by the bottom drawer for a moment, staring up at the tortoise-

shell cat watching her. Then she suddenly started beating her
fists against the file cabinet in frustration. Alarmed, Godfrey
jumped away.

Nicole used the scarf to wipe the part of the cabinet her fists
had touched. She stood up and hesitated. Then she went back
to the desk and very carefully wrapped both pieces of the
broken Hermes in her scarf, knotting the ends tightly. Once
more she hesitated; then, shuddering, she put down the scarf
and picked up Uncle Vincent's right hand. She managed to
get the dead man's stiffening fingers around the automatic
pistol and used his forefinger to press the trigger.

At the sound of the report, Godfrey shot under the sofa,
trembling all over. The bullet had gouged a shallow furrow
along the top of the desk before disappearing in the direction
of the fireplace. Nicole quickly picked up the scarf with its
incriminating contents, turned out the lights, and left the library, closing the door behind her just as the clock on the
mantelpiece struck two.

Simon and Dorrie Murdoch crept stealthily along the outside
of the terrace wall surrounding Vincent Farwell's house. Each
was dressed in black turtleneck sweater, black trousers, black
shoes and gloves. Dorrie wore a small backpack made of navy
blue nylon. She didn't have a black one.

"This is insane," Simon muttered.

"Ssh." Dorrie was looking for a good place to climb the wall.

"I don't know what's got into you, darling," Simon complained. "You come rushing in yelling that we've got to *do*
something, you drag me out of the shower, you make me dress
in this ridiculous outfit—"

"You're supposed to wear black when you break into someone's house. Everybody knows that."

"We'll go to *jail!*"

"No, we won't. Here." Dorrie had found the part of the wall
she wanted to climb; it looked no different from the rest of the
wall to Simon. "Give me a leg up," she commanded.

Simon locked his fingers together and held his hands for
Dorrie to step in. He flipped her up as high as he could, and
she scrambled to the top of the wall. "Now what?"

"Wait." She dropped down on the other side.

He waited. Before long a rope came sailing over the top of

the wall and dangled down on Simon's side. "I'm supposed to climb that, I assume," he muttered.

He managed it, although the rope began to slip a little just as he reached the top. He dropped down beside Dorrie and saw she'd tied the rope to the leg of a heavy wrought-iron bench. The streetlights caused the wall to cast a heavy shadow over about half the terrace, but beyond the shadow visibility was good. Dorrie picked up her backpack and started to creep along the outside of the house.

"Wait a minute," Simon stopped her. "Have you forgotten Uncle Vincent's alarm system? Exactly how do you plan to get in?"

"I thought of that." Dorrie opened the backpack and pulled something out.

Simon looked at the aerosol canister she'd handed him. "Redi-Whip?"

She nodded. "You know how on television burglars are always spraying the alarm box with a white foam—to shortcircuit the wires or whatever? All we have to do is find the box and give it a squirt."

Simon felt his head reeling. "I think that's shaving foam, darling."

"But you use an electric razor," she explained patiently. "Whipped cream was all we had. Come on—help me look for the box."

Two circuits of the house failed to turn up any conveniently located alarm box. The Murdochs ended up by the double doors leading to the library, their ultimate destination. Simon folded his arms and arched an eyebrow at his frustrated-looking wife. "What now, Madame Burglar?"

"Maybe the alarm isn't turned on. We could try the doors and see. If it is turned on, we just get out of here fast and try to think of something else."

"What if it's a silent alarm? The kind that's hooked up to the nearest police station?"

"But it's not, darling—remember the time Gretchen set it off by accident? Made one hell of a racket."

Simon remembered. "But before we try the doors—hold on." He put down the can of Redi-Whip and grabbed the edges of a rectangular wrought-iron table and, with much groaning and straining of muscles, carried it over and put it down flush against the wall. "In case we do have to make a quick getaway," he said.

"Darling, that's brilliant!" Dorrie beamed at him. "Do you think you can jimmy those doors open with a screwdriver? The backpack wasn't big enough to hold a crowbar."

"Let's try the doorknob first." Simon reached out and turned the knob; the door swung open easily. No alarm went off.

"Hallelujah!" Dorrie cried softly, and dipped into her backpack again. "Here—I brought one for each of us."

Simon took the flashlight she handed him. "Why don't we just turn on the lights?"

Dorrie was scandalized. "You *never* turn on the lights! The idea!"

"But with that wall blocking the view—"

"No. No lights. Absolutely not." Her voice was firm.

Simon shrugged and turned on his flashlight, pointing the beam downward. He stepped into the library, Dorrie close behind. He played his light over the Sultanabad carpet and was startled when two yellow eyes suddenly blinked at him in the light. "The cat's in here," he told Dorrie. "Don't step on him."

"Simon." Her voice was high and tight.

He looked to where her light was shining—and saw Uncle Vincent slumped over the desk in his own blood, grasping an automatic pistol in his right hand. "I think," Simon said slowly, "we had better turn the lights on."

"I'll do it." Uncle Vincent disappeared as Dorrie's light moved down to the carpet. She crossed the room and flipped the light switch. "My god," she said as Simon stepped up to the desk and bent over the corpse. "Is he . . . ?"

"He certainly is." Simon straightened up. "Most decidedly so."

Dorrie stared at the gun. "Did he shoot himself? Why would Uncle Vincent commit suicide?"

Simon wrinkled his nose fastidiously and bent again for a closer look. "Don't bullets make neat little round holes?"

"I think so. They ought to."

"Well, I don't see anything like that. It looks to me as if someone just hit him over the head with something."

Dorrie gathered up her courage and went to the desk to see for herself. "You're right—that's what it does look like."

"We'd better get out of here."

She put a hand on his arm. "Not yet. We came here to get that promissory note—now it's more important than ever. Do you want to take the desk or the file cabinet?"

Bravely, Simon chose the desk. Their search failed to turn up the ever-elusive promissory note; they even looked in the drawers of the two end tables in the room.

"You know what this means, don't you?" Dorrie asked, dropping down on the sofa. "Whoever killed Uncle Vincent took it."

"Dorrie, I think we should leave. Right now."

"Wait, Simon—let's think this through. It must have been Lionel, don't you think?"

"Or Nicole. She has almost as big a vested interest in Ellandy's as you and Lionel." Simon sat on the sofa beside his wife. "Lionel's the more likely one, though, I should think."

Dorrie nodded. "And if it's that obvious to us, it will be equally obvious to the police. What happens then?"

Simon spread his hands. "Then they lock him up for the rest of his life. If he were a mass murderer, he'd get off with six or seven years." Just then Godfrey Daniel jumped up into Simon's lap and dug in his claws before he could be pushed away. "Ow! Blasted animal." Simon tried unsuccessfully to disengage the claws, but Godfrey held on with determination; Simon gave up and accepted the situation. "Lionel will go to jail, and since a felon is not permitted to profit from his crime—I think that's the way that goes—the loan will be called in and—"

"Called in by whom?"

"By whoever is appointed executor of Uncle Vincent's estate, I should imagine."

"But how can the executor call in the loan if he doesn't have the promissory note?" Dorrie persisted. "Simon, Ellandy's just may be off the hook. I'll bet Lionel's already destroyed the note by now."

Simon shook his head. "How he hopes to get away with it, I'll never know."

Godfrey meowed harshly, tired of being ignored. Dorrie stretched out a hand and stroked the cat's back. "Yes, that's the difficulty, isn't it? If he *doesn't* get away with it, Ellandy's is doomed."

A suspicion began to dawn in Simon's mind. "Dorrie . . ."

"Look around you. Look at this room—everything in place. It doesn't look at all as if, say, an ordinary, everyday sort of burglary has taken place here, does it?"

Simon noticed she herself avoided looking in the direction of the desk. "Darling, if you have in mind what I think you have in mind—"

"Say we make this place look as if a burglar broke in and Uncle Vincent surprised him. Uncle Vincent managed to get his gun out of his desk drawer, but the burglar was too quick for him. He bashed Uncle Vincent on the head and then made his escape! How does that sound?"

"Dorrie, my love—are you absolutely certain you want to aid and abet a killer? Think about it."

Dorrie thought about it seriously for several minutes. "Yes," she said.

Simon's half-smile returned, the first time since they'd found Uncle Vincent in his defunct state. "And I suppose there's no chance of talking you out of it?"

"No chance in the world." She jumped up from the sofa. "Come on—let's do it."

"I will if this blasted cat lets me get up." Godfrey permitted it. Dorrie was already busy pulling out desk drawers and emptying the contents on the floor. "Wouldn't a burglar actually *take* something?" Simon asked.

"Oh—yes, he would, wouldn't he? Why don't you take that little jade horse? And that pearl inlay box on the end table. Whatever looks worth stealing." Dorrie gritted her teeth and awkwardly removed Uncle Vincent's expensive watch from his left wrist, needing to take off one glove to do so.

"What about the Degas?" Simon suggested.

Dorrie considered. "Too awkward. We have to carry all this stuff, you know." She put her glove back on.

"Billfold—I'll bet the old boy carried his billfold with him around the house." Simon went through the dead man's pockets and found the billfold. "Aha!"

"Don't forget the credit cards."

Simon removed the cash and the credit cards and dropped the billfold in a conspicuous place on the carpet. Godfrey Daniel immediately pounced on the billfold and started knocking it around the floor with his paws. "Leave that alone, you wretched

creature!" Simon hissed. "Do you want to spoil our evidence?"
He toed the billfold under the desk where the cat couldn't get
at it.

Dorrie threw a couple of the sofa cushions on the floor. "It
still doesn't look messed-up enough." She pulled open a file
drawer and started tossing papers up in the air. Godfrey loved
that; he stood on his hind legs and batted at the falling pages.
"Darling, shouldn't those terrace doors look as if they'd been
broken open?" Dorrie asked. "There's a screwdriver in the
backpack."

"I've got a better idea." Simon stepped out onto the terrace,
turned his head away, and thrust a gloved fist through the glass
panel nearest the doorknob.

The sound of breaking glass made both cat and woman start.
"Oh my—that did make a bit of noise, didn't it?" Dorrie caught
sight of a black, orange, and white tail twitching nervously
from beneath the sofa. "Do you suppose anyone heard?"

"We'd better leave—come on."

She glanced toward the mantelpiece. "What about that clock?
It's worth several thousand at least."

"Leave it—we've got more than we can carry now. Oh . . .
the lights. The lights were off when we got here."

Dorrie frowned. "Would a burglar who'd just killed a man
stop to turn off the lights?"

"You're right. Let's go." Simon went out on the terrace,
wondering how they were going to get all their loot over the
wall. "We'll have to toss this stuff over, I suppose, one piece
at a time. Or—wait a minute." The walled terrace encircled
only three-fourths of the house, leaving the front entrance
clear. At each end of the terrace was a metal gate—locked
from the outside only. "Darling, see if you can lift the latch
on that gate. My arms are full."

Dorrie managed to get the heavy gate open and held it while
Simon passed through. But when she tried to prop it open—
to make it appear as if the burglar had left in a rush—it swung
to behind her and fastened with a noisy click.

"Oh well," said Simon. "The police will figure that's what
happened to the burglar, too."

The latch on the library door clicked and the door itself
slowly began to inch open. Godfrey Daniel was instantly alert.

Malcolm Conner peered into the room, and grimaced at what he saw. He stepped inside and closed the door behind him. Malcolm stood quite still for a few moments, gazing in confusion at the glorious disarray around him. He took in the gaping file cabinet drawers, the papers scattered everywhere, the sofa cushions on the floor, the desk drawers pulled out and turned upside down.

Finally he focused his attention on Uncle Vincent. He crossed over to the desk and pulled Nicole's scarf out of his jacket pocket. Carefully he untied the knots; and using the scarf to handle each piece, he placed half the broken alabaster Hermes on the desk and the other half on the floor.

Malcolm stepped back to examine the effect. Satisfied, he stuffed the scarf back in his pocket and left, absent-mindedly switching off the lights as he went.

Bored, Godfrey went back to sleep.

The lights clicked on. Godfrey yawned and resettled himself, waiting patiently to see what this one was going to do.

Lionel Knox leaned against the closed library door, gazing in horror at the scene before him. "Jesus Christ," he muttered. Slipping off one glove, he quickly crossed to the desk and felt for a pulse in Uncle Vincent's left wrist. Finding none, he stood in a brown study for a while, barely aware of the cat rubbing against his leg.

Lionel put his glove back on. He hunkered down and picked up a piece of paper from the floor and glanced at it. He dropped it, picked up another. Godfrey leaped to the back of the sofa, catching Lionel's eye. "What happened here, Godfrey?" he asked. The cat blinked at him.

Methodically Lionel started working his way through every piece of paper in the room. He'd look at each one only long enough to see what it was and then go on to the next. The job took him nearly half an hour, and when he finished he still didn't have what he was looking for.

Lionel sat on the floor thinking, his forearms resting on his knees. Godfrey trotted up between the man's knees and raised his head to be petted; Lionel obliged. "I think I know what happened," he told the cat.

With a new sense of purpose, Lionel got up and went around

behind the desk. Gritting his teeth, he took hold of Uncle Vincent's shoulders and pulled him back so that the dead man was sitting more or less upright in the wheelchair. Lionel grasped the chair's handgrips and wheeled Uncle Vincent out to the middle of the room. There he unceremoniously dumped the corpse on the floor. "Sorry, Uncle Vincent," Lionel muttered. "It's necessary." He fetched the automatic from the desk and shoved it under Uncle Vincent's body.

He went back to the desk again and picked up the blood-stained blotter—and caught sight of the manila folder that had been underneath. *Bernstein, Paul*, the tab read in Uncle Vincent's spidery handwriting—the private investigator's report. Lionel read through the typewritten report and glanced again at the revealing photographs that accompanied it. He took both the folder and the blotter to the fireplace where he put a match to them; soon both pieces of evidence were going up in flames. Lionel stepped backward away from the fire—and trod on Godfrey Daniel's tail.

The cat let out a scream to wake the dead; Lionel jumped a foot and Godfrey scooted to safety. Lionel's mouth had turned dry; someone must have heard that godawful noise. He looked around the room hastily, thinking there was something else that needed to be done. But the cat's cry had disconcerted him; he couldn't concentrate. When he felt he couldn't safely linger any longer, he switched off the lights and opened the library door a crack.

And heard someone coming down the hall stairway.

Lionel quickly shut the door again, and—because he couldn't think in the dark—switched the lights back on. A small black-white-orange face watched him anxiously from under the sofa. There was only one other way out of the library. Lionel raced across the room—jumping over Uncle Vincent—and pushed open the double doors.

The first thing he saw on the terrace was the wrought-iron table shoved up against the wall. He leaped up on the table and vaulted to the top of the wall—no mean feat for a man so unathletically disposed as Lionel Knox. He dropped down on the other side of the wall, twisting an ankle as he fell.

The first light of dawn was beginning to show as Lionel got up and limped painfully away.

* * *

Gretchen Knox was walking down the hallway from the bath-room when she heard the scream. She'd only just removed her earplugs after several hours of blissful silence, and the sudden noise unnerved her.

The cat, she thought, *it must be the cat*. But the scream had had an almost human sound to it; and even if it were Godfrey Daniel, why would he let out a yowl like that unless something had happened to him?

Gretchen knew she wouldn't get back to sleep without find-ing out; it was almost morning anyway. She went down the stairs, calling the cat. A faint answering *meow* sounded from the library.

She opened the library door, and a black, white, and orange blur streaked out past her. But Gretchen didn't notice; she stood transfixed by the sight of the dead body lying in the middle of the floor. *What on earth?* She came out of her shock and hurried over to the corpse; one touch was all she needed to tell her he was thoroughly dead. "Oh, damn it, Uncle Vin-cent!" she said crossly.

Her first instinct was to go back and shut the library door. "Now why did I do that?" she murmured. To give herself time to think, obviously. She picked up one of the sofa cushions from the floor, put it on the sofa, and sat down. For the first time she took in fully the utter mess the room was in. She sat there scowling, trying to figure out what it all meant.

She looked over the room carefully, foot by foot. Gradually the scowl lines began to disappear from her face. Then she was almost smiling. Then she *was* smiling. She jumped up and started gathering the papers up from the floor, thrusting them any which way into the file folders. When she had all the papers collected, she put the folders back into the file cabinet.

Next she replaced the other sofa cushions. She closed the double doors leading to the terrace, being careful of the broken glass. Then she put the desk drawers back, filling each one with the pens and paper clips and other paraphernalia that had been dumped on the floor. That done, she stood in the middle of the room and examined it again—and noticed a few things missing. She ran out of the room and came back a few min-utes later carrying an ivory owl, a Donovan ironstone vase, an eighteenth-century music box, a small silver luster jug, and a brown and white sardonyx ashtray. These items she placed at appropriate places around the room.

Once again she surveyed the room. At last she gave a satisfied little nod and left the library, turning out the lights and closing the door behind her. She started up the stairs and then changed her mind and used Uncle Vincent's elevator instead. She'd just reached her own door on the second floor when the alarm clock went off in Mrs. Polk's room on the floor above.

Barney wasn't in his room. *How vexing!* Mrs. Polk thought. Just when she needed him the most!

She searched the house quietly, not wanting to wake Miss Gretchen. She found the manservant in the kitchen, asleep on one of the breakfast nook benches—shameful! Mrs. Polk shook his shoulder, rather roughly. "Barney! Wake up!" she hissed. "Do you hear me, Barney? Wake up!"

Bjarne Pedersen fought his way up out of a Valium-and-alcohol stupor. He was vaguely aware of Mrs. Polk's high voice calling him from a long distance away. He felt hands tugging at him, forcing him into an upright position.

Then the hands and the voice went away, and Bjarne's head drooped forward on his chest. But not for long; after what seemed only a second or two the hands and the voice were back, and with them the smell of coffee. He managed to get one eye open enough to see Mrs. Polk's anxious face peering into his.

"Drink the coffee, Barney!" Mrs. Polk urged him. "Something terrible has happened and I need you!" When he made no move to take the cup, she held it up to his lips. "Hurry, Barney! There's not much time! Miss Gretchen will be waking up any minute now!"

A tea-drinker by preference, Bjarne had to down two cups of the noxious stuff before Mrs. Polk would tell him what the "terrible" thing was that had happened. And when she did tell him, it was terrible indeed. Now shocked fully awake, Bjarne lurched to his feet and stumbled after the housekeeper to the library.

There it was—the thing he'd feared the most. Mr. Vincent lay sprawled on the floor, head bloodied and ugly, as dead as they come. All Bjarne's fears about his future came rushing to the front, and he had to squeeze back the tears. When he could speak, he said only one word. "Police?"

"I haven't called them yet," Mrs. Polk said tightly. "There's something I want you to do first. It's not decent to leave him there like that—contemptuous, somehow. He should be behind his desk, where he belongs. Pick him up, Barney."

A phrase from a thousand television shows floated into Bjarne's head. "Isn't that, uh, tampering with the evidence?"

"I don't care," Mrs. Polk said rigidly. "I don't want anyone to see him like that. And what difference could it make anyway? He's just as dead either place."

Bjarne wasn't up to arguing with her. Besides, in a way she was right; there was something obscene about leaving Mr. Vincent sprawled out like that. Bjarne found no pleasure in seeing a once-powerful man brought low. He stooped down and wrestled the dead man back into the wheelchair.

Mrs. Polk gasped. "Look!" She pointed to the automatic pistol on the floor. "That must be the gun that killed him! It looks like Mr. Vincent's gun, doesn't it?"

It did. But the wound on Mr. Vincent's head didn't look like a gunshot wound to Bjarne—not that he had all that much experience with bullets and the kinds of holes they made. "Better bring it along," he told Mrs. Polk.

Bjarne wheeled the body to behind the desk; when he stopped the chair, Mr. Vincent slumped forward across the desk top, his right arm extending stiffly out to the side. Mrs. Polk approached, gingerly carrying the automatic by the barrel between thumb and forefinger. She placed the gun on the desk top just a few inches beyond Mr. Vincent's outstretched right hand.

"You left your fingerprints," Bjarne said, and wiped the barrel clean with his handkerchief.

Mrs. Polk sighed. "Now we're ready to call the police," she said.

5

A *good old house*, Lieutenant Frederick Toomey thought. Well maintained, not cuted up by restorers and the like. Toomey puffed his way up the front steps. He was a shortish man who grew a little rounder every year; he'd bought his last suit one size too large in the mistaken notion that others would think he'd recently lost weight. His protruding eyes were heavily lidded and his lank hair had never once been blown dry. He did not cut a dashing figure. The uniformed officer stationed at the door nodded him in.

The inside of the house was even better. Furnishings that were solid and expensive without being ostentatious. Paneled walls and high ceilings. The kind of place Lieutenant Toomey wanted to own himself someday, but knew he never would. He followed the sound of voices to the library.

The crime lab boys were there, and Dr. Oringer from the medical examiner's office. Lieutenant Toomey's captain had told him a detective was already at the site, and Toomey groaned when he saw it was Sal Rizzuto. Rizzuto wasn't a bad cop, but he had one habit that drove Lieutenant Toomey wild. He deliberately spoke bad English; he thought it made him sound cool, man. Street-wise.

Avoiding Sergeant Rizzuto for the moment, Toomey headed toward Dr. Oringer. "Hello, Doc. What can you tell me?"

"Morning, Fred. Well, he was killed by a blow on the head, struck from the front—looks as if the murder weapon's that broken statuette over there. Position of the wound indicates a right-handed killer. Time of death—midnight or before."

"Midnight or before? Can't you pin it down more than that?"

Dr. Oringer gestured toward the fireplace. "Tell me what time that fire went out and I can. You know how an overheated room delays the onset of rigor. When it wears off I can run some tests and tell you more."

The only thing Toomey knew about the victim was his name. He took a quick look at the corpse before it was zipped up into the body bag. "How old was he, would you say?"

"Late seventies. He was paralyzed from the waist down. The housekeeper says stroke."

Toomey had noticed the wheelchair. And now it was going to be up to him to catch the big, brave soul who'd struck down a helpless invalid.

Dr. Oringer left with the body. Sal Rizzuto strutted over, an open notebook in his hand, working hard at appearing blasé. "Mornin', Lieutenant," he said casually, as if he started every day with a murder investigation. "Looks like the victim surprised a burglar in the act. Fairly cut-and-dried. Farwell pulled a gun but the thief got the jump on 'im—conked 'im with that there statuette on the desk."

The top of the desk held both pieces of the broken statuette in separate plastic bags as well as Vincent Farwell's gun, similarly encased in plastic. A tape outline marked the position where the upper half of the body had lain. Toomey noticed the gouge mark the bullet had made along the surface. "Must have been a pretty hard blow to break that statuette," he remarked.

"Naw, that stuff's alabaster," Rizzuto said surprisingly. "Carves easy, breaks easy. Prolly wouldna killed a younger man."

Toomey raised a mental eyebrow and said, "I wonder if our killer knew that. But he might not have had time to think—just grabbed the nearest thing that looked like a weapon and struck out. What else have you got?"

"Farwell's billfold under the desk—cash and credit cards missin'. Marks of a stretch band on the victim's left wrist—watch was taken. Might be other things gone, too. The housekeeper was too strung out to talk when I got here. Her and the valet or butler or whatever he is, they're in the kitchen."

Toomey nodded, staring at the painting on the wall. "Wonder why he didn't take the Degas?"

Rizzuto shrugged. "Must be a copy."

"Or that music box on the end table? That's got to be worth a nice piece of change."

"He just got spooked and took off after he killed the old guy. He was interrupted, like."

"He wasn't too spooked to stop and take the victim's watch and clean out his billfold."

"Yeah, thass right. Well, maybe he dint think the box was worth nothin'. Look, we found a coupla other things." Rizzuto went over to one of the men from the crime lab and came back with three plastic bags. "This here's a page from a letter. It was underneath the sofa."

Toomey took the plastic bag and read the first page of a letter to Vincent Farwell from his insurance agent. Farwell had evidently inquired about increased coverage for his household goods, and the letter was a response explaining terms. "What are these little prick marks up in the corner?"

"Huh." Rizzuto peered closer. "They look like pinholes."

Toomey pursed his lips. "Some of my album covers at home have little holes in them just like those. Is there a cat in this house?"

The other man shrugged. "I dunno." He handed Toomey another plastic bag. "Here's somethin' else."

Toomey read the name on the instrument inside: *Infralux.* "What is it?"

"An appliance."

"I can see it's an appliance, Rizzuto. What's it for?"

"Beats me. It was on the floor behind that leather chair. But there ain't no outlet in that wall there."

"Mm. A piece of paper under the sofa. An appliance out of place. Sloppy housekeeping? What's in that last bag?"

"The bullet. Thirty-eight caliber, looks like, same as Farwell's gun. You can see where the bullet hit the desk and changed trajectory so it went off toward the fireplace, where it got deflected to over there behind the sofa."

"Interesting. He would have had to be pointing the gun almost parallel to the desk top when he fired—and only slightly downward. Rizzuto, bring me a chair." Toomey sat down behind the desk on the chair the Sergeant brought. "You're the killer—stand in front of the desk. Okay, now come at me."

Rizzuto pantomimed grabbing something from the desk and raising it over his head to deliver a blow, while Toomey jerked open a desk drawer and pulled out a pencil he pointed toward the Sergeant. At no time was his hand aiming along the direction of the furrow made by the bullet.

"He musta put the gun down," Rizzuto said. "Without lettin' go of it, I mean."

"Which would suggest he knew his killer. Another possibility is that he fired the gun spasmodically after he'd already been hit and slumped forward. Didn't anybody hear the shot? How many people in the house?"

"Three. Farwell's niece, name of Gretchen Knox—she's up in her room. And the housekeeper and the valet."

"Which one found him?"

"The housekeeper. Mrs. Polk."

"Then I'll talk to her first. Unless there's something else?"

"Matter of fact there is. All sorts of goodies, out on the terrace. A table with a scrape mark on the top, a rope thrown over the wall, and," Rizzuto grinned, "a can of Redi-Whip."

"*Redi-Whip?*"

"Yeah, you know, that whipped cream that comes in aerosol cans? There's a can of it sittin' on the terrace floor, right outside those double doors there."

"I know what Redi-Whip is," Toomey said grumpily. "What's it doing out on the terrace?"

Just then one of the men from the crime lab called out, "Everything's dusted, Lieutenant. Go ahead and touch." Toomey waved a thank-you as the men packed up their gear and left.

Rizzuto was standing by the terrace doors. "Here's how he got in," he said, pointing to the broken glass.

Toomey walked over and looked at the door. "The bolts weren't shot?" He pointed to the two inside bolts, one at the top of the door and the other at the bottom. He tried the door knob, which turned easily. "Wasn't the door locked?"

Rizzuto scowled. "Musta been. That little lock-button in the middle of the knob woulda popped out when he reached through from outside and turned it."

"But how did he pull back the bolts? You can't reach either one from the broken pane. Try it."

Rizzuto thrust an arm through the hole left by the broken glass and stretched first upward and then downward. He couldn't touch either bolt. "The old man musta forgot to shoot the bolts. Or the housekeeper."

"Curious," Toomey murmured.

Rizzuto pointed to the can of Redi-Whip sitting on the terrace floor. "No prints, they said. Just smears."

Toomey picked up the can and gave it a vigorous shake before squirting a little cream out on his finger. It tasted all right.

"The crime lab guys dint see no reason to take it in," Rizzuto explained.

Toomey nodded and slipped the can into his jacket pocket, heartily wishing the Sergeant would realize Vincent Farwell's house was not an appropriate setting for make-believe street talk. "Is this the table you meant?" The wrought-iron table had been painted white, and right in the middle of the top was a scuffed place—made by the foot of a man in a hurry to get away?

"He came in over the wall by the rope around to the side of the house," Rizzuto said, "but he went out this way, by jumpin' up on the table."

"Losing his Redi-Whip in the process," Toomey murmured. "Show me this rope."

Sergeant Rizzuto led him along the terrace to the west side of the house, where he pointed to the rope tied to a leg of a wrought-iron bench.

Toomey grunted. "So there were two of them." Rizzuto looked blank. "The rope's hanging down on the outside. One guy alone wouldn't climb the wall and then toss the rope over for himself, now, would he? There had to be two. One boosted the other over, and that one fixed the rope." Toomey was annoyed; Rizzuto should have spotted something that obvious. "Why'd the crime lab boys leave the rope?"

"For you to see," Rizzuto said a touch sullenly. "They cut off a piece to check, but they said it looked like common manufacture."

Toomey started back toward the library but paused before going in. "That's a funny place to keep a table, isn't it? Right outside these doors, shoved up against the wall like that?" He bent over to inspect the concrete floor of the terrace and soon found what he was looking for. "Look here—scratch marks. Four of them. This is where the table usually sits."

Rizzuto shrugged. "So he moved the table to climb over the wall. *They* moved it," he corrected himself.

"Let's try it."

Toomey grunted as they picked up the heavy table and

carried it to its original position; Rizzuto, both younger and stronger, had no trouble with it. "Now back," Toomey said. He grunted again as they put it back against the wall where they'd found it.

Toomey pulled out a handkerchief and patted his forehead. "Not exactly a speedy maneuver, would you say?" he commented. "If they were in such an all-fired hurry to get away, why'd they stop to move this heavy table? It would have been quicker to use the rope." Toomey looked around. "Or," he said, walking to the metal gate at the end of the terrace, "why not just go out this way?" The latch lifted easily to his touch.

"Maybe they dint know about the gate. Maybe it was too dark to see. Maybe they just got rattled."

"Maybe," Toomey said noncommittally.

"Aw, hell!" Rizzuto exclaimed. "I forgot to tell you. Somethin' was burned in the fireplace not too long ago. They found a piece of blotter."

"Blotter? Like a desk blotter?"

"Yeah, that's what it looked like. It'll be in the lab report."

Toomey mulled that one over as he walked back inside. "Now why would the killer stop and burn the desk blotter? Did Farwell write something on it—a name, a telephone number? Could he have known his killer?"

"Maybe Farwell burned it himself. Or the housekeeper—when she was puttin' out a new one."

"That's possible," Toomey admitted. "I'll talk to the housekeeper now. Bring her in here, will you, please?"

Sergeant Rizzuto left and returned in a few minutes with a neatly dressed, fiftyish woman with faded blond hair. "Mrs. Dorothy Polk," Rizzuto said.

"Mrs. Polk, I'm Lieutenant Toomey," he said, wishing Rizzuto would learn to complete his introductions. He offered his condolences, seated her in a chair, and pulled up another chair for himself. Under Toomey's gentle questioning, she related how she had come into the library to straighten up from last night, turned on the lights, and found Vincent Farwell dead at his desk.

"The lights were off when you went in?"

"Yes, I couldn't see very well. This side of the house doesn't get the sun until afternoon." She told how she'd called the police and then wakened the other two in the house.

"That would be Mr. Farwell's niece, Gretchen Knox? And . . . ?"

"Barney, Mr. Vincent's manservant. Barney Peterson."

"Mrs. Polk, did you lock the library doors last night?"

"That's Barney's job. Every night he checks the windows and doors, and turns on the security alarm."

"Security alarm? Was it turned on last night?"

Mrs. Polk looked uneasy. "I don't know, Lieutenant. Barney . . . well, Barney's been known to take a drink or two. And he wasn't in his room when I went looking for him this morning. I found him asleep in the breakfast nook, in the kitchen. In his clothes! He hadn't been to bed at all."

"So he might not have locked up and turned on the alarm? Hm. Mrs. Polk, Mr. Farwell fired his gun last night. Didn't you hear the shot?"

She shook her head. "My room's on the third floor of the house, way at the back. I can't hear anything back there, not even street noises."

"I see. Did Mr. Farwell always keep a gun in his desk?"

"Yes, sir. And another one in the table beside his bed."

"What floor is Mr. Farwell's room on?"

"The second."

"And Barney's?"

"His room is right next to Mr. Vincent's—in case Mr. Vincent needed him during the night, you know. Miss Gretchen's room is on the second floor too. I'm the only one on the third."

"What time did you go to your room last night?"

"Right after I served the drinks to Mr. Vincent's guests. It must have been before eight-thirty. I remember I had a little while to wait before a nine o'clock show I wanted to watch came on."

Toomey had perked up at the word "guests". When asked, the housekeeper gave them the names of the visitors who had been there the night before, all six of them. Rizzuto wrote the names in his notebook.

"You included Gretchen Knox," Toomey said. "Doesn't she live here?"

Mrs. Polk smiled. "Oh, no sir. She and Mr. Lionel have a lovely house of their own. Mr. Vincent gave it to them as a wedding present."

"But she decided to stay here last night? Without her husband? Why?"

"I'm sure I don't know, sir," she said primly.

Very proper, Toomey thought. "Mrs. Polk, do you take care of this great big house all by yourself?"

"I have day help. But Barney and I are the only ones who live here."

Toomey nodded. "When was the last time the library was cleaned?"

"Yesterday. I cleaned it myself. So it would look nice for the guests, you know."

Toomey couldn't think of any tactful way to ask his next question. "Did you clean under the sofa?"

"Of course." Mrs. Polk looked mildly insulted. "Barney moved the sofa for me and then moved it back when I was finished."

"I ask because we found a sheet of paper there. The first page of a letter."

"Well, it wasn't there when I finished cleaning!" she said firmly, and both the policemen believed her.

Rizzuto cleared his throat. At Toomey's nod, he asked, "Do you know what an Infralux is, Mrs. Polk?"

"Why, it's one of those things for Mr. Vincent's arthritis. We keep one in every room."

"There was one on the floor over there in the corner," Rizzuto said.

The housekeeper looked surprised. "What was it doing there? It belongs in the desk." Just then a black, white, and orange cat trotted into the room and positioned himself in front of Lieutenant Toomey, eyeing him suspiciously. "That's Godfrey Daniel," Mrs. Polk said. "Mr. Vincent spoiled him rotten."

Toomey patted his knee. "Here, kitty!" Godfrey majestically turned his back and sat down. The Lieutenant sighed and picked up the questioning where he'd left off. "When you cleaned, did you take a blotter off the desk?"

"No, sir—it didn't need changing." She glanced over at the desk and saw the bare top. "Why, it's gone!"

"When you do change blotters, what do you do with the old one? Do you burn it?"

She gave Toomey a *what-a-crazy-idea* look and said, "No, I throw it out with the rest of the trash."

Toomey let the question of the blotter go, and asked the housekeeper whether there was a safe in the room somewhere.

"Not in here," she said, "but there's one in Mr. Vincent's bedroom."

"Why his bedroom? Why not right here where he worked?"

"Oh, that wall safe upstairs was put in a long time ago—before Mr. Vincent had his stroke. He was still going out to his office every day then. It's only since his stroke that he started using this room so much."

Toomey nodded. "Does the safe have a combination lock?"

"Yes, but I can't open it for you, if that's what you want."

"Who can?"

Mrs. Polk looked puzzled. "Why, I don't know—I suppose Miss Gretchen might."

Abruptly Toomey reached in his pocket and pulled out the can of Redi-Whip. "Yours?"

Her eyebrows rose. "No. We don't have any whipped cream in the house."

"You're sure?"

"Of course I'm sure," Mrs. Polk said, getting a little tired of all the questions. "Mr. Vincent can't—*couldn't* eat rich foods, and Barney doesn't like sweets, and, well, I'm trying to watch my weight. There's no whipped cream in this house. What's that owl doing in here?"

"Pardon?"

"That owl. It's supposed to be in the dining room." She got up and walked over to the end table where an ivory owl rested. "And that music box—it should be in the living room. And where's the jade horse?" She looked around, examining the room closely. "Why, this isn't right—this isn't right at all!"

"What isn't right, Mrs. Polk?"

She explained that certain objects that were supposed to be in the room were missing, and other objects from other rooms of the house had mysteriously taken their place. Toomey asked her to check in the other rooms for the missing objects, in case someone had just swapped them around. "Before you leave—is there anything else out of place that you can see? Any little thing at all?"

Mrs. Polk pressed her lips together. "Lieutenant, there's one very big thing out of place. I don't know if it means anything . . . but Mr. Vincent's elevator was at the second floor when I got up this morning. Just where it is every morning."

Neither Toomey nor Rizzuto got the point.

"Don't you see?" the housekeeper said. "The elevator was on the second floor, but Mr. Vincent was still on the first floor. Right there." She gestured awkwardly at the desk. "It's a house rule that the elevator always stays on the same floor where Mr. Vincent is."

"I see," Toomey said. "You had walked up to the third floor, and Barney Peterson evidently spent the night in the breakfast nook. That leaves Mrs. Knox."

Mrs. Polk shook her head. "Miss Gretchen knows the rule. She never used Mr. Vincent's elevator. Lieutenant, if you're finished with me, I'll go look for the jade horse and the other things. This doesn't make any sense."

Toomey agreed that it didn't, and thanked her for her help. When she'd gone, he turned to Rizzuto and said, "Curiouser and curiouser." He sat down heavily on the sofa. Godfrey Daniel, who by now had decided that Lieutenant Toomey was acceptable, jumped up beside him and allowed himself to be stroked. "Were you in here last night, kitty?" Toomey asked. "What did you see?"

"Meow," said Godfrey.

"That's what I thought," Toomey sighed. "Rizzuto—anything?"

"Well, aside from the knick-knacks Mrs. Polk is lookin' for, I s'pose the blotter. Maybe the old man did have somethin' written on it."

"There was something else on it. Blood. Look at that desk —not a drop of blood anywhere. The gash in Farwell's head was a nasty one. So where's the blood?"

Rizzuto stared at him. "That's crazy, Lieutenant. Why'd anyone get rid of the blood but leave the body?"

"Why indeed," Toomey murmured. "Then there's the interesting fact of the elevator's ending up on the wrong floor."

"That don't mean nothin'," Rizzuto said dismissively. "One of the visitors coulda taken it up last night. To use the bathroom, maybe."

"I wonder why Mrs. Polk called the police before she woke up the other two. You'd think she'd tell the niece first, wouldn't you? We might as well see the niece now."

Gretchen Knox turned out to be a tall woman in her early thirties with shoulder-length reddish-orange hair. A pleasant face, Toomey thought, marred by a rather pouty mouth. She wore pearls just about every place it was possible to wear pearls. Toomey observed the amenities, noticing she was nervous but not particularly grief-stricken. "Were you close to your uncle?" he asked.

"I lived with him for ten years," Gretchen said.

Translation: No, Toomey thought; she wouldn't have avoided a direct answer if they'd been close. "Mrs. Knox, let me get a few business matters out of the way first. Do you inherit Mr. Farwell's estate?"

"Yes, I do," she said. "I never saw any will or anything, but Uncle Vincent told me I was his heir."

"Who was Mr. Farwell's attorney?"

"Mr. Dann. Richard Dann—he's in the Crafton Building." Sergeant Rizzuto wrote down the name and address in his notebook.

Toomey said, "Mrs. Polk told us there's a safe in your uncle's bedroom. Do you have the combination?"

"Oh—I'd forgotten about that safe. No, Uncle Vincent never told me the combination."

"Does anybody know it?"

"Well, Mr. Dann might. The attorney." Godfrey Daniel jumped up in her lap; Gretchen began to stroke him in an absentminded way. Toomey noticed her hair was almost the same shade as the orange part of the cat's fur.

"All right, now I want to ask you about last night," Toomey said. "You know your uncle fired his gun, don't you? Didn't you hear the shot?"

Gretchen made a vague gesture with her hands. "I was wearing earplugs, Lieutenant. I'm very sensitive to noise, and the night sounds were making me nervous. I couldn't hear anything once I put the earplugs in."

"What time was that?"

"Oh, it was early—I didn't look at my watch, but it must have been before eleven."

Rizzuto cleared his throat again, asking for permission to interrupt. "Mrs. Knox, that Degas on the wall—it's a copy, right?"

"It certainly is not! It's an original. Why do you ask?"

"An original Degas—and a burglar leaves it behind?"

"Maybe he didn't know anything about art. Then you think it was a burglar who killed Uncle Vincent?"

Toomey said, "We don't know for certain. But a few things seem to be missing from the room, and your uncle's money, credit cards, and wristwatch were taken."

Her surprise was genuine, and perhaps greater than might have been expected. "I didn't know that," she said faintly.

"You stayed here last night instead of going to your own home. Do you mind telling me why?"

It was obvious that she did. "I . . . my husband and I had a disagreement last night. It's a personal matter, Lieutenant, and I really don't want to talk about it."

Toomey started to pursue it but then changed his mind and asked her if she knew why the elevator was on the second floor.

"Why shouldn't it be on the second floor?"

"How did it get there?" Toomey asked. "Your uncle certainly didn't take it up. Who did? You?"

A change came over her that was obvious to both policemen. She tensed up, clasping her hands so tightly around the cat in her lap that he wriggled free and jumped to the floor in annoyance. *My, my,* Toomey thought, *is the lady on the verge of telling an untruth?* Gretchen's voice was a full octave higher when she spoke. "No, I never use the elevator. I don't know how it got up there."

"Perhaps one of the guests last night took it up?"

"Perhaps . . . I don't know . . . yes, that must be what happened."

"Why was everyone here last night, Mrs. Knox? It couldn't have been a social evening. Mrs. Polk evidently served only one round of drinks and then went to her room. What was going on?"

Gretchen hesitated. "It was a business meeting. It didn't last very long."

"How long?"

"Less than an hour, I'd say."

"What kind of business did you talk about?"

"My husband's jewelry business. His and Dorrie Murdoch's —they're partners. Ellandy Jewels."

"Spell it?" Rizzuto asked, pencil poised.

She spelled it. "For Lionel and Dorrie, ell and dee."

Rizzuto grimaced. "Okay—you and your husband Lionel. Dorrie Murdoch and her husband Simon. Who are these other two people—Nicole Lattimer and Malcolm Conner?"

"Nicole is a designer at Ellandy's—they may make her a partner, if she gets her way. She usually does," Gretchen explained a touch waspishly. "Malcolm Conner is Ellandy's attorney. He's also Dorrie's brother."

Toomey asked, "What did your uncle have to do with Ellandy Jewels?"

"He lent them money."

It was like squeezing water from a stone. "What about this loan, Mrs. Knox? What needed discussing?"

Again that vague gesture with the hands. "I don't know whether I should talk about business matters—"

Just then a door slammed and a voice called out, "Gretchen! Gretchen—where are you?"

She rose quickly to her feet. "In the library!" she called back.

Lionel Knox appeared in the doorway—a large man, harried-looking, walking with a limp. Lionel took a tentative step toward his wife, and then she resolved his doubts by running into his arms. Gretchen buried her head in Lionel's shoulder and let loose a flood of tears she hadn't even known needed shedding.

But Lieutenant Toomey wasn't watching the touching reunion. His full attention was on Godfrey Daniel—who was standing with his back arched, hair on end, hissing and spitting like a jungle tiger ready to fight to the death.

6

"It's a hell of a thing to happen," Lionel Knox was telling Lieutenant Toomey earnestly. He and Gretchen were seated together on the sofa, the very picture of a happily reconciled couple. "When Gretchen called and told me, I had trouble believing it. Was it a burglar who killed him?"

"Possibly," Toomey said. "There are a few questions that still need answering before we'll know. Mrs. Knox, I know seeing your uncle like that this morning must have been distressing, but did you notice anything missing from this room?"

"I didn't see my uncle this morning," Gretchen said. "Polka Dot wouldn't let me come in."

"Polka Dot?" Rizzuto asked.

"Mrs. Polk, the housekeeper. Her first name's Dorothy. She told me I didn't want to see—and I wasn't much inclined to argue with her."

"Yeah, she likes to take care of things her own way," Lionel said. "She's already been hard at work even today."

"What's that?" Toomey asked.

"Oh, I just meant she's already cleaned this room—in spite of what's happened."

"Mrs. Polk hasn't cleaned in here yet. What made you think she had?"

Lionel had the look of a man who's just realized he's made a mistake, while Gretchen started nervously twisting her fingers and trying not to look at her husband. Lionel looked desperately around the room for a liferaft; *Here comes a whopper*, Toomey thought. "The glasses," Lionel said in a rush. "We all had drinks last night and now the glasses are gone. I thought Mrs. Polk had cleared them away."

"The men from the crime lab took them," Rizzuto said.

Toomey looked daggers at his subordinate; Rizzuto had said

nothing about glasses. Just then Godfrey Daniel jumped up in Toomey's lap, still bristling at Lionel. "This cat doesn't seem to like you, Mr. Knox," the Lieutenant said.

Gretchen waved a hand dismissively. "Godfrey will spit at you one minute and then come beg to be petted the next. You never know what mood he's going to be in."

Toomey placed a calming hand on the cat's back and said, "Mr. Knox, now that you're here, suppose you tell me about this loan for Ellandy's you were all meeting about last night."

Lionel took his time answering. "Uncle Vincent had already made us the loan," he said slowly. "We were asking him for an extension, for more time to repay."

"Did he agree?"

Lionel licked his lips and shifted his weight edgily. Instead of answering, he glanced at his wife.

"He didn't decide," she said suddenly.

"That's right," Lionel said with relief. "He just put us off."

"Mm. What time did the meeting break up?"

"Oh, I don't know—around nine, I think," Lionel said. Gretchen nodded.

"Was the fire burning when you left?"

They both stared at him blankly. "It was burning when we got here," Lionel said. "I remember Uncle Vincent told me to move, I was blocking the fire. I guess it was still burning when we left."

"I don't remember," Gretchen said. "Is it important?"

"If the room was overheated," Toomey explained, "the onset of rigor mortis would have been delayed. I'm sorry to have to say this," he added quickly, noting Gretchen's look of distress, "but it's necessary. Since your uncle's desk is so close to the fireplace, the heat would have made a difference."

They both looked confused. "What does the desk have to do with it?" Lionel asked.

Toomey reminded himself that neither one of them had seen the corpse. "That's where he died. At the desk."

"*At the desk?*" both Knoxes said, astonished.

"At the desk," Toomey repeated, astonished at their astonishment. "The body was found slumped forward on the desk top. Why? Did you expect it to be found somewhere else?"

Gretchen shook her head vigorously while Lionel hemmed and hawed, "Uh, no, Lieutenant, not at all."

"Where did you expect the body to be?" Toomey persisted.

"Nowhere in particular," Gretchen said in a high voice.

"It was just a surprise," Lionel said, "finding out *where*. I hadn't had time to think about that part of it, I guess. It's hard to imagine Uncle Vincent just sitting there quietly at his desk and letting himself be killed."

"Yes, that's it!" Gretchen said eagerly.

Toomey and Rizzuto exchanged a look. "You think he would have fought back?" Toomey asked the Knoxes. "A man in a wheelchair?"

"He would have done *something*," Gretchen said, her voice gradually coming back down to normal.

"He did do something," Toomey said. "He pulled a gun on whoever was threatening him. He just wasn't fast enough."

"Oh, poor Uncle Vincent!" Gretchen wailed.

At that moment Mrs. Polk appeared in the doorway. "Excuse me for interrupting, Lieutenant, but I can't find the missing things anywhere. The things that are in here belong in other places."

"Just leave them where they are for the time being, Mrs. Polk," Toomey said, "and thank you."

The housekeeper gestured toward the double doors leading to the terrace. "Are you finished examining that broken glass, Lieutenant? Would it be all right if I called a glazier to come replace it?"

Toomey, who hadn't examined the broken glass at all, told her it would be all right. Mrs. Polk gave Gretchen an encouraging smile while ignoring Lionel altogether and left.

"What missing things?" Lionel asked.

"A few *objets d'art* that should be in this room but aren't. A jade horse, for one thing."

"Then it was a burglar!"

Toomey made a noncommittal noise and pulled out his can of Redi-Whip. "Ever see this before?"

Gretchen blinked. "I've seen Redi-Whip before, yes."

"Anything special about that can?" Lionel asked.

"We found it out on the terrace—right outside the doors."

"Funny place to keep whipped cream," Lionel shrugged. Neither of them seemed particularly interested.

Toomey tried a different tack. "Mr. Knox, did anybody use the elevator while you were here last night?"

"Uncle Vincent's elevator?" Lionel laughed. "Not on your life! Not if he wanted to live to talk about it. Nobody used Uncle Vincent's elevator but Uncle Vincent."

Toomey noticed that Gretchen was doing her nervous hand-twisting routine again. "Perhaps someone used it without his knowing it? Can you hear the elevator from in here?"

"Yes, you can," said Lionel, "and nobody used it. No one left the room, for one thing. Oh, Mrs. Polk was in and out a couple of times serving drinks, but the rest of us stayed in here the whole time. Lieutenant, do you suppose we could continue this later? I've got to get in to Ellandy's—my partner doesn't know about Uncle Vincent, and we're going to have to find out where we stand legally—on the loan, I mean."

Toomey said that would be all right. "I'd like to drop in at Ellandy's myself—I'll need to talk to Dorrie Murdoch and Nicole Lattimer. Do you plan on going straight there?"

"I'm going to drive Gretchen home first." In response to a question from Rizzuto, Lionel supplied Ellandy's address as well as his and Gretchen's home address and phone number. "I'll be at Ellandy's in forty-five minutes or an hour, Lieutenant."

"Somebody will be around later to fingerprint you," Toomey told the Knoxes. "We need to eliminate all of you we know were here last night, to see if any unaccounted-for prints remain."

Gretchen went out to tell Mrs. Polk they were leaving; Godfrey Daniel abandoned Lieutenant Toomey's lap and followed her out. Toomey stopped Lionel at the door. "I notice you're favoring your left leg. Have an accident?"

"Oh, I turned my ankle yesterday. A nuisance."

"Mr. Knox—what did you and your wife argue about last night?"

"That's between my wife and me, Lieutenant," Lionel grinned. "Besides, it's patched up now." He limped on out.

Rizzuto sniggered. "Playin' around."

Toomey rounded on his sergeant and chewed him out soundly for not informing him about the drinking glasses that had still been in the library when the police first arrived. Rizzuto replied sullenly that they'd show up in the crime lab photos and what was all the fuss about—after which Toomey bawled him out again, this time for his attitude.

Then, as much to keep Rizzuto from sulking as for any other reason, Toomey asked him what he made of the Knoxes.

Rizzuto perked up. "She's lyin' about that elevator, for one thing. For another, she don't like Nicole Lattimer at all."

Toomey grunted in approval, pleased that Rizzuto had picked up on both. "Remind me to check with the others about whether anyone left the room during the meeting. I'm inclined to believe the husband—no one used the elevator last night. And if neither of the servants used it, that means Gretchen Knox did—later, after everyone had gone. The only reason she would have used it is that she knew her uncle would *not* be using it."

Rizzuto asked the obvious. "Think she did it?"

"I think she knows more than she's telling. She was obviously surprised to hear the body had been found at the desk instead of somewhere else—they both were."

"Yeah, and another thing," Rizzuto said, "there's somethin' fishy about that loan."

"You can make book on it. Let's see what the other partner has to say. You know, Lionel Knox was expecting to find something in here that's not here now—remember all that talk about Mrs. Polk's having already cleaned up? He just pretended he was talking about the glasses—a fast-thinking cover-up, but not very convincing. I wonder what he thought he'd find? Those two are lying in their teeth."

"Protectin' each other?"

"Possibly. There's one other little thing that's been bothering me. How did Mrs. Polk know Gretchen Knox was staying the night here?"

"Huh?"

"Mrs. Polk said she went up to her room on the third floor well before nine o'clock. Gretchen Knox couldn't have gone to her room on the second floor until nine at the earliest, the time the meeting broke up. Yet Mrs. Polk said that this morning she called the police and then went to wake the other two."

Rizzuto's eyes gleamed. "Yeah—how'd she know there was *two* other people in the house? Acourse, the niece coulda gone up to the third floor and told Mrs. Polk she was stayin'. She coulda did that."

It was the *coulda did* that did it. "Rizzuto," Toomey said in annoyance, "where did you ever get the idea that talking like a grade-school dropout made you sound tough? Look, go out to the kitchen and ask Mrs. Polk about Gretchen. Don't tell

her why you want to know. Just ask her if she spoke to her
Miss Gretchen anytime *after* the meeting last night. And you
might as well send in the manservant."

Rizzuto nodded and left the library. A minute later, Bjarne
walked in. "You wanted to see me?"

"You're Barney Peterson?"

"I am," said Bjarne Pedersen, thinking that this overweight,
droopy-eyed policeman bore a startling resemblance to Peter
Lorre in his later, more corpulent years.

Lieutenant Toomey introduced himself and told the other
man to sit down. Toomey got the preliminaries out of the
way—how long Bjarne had been working for Vincent Farwell,
what his duties were, and so forth. "I understand you were
sailing three sheets to the wind last night," Toomey said.

Bjarne's face took on a pinched look. "I was very stupid last
night. I didn't drink *that* much—it was the pills what did
me in."

"What pills?"

"Valium. I took only two. Whenever a lot of people came
here, Mr. Vincent would always be, well, difficult afterwards.
I thought he'd be easier to handle if *I* was relaxed."

"You took two, you say. What dosage?"

"I don't know. Whatever those are, in Mr. Vincent's bottle."

Toomey stared at him. "You're right. You *were* stupid. Mix-
ing alcohol and Valium—and you don't even know the dosage?"

Bjarne rubbed both eyes with his fingertips. "I'm still groggy."

"I'm not surprised," Toomey grunted. "I don't suppose you
know what time it was when you passed out?"

"It was after all the guests got here but before anybody left.
That's all I can tell you."

"Between eight and nine, then. Did you manage to lock up
and turn on the alarm first?"

Bjarne shook his head, and then winced. "I was waiting for
everyone to leave. There'd be no point—" Then it hit him.
"Oh god. Oh my god. Because I didn't lock up, that burglar
—oh, good god!"

"Hey, are you all right?" Toomey asked. The manservant
looked as if he was going to throw up.

Bjarne let out a cry that brought both Rizzuto and Mrs. Polk
running. "It's *my* fault!" Bjarne moaned. "Because I got drunk
last night, Mr. Vincent is dead! He's dead because of me!

Because of *me!*" The realization that he himself had made possible what he feared the most thoroughly devastated Bjarne. He slid off his chair on to his knees and buried his face in his hands. His whole body shook with sobs.

Mrs. Polk took charge while the two policemen looked on helplessly. "Now, Barney—that's no way to carry on." She urged him to his feet. "You come with me. Go wash your face and I'll fix you a pot of tea. Come along, now." Crushed, Bjarne let her lead him away.

"Whew!" Rizzuto said when they were gone. "Ain't that carrying *responsibility* a little far?"

Toomey grunted. "Well, he was responsible. It'll be interesting to see whether he starts making excuses once he's recovered from his attack of *mea culpa*. What about Mrs. Polk? Did Gretchen Knox tell her last night she was staying over?"

"She says she and 'Miss Gretchen' dint speak again after she served the drinks. You know, Lieutenant, she coulda just heard her movin' around."

Toomey put on an expression of mock surprise. "But she can't hear anything from her room, remember? Mrs. Polk isn't being straight with us. None of them is, except Barney Peterson, and he went to pieces on me. And we still have half the people who were here last night to talk to!"

"They won't know nothin' about the burglary," Rizzuto stated flatly. "And somebody did break in here last night, no matter how many lies the Knoxes tell."

"That's true—they did. And a most unusual pair of burglars we have here, wouldn't you say? Look at what the physical evidence tells us happened. The first burglar boosts the second up over the terrace wall, and Burglar Number Two fixes a rope for Burglar Number One to climb. They creep around the house until they come to the double doors leading to the library. They look into a lighted room and there is Vincent Farwell himself in full sight—"

"How d'you know the lights was on?" Rizzuto asked.

"Farwell wouldn't be sitting at his desk in the dark, now, would he? So the lights are on. Ignoring the fact that they themselves are fully visible to the room's occupant, the burglars forcibly break through the terrace doors—doors that are not even locked, incidentally. Vincent Farwell responds to this unseemly intrusion by drawing a gun and shooting his desk.

No one hears the shot, because Mrs. Polk is too far away, Gretchen Knox is wearing earplugs, and Barney Peterson is zonked out on pills and alcohol."

"Then they kill 'im."

"Then one of the burglars picks up the alabaster statuette and bashes Farwell with it, breaking both the statuette and Farwell's head in the process. One of them lifts the body a bit while the other pulls out the blotter and takes it to the fireplace and burns it. Then one burglar removes one page of a letter from the file cabinet and puts it under the sofa for the cat to play with. The other burglar finds the Infralux in the desk, decides he doesn't like the color, and tosses it over into the corner."

Rizzuto snorted.

"That taken care of," Toomey continued, "they proceed to steal the jade horse and other undoubtedly overpriced small items scattered hither and yon about the room. Their next move is to gather up *other* expensive items from *other* rooms in the house and substitute them for the ones they've stolen —hoping the original set would not be missed, no doubt."

"Aw, Lieutenant."

"They ignore the Degas because they don't care for the impressionist school. They take Vincent Farwell's watch, money, and credit cards. They drop the empty billfold on the floor and kick it under the desk. Then one of them goes out to the hall and sends the elevator up to the second floor. Finished at last, they turn out the lights in order to save on electricity. They go out through the double doors, avoiding the broken glass in the dark as best they can. Out on the terrace once again, they decide to leave their can of Redi-Whip as a thank-you present. They put down their loot long enough to move the wrought-iron table over against the wall. At that point they part company, one using the table to climb over the wall, the other walking out through the terrace gate. And that's the end of it. As you said, Rizzuto, cut and dried."

"Who, me?" Rizzuto said. "Never."

" 'The Case of the Body in the Library'," Toomey sighed. "Too bad the library door wasn't locked from the inside—that's all that's missing. I'm going to pay a visit to Ellandy Jewels, but I want you to stay here, Rizzuto. There are some things that need doing. First, that one page of a letter from Farwell's insurance agent—I want you to look in the file cabinet and find the rest of the letter. It probably doesn't mean anything, but we ought to check it out."

"Okay."

"Then I want you to call Farwell's attorney, ah—Dann, Richard Dann—and ask him if he has the combination to the wall safe upstairs. Then get somebody from headquarters over here with a thirty-eight and a box of sand to fire it into. I want you to find out if the shot can be heard in Mrs. Polk's room or not. Got all that?"

"Yep. Where'll you be when you finish at Ellandy Jewels?"

"Depends on what I find out there. I'll call you."

"I'll be here," Rizzuto said.

Lionel Knox pulled the car over to the side of the street long enough to give Gretchen a big hug and a kiss. "You were terrific back there!" he laughed happily. "Saying Uncle Vincent hadn't made up his mind about the loan! How can I ever thank you?"

"Oh, I'll think of a way," she smiled coyly.

"If that sleepy-eyed police lieutenant and his subliterate sergeant find out that Uncle Vincent turned us down—you know what that means, don't you? That means we'd all be suspects."

"I thought of that," she said.

Lionel pulled back out into the line of traffic. "I've got to make some phone calls from home. I'll have to let the others know what happened to Uncle Vincent and say we're telling the police he didn't give us an answer on the loan."

"Do you think they'll go along?"

Lionel considered. "I think so. Malcolm might take some persuading."

Gretchen cleared her throat. "Lionel. There's something we've got to talk about. You were surprised when the Lieutenant told us Uncle Vincent's body was found at his desk."

"So were you!" he shot back. When she didn't say anything, Lionel sighed. "I guess I'd better tell you. I was there last night—or early this morning, rather. And no, I didn't kill him. After the meeting, the five of us were talking about what we should do, and someone suggested stealing Uncle Vincent's copy of the promissory note. We sort of dismissed the idea as impractical, but after I got home I started thinking about it. I couldn't sleep, and the more I thought about stealing the note, the more it seemed as if that was the only possible solution to our problems. So I went back to the house."

"And found Uncle Vincent."

"And found Uncle Vincent—at his desk. But Gretchen, I moved him! He was in the middle of the floor when I left! How'd he get back to the desk?"

"Why did you move him?"

"Well, the study was in a terrible mess—that's another thing, there were papers all over the place! The file cabinet had been completely emptied, and Uncle Vincent's papers were scattered everywhere. But they were gone when I came back just now, and Lieutenant Toomey said Mrs. Polk hadn't cleaned in there. Do you suppose the police took all those papers?"

"No," Gretchen said in a small voice. "I picked up the papers. I put them back in the file."

"*You!* Then you were—"

"You first. Finish telling me what you did."

"Well, you know what a mess the library was in, then. I couldn't find the promissory note—I looked at every piece of paper in that room. So it seemed to me that whoever had killed Uncle Vincent had come there for the same reason I had, and had *found* the note. So who was it? I felt sure it had to be either Dorrie or Nicole. Which one would you pick?"

"Not Dorrie."

"Definitely not Dorrie. And if Nicole had turned herself into a killer to help Ellandy's, I'd be damned if *I* was going to give her away. She probably didn't mean to kill him at all—he must have surprised her."

"But why'd you move Uncle Vincent?"

"Oh, that was one of those brilliant ideas that seem a lot less brilliant in the clear light of day. The scene just didn't look right, you know? There was that broken glass that made it appear as if a burglar had broken in—"

"How did you get in?" Gretchen asked suddenly.

"I just took your spare set of keys and unlocked the front door. Anyway, if a burglar did break in, Uncle Vincent wouldn't just sit there calmly at his desk and watch, would he? He'd be roaring out in his wheelchair and waving his gun and yelling for Barney—but he wouldn't just sit there. So I moved him out to the middle of the floor to make it look as if that was what happened."

"And that's where he was when I went in—in the middle of the floor. But go on."

"Well, the blotter was all bloody. And since it might be kind of hard to explain how a man who died in the middle of the floor managed to bleed all over his desk, I burned the blotter in the fireplace."

"Ugh," said Gretchen.

Lionel thought it best not to mention burning the private investigator's report as well. "Then I took Uncle Vincent's gun and tucked it under him, and—*Christ!*"

Gretchen jumped. "What?"

"I just remembered what else I should have done. I meant to take away the two pieces of the Hermes—the, er, murder weapon. In case Nicole left her fingerprints. But then I stepped on Godfrey Daniel's tail—that's why he was giving me the hate treatment this morning. But last night he let out such a yowl that I got rattled and took off."

Gretchen nodded. "I heard him. I went downstairs to find out what was wrong."

"All right—why did you pick up the papers?"

Gretchen was silent a moment, and then said in a shaky voice, "I'm not too proud of this, Lionel. When I saw the room, it seemed to me that someone had tried to make it look as if a burglary had taken place—all those papers on the floor! Ordinary burglars don't go through file cabinets, for heaven's sake. And even the things that were taken—the jade horse and the like. They're all small things, things you can slip into a pocket or carry easily. The Degas and Uncle Vincent's six-thousand-dollar Georgian clock—they weren't touched. No real burglar would have left them behind."

"So you concluded one of us had done it?" Lionel asked. She nodded. "You thought I had done it?" he persisted.

"You or Nicole or possibly Simon."

"Simon! Why Simon?"

"Because I couldn't see Dorrie doing it, but it's the sort of gesture Simon might make—you know, taking drastic action to rescue his lady fair. A romantic kind of gesture."

"You've got a strange idea of romance, Gretchen my love. But go on."

"This is the part I'm not too proud of," Gretchen said. "You've got to remember I'd just found out about you and Nicole, and I was hurt and confused and . . . and I wanted to make trouble for you. Yes, I did! So I decided to make it look as if a burglary had *not* taken place. Then when the police found out about the loan . . . well, I put all the papers back in the file and brought in the ivory owl from the dining room and a few other things to make it look as if nothing had been taken."

"I see," Lionel said, taken aback.

"But then this morning Lieutenant Toomey told me that Uncle Vincent's watch and money had been taken too—and Lionel, it hit me for the first time that it might really have been a burglar after all! So that's why I said Uncle Vincent hadn't decided about the loan. To try to undo any damage I might have done. I'm truly sorry, Lionel. I should have left things alone."

"It might not matter in the long run," Lionel said, thinking. "If our burglar was indeed Nicole Lattimer, I'm sure she's had the sense to destroy the promissory note by now. Then we'll all be in the clear."

"If she found it," Gretchen said. "It might be upstairs in the wall safe."

"*Wall safe?*" Lionel yelled, and had to swerve to avoid hitting another car. "What *wall safe?*"

"There's one in Uncle Vincent's bedroom. I'd forgotten all about it until Lieutenant Toomey asked me if I knew the combination."

"Do you?"

"Of course not. Uncle Vincent never told me things like that."

Lionel thought about it. "Wait a minute, now—it won't make any difference. So long as we all stick to the story that Uncle Vincent postponed making a decision about extending the loan, it won't matter whether the promissory note is found in the safe or not. So that's all right. The only question left is—how did Uncle Vincent get back to his desk?"

"Yeah," said Gretchen. "That's weird."

They drove in silence for a few minutes. "He *was* dead,"

Lionel said worriedly. "I know he was dead. I felt for a pulse."
He pulled into the driveway of their house and cut the engine.
"I'll make a few fast phone calls and then be on my way."

"Lionel?"

"Hm?"

"If it had been Dorrie—would you have covered up for her
the way you did for Nicole?"

"I'd have covered up *better* if it had been Dorrie," Lionel
said grimly. "Dorrie's my partner—what happens to her, happens to me. Don't think what you're thinking, Gretchen. There
is absolutely *nothing* between Nicole and me. Nothing. You're
the only woman in my life."

That helped a great deal; Gretchen smiled and decided to
say no more about it.

For the time being.

7

Dorrie Murdoch put down the telephone and sat thinking for a few minutes. Then she left her office and walked down the hall to Nicole Lattimer's office. She went in, shut the door behind her, and told Nicole that Uncle Vincent had been murdered.

The two women stared at each other a long time, both of them trying hard to look surprised and shocked. Finally Nicole remembered to ask questions. "How? When? Who? Why?"

"In the library," Dorrie said, answering the unasked *Where?* "Lionel just called and told me. Someone broke in last night and hit him over the head and killed him. They don't know who."

"A burglar?"

"Sounds like it. Lionel didn't give me many details—he just said the police would be here soon to talk to us. But there's something else. Evidently Lionel and Gretchen have made up their differences, because *she* told the police that Uncle Vincent simply delayed giving us an answer on the extension of the loan. She said he hadn't decided yet!"

A smile started slowly and then spread all over Nicole's face. "Does that mean what I think it means?"

Dorrie smiled back. "The least it means is that we'll have a little time. Lionel says we all have to tell the same story. If the police find out Uncle Vincent refused to grant us an extension, they're going to suspect one of *us* of killing him!"

"But I thought it was a burglar."

"I'm sure it was—but why take chances? Just say Uncle Vincent postponed giving us an answer and we'll be all right."

"What about Malcolm and Simon?"

"Lionel's calling them. Simon's no problem, but Malcolm might balk. He's always been such a stickler for doing things the proper way—even when he was a little boy, he was like that."

"I don't think Malcolm will object this time," Nicole said evenly. She looked questioningly at Dorrie. "It's all right, then? It really is all right? We're not going out of business in two weeks?"

Dorrie laughed. "We are *not* going out of business in two weeks!" she sang, and Nicole laughed with her. On impulse the two women joined hands and did an impromptu little dance. Dorrie was the first to realize that their behavior might be interpreted as a tad unseemly. "Poor Uncle Vincent," she said soberly.

"I'd better practice saying that," Nicole remarked dryly. "I should be sorry he's dead, but I'm not. Uncle Vincent was a troublemaker, and I'm not going to miss him one little bit."

"Nicole," Dorrie said reprovingly, mostly because she felt she was supposed to. "We'll have to find out from Malcolm just where we stand now on the loan."

"Well, let's see. We'll have to pay the estate—unless that promissory note magically disappears."

"Oh, wouldn't that be nice!" Dorrie sighed. "I don't like being a deadbeat . . . but a million and a half? Well."

"Maybe we should have stolen the note after all," Nicole said slyly.

Dorrie looked at her out of the corner of her eye. "I'm beginning to wish someone had."

"Yes, that would solve the problem, wouldn't it? Especially now that Gretchen seems to be on our side again."

It hit them both at the same time. "Gretchen!" Dorrie cried, appalled. "She inherits!"

"Everything," Nicole gasped. "Including debts owed to Uncle Vincent!"

"That means—"

"It means that Ellandy Jewels owes one and a half million dollars to *Gretchen Knox*! Plus interest!"

"Aaaaaoooooowwwww!" Dorrie wailed.

"Ditto," Nicole said grimly.

"I *hate* owing Gretchen Knox money!"

"And *Gretchen* hates *me*," Nicole muttered. "Oh my."

The two women stared at each other aghast, their earlier ebullient mood completely shattered.

* * *

Simon Murdoch's left eyebrow climbed higher and higher as he listened to what Lionel Knox was telling him over the telephone.

There was a silence. "Simon?" Lionel asked. "Are you still there?"

"Still here, and trying to absorb everything. So was it a burglar or not?"

"It must have been, but the police aren't saying definitely. They're going in to Ellandy's to ask questions—which means they'll get around to you eventually. Just remember to say Uncle Vincent wouldn't give us an answer on the loan extension."

"Right, no problem. Do the police actually suspect one of us?" Simon asked.

Lionel hesitated. "I think they're just tying up loose ends. The man in charge is a Lieutenant Toomey—he seems reasonable enough, but he keeps asking questions. If he finds out Uncle Vincent refused to renew the loan, though, then he *will* suspect one of us."

"And we can't have that, can we?" Simon murmured smoothly. "Don't worry about me, Lionel—I won't give anything away. But what about good old straight-arrow Malcolm? Are you saying he's actually agreed to tell a falsehood to legally appointed enforcers of the law? Incredible."

"I haven't talked to Malcolm yet," Lionel admitted. "I was putting him off 'til last."

Simon chuckled. "Good luck."

"I'll need it," Lionel said glumly. He hung up and sat marshaling his arguments for a minute before he punched out the number of Malcolm Conner's law office.

A secretary passed his call on to Malcolm, and Lionel began his spiel. "Hold on to your hat, Malcolm, I've got something big to tell you. Uncle Vincent was murdered last night. He—"

"I know. Nicole just called me."

"Oh." Lionel felt deflated. "Well, then, did she tell you we've all agreed to say that Uncle Vincent hadn't yet decided about extending Ellandy's loan?"

"Yes, and I agreed too."

"Because if we don't, the police are going to start thinking that—"

"Lionel, you're not listening. I said I agreed. I'll tell the same story."

"Oh. Well, uh, thanks, Malcolm."

"Is there anything else?"

"Uh, no." There was a click on the line. Lionel replaced the receiver and sat staring at the telephone, somewhat puzzled.

"Dorothea Conner Murdoch," Dorrie said, and gave Lieutenant Toomey her home address and phone number.

The Lieutenant did not like Ellandy Jewels; the place threw him off stride. The showroom, instead of being one nice even floor with ordinary display cases arranged in nice even rows, was instead divided into different levels. Each level had its own lighting scheme, its own décor. The jewelry itself was displayed with more pomp and circumstance than the Crown Jewels in the Tower of London. And with about the same amount of security, both human and electronic.

Even when he'd finally gotten himself oriented, Lieutenant Toomey still didn't like the place. It made him feel like a peasant. Not one of the pieces of jewelry he'd looked at had had anything as crass as a price tag attached to it. And he'd bet that any one of the chairs placed on the various levels for the customers to sit on cost more than all the furniture in his living room put together. Ellandy Jewels was definitely not a place for dropping in and doing a little comparison shopping for a bargain bracelet for Aunt Sophie's birthday.

He'd found Dorrie Murdoch on one of the "consulting" levels—no jewelry on display, just a table and two chairs. Dorrie herself was as carefully made up as a model, Toomey noted. She was wearing a soft green pantsuit made of some rich material he couldn't identify. Her hair was an unusual shade of blond, carefully coiffed. All in all, the female partner of Ellandy Jewels looked every bit as expensive as her surroundings.

"A great deal of our business is for custom-designed pieces," Dorrie explained when asked about her work. "Perhaps someday that's all we'll do. A man who just left—he wanted something special to give his wife for their anniversary." Dorrie gave Toomey a satisfied smile. "He decided on diamond earrings. His wife has a round face and a rather short neck, so I'll take that into consideration in my design."

"So it helps to know what the wearer looks like?"

"It's essential. I've never met this woman, so when her husband phoned for an appointment I asked him to bring in a photo. But every piece here is unique, custom-designed or not. Owning the only one of something appeals to a lot of people. It's a status thing, Lieutenant. The man who ordered the diamond earrings—he was *determined* to have something especially designed for his wife, even though I can't have it in three days as he wanted. Heavens, it takes longer than that just to cut the stones!"

"Really?" Toomey said. "It takes three days to pick up a mallet and tap a wedge or whatever it is?"

"You're thinking of cleaving. Most diamonds are sawed these days instead of cleaved—we don't even employ a diamond cleaver. When we have a stone that needs to be cleaved, we contract the job out."

"What's the difference?"

"Cleaving works with the gain, sawing goes against the grain. Sawing takes more time. You can also cut diamonds with a laser beam. But that's a rather more expensive operation, and we haven't decided whether to invest in the necessary equipment yet or not."

"How much did Vincent Farwell lend Ellandy Jewels?" the Lieutenant asked suddenly.

"A million and a half. Why?"

"And you can't pay it back?"

"We can, but it would put us back so far it would pretty much wipe out the benefit of getting the loan in the first place. We were prepared to make a partial payment—look, Lieutenant, why don't you talk to Lionel Knox about this? He handles the business end of Ellandy's."

Toomey asked her about the preceding night. Dorrie said they were all at Uncle Vincent's house by a few minutes after eight, they talked business for the better part of an hour, Uncle Vincent said he'd let them know about extending the loan, and they all left around nine, except Gretchen Knox who stayed over. No, no one left the room or used the elevator. And she was sorry, but she didn't remember whether the fire was burning when they left or not.

"Where did you go after the meeting?" Toomey asked.

"Well, Nicole Lattimer and Lionel and I came in here to do some work, and Simon and Malcolm just went on home."

"Simon Murdoch—your husband? And Malcolm Conner is your brother?"

"That's right."

"How late did you and Ms. Lattimer and Mr. Knox stay here last night?"

"Oh, it was after midnight when we left. I don't know the exact time."

Toomey asked for Simon's and Malcolm's business addresses, warned her to expect a fingerprint man, and then said he wanted to talk to Nicole Lattimer. "I understand there's some chance she might be made a partner in Ellandy Jewels?"

"It's almost a certainty," Dorrie said emphatically. "Lionel just wants to get this loan paid off first. If Nicole had the money to buy in, there wouldn't be any problem. As it is, her contribution would be her designs—the same arrangement I have with Lionel."

"And you don't object?"

"Object? Certainly not, Lieutenant—I'm one hundred percent in favor of it! We might lose Nicole if we don't make her a partner, and she's far too talented to let get away."

"Where is she now?"

"I think she's back in the workshop," Dorrie said. "Nicole's come up with a new diamond cut and she wants to see it through the process herself. This way." She got up and walked through a curtained-off alcove, identifying Toomey to a discreet-looking guard on the way.

The workshop was a surprise. Toomey had expected to find a roomful of little old men hunched over their workbenches, grinding away at whatever precious gems had been entrusted to their personal touch. There were a few craftsmen at work (none of them old), but the first thing that caught Toomey's eye was the long row of high-tech machines busily humming away.

"Here she is," Dorrie said, and made the introductions.

When Toomey had been looking over the jewelry on display, he'd noticed two distinct styles. One might have been called "traditional". Traditional for kings and queens, that is—elegant ornamental pieces that made one think of castles and courtiers and royal balls. The other style was boldly modern, its pieces strong accents to be worn with today's clothing. Toomey had tentatively pegged Dorrie as the designer of the traditional jewelry—or perhaps "classical" was the preferred word. When he met Nicole Lattimer, he knew he was right.

Nicole, for some reason, was dressed as a gypsy. A *rich* gypsy. Her dark hair was partially covered by a brightly colored designer scarf tied at the nape of her neck, and ruby-studded geometric shapes dangled from her ear lobes. An off-white linen shirt that would have shocked Toomey if he'd known the price, a heavy wine-colored skirt, and wine-colored boots completed the ensemble. Toomey couldn't decide whether the clothing complemented Nicole's dark eyes and prominent cheek bones or if it worked the other way around. Either way, Nicole Lattimer was A Presence.

"How's the new cut going?" Dorrie asked.

"It's in the Piermatic," Nicole smiled and held up crossed fingers. "We'll know soon."

"I can't wait to see it. But for now I'll leave you to Lieutenant Toomey." Dorrie touched Nicole lightly on the shoulder and was gone.

"What's a Piermatic?" Toomey asked.

"It's the last step in the cutting process," Nicole said. "Here, I'll show you." She led him to six machines equipped with sawwheels; all were in use. "The rough diamond is first cut here, creating the uppermost facet of the finished stone—it's called the table facet."

"Are those ordinary metal saws?" Toomey asked. "I thought only diamond could cut diamond."

"That's true. The cutting edge of the saw is coated with diamond dust. It's the dust that does the actual cutting, by abrasion—the sawwheel just provides the movement. From here the stone goes to a bruting machine," she pointed, "where the girdle is applied. That's like an equator circling the stone, separating the crown from the bottom part. This machine is a fairly new development and it can't handle all the stones we feed it. We still employ a human brutter to do the jobs the machine can't."

"That's nice," said Toomey.

"Next the stone has to be faceted. Say you're cutting a brilliant—that's the most popular diamond cut. Normally it would take four men to do the job. The top blocker would apply the eight basic facets on the crown, and then the bottom blocker would take care of the eight below the girdle. For a small stone, that would be the end of it—it'd be sold as an eight-cut. But a larger stone would go on to the top brillianteer, who'd add twenty-four more facets to the crown. Then the bottom brillianteer would add another sixteen. That's the old way of doing it," Nicole smiled.

"And the new way?" Toomey asked, recognizing a cue when he heard one.

Nicole patted the machine she was standing next to. "The Piermatic. Does the work of all four faceters. You set a diamond into a holder and its profile is projected onto a graph, which tells you what angles to program the Piermatic to cut. The machine does the rest."

It suddenly hit Toomey what she was talking about. "The automated manufacture of diamonds?"

"That's exactly what it is. A lot of cutting and polishing operations still do it the old way, but the machines are gaining ground."

"I'm amazed," Toomey said. "I had no idea all this went on behind jewelry stores!"

"Oh, it doesn't, usually—very few retailers have their own manufacturing operation. This is a big venture for us. It's what we needed the loan for."

Toomey noted the proprietorial "we".

Just then a red light on the Piermatic went on; Nicole removed a finished diamond from the machine. She placed the stone on a small table covered with black velvet and switched on a strong light. "Color is good," she said, "but it's not very brilliant. That's always the problem, trying to balance color and brilliance—you usually end up sacrificing one for the other. I was trying an extreme angle on a cut-corner triangle shape, and I lost something. Damn."

"A failure?"

"No, it's still a perfectly good diamond—we'll have no trouble selling it. It's just not the roaring success I was looking for. All right, I'm finished here, Lieutenant. You want to ask me questions? Let's go to my office."

As he followed her out of the workshop, Toomey spotted a small room that had been built into the corner of the main room, barely larger than a closet. He asked Nicole about it.

"That's the X-ray room, for testing pearls," she said in a dismissive manner. "I don't do pearls."

Nicole's office was as dramatic as a stage set. The rug was black, the walls were white, and the furniture was all black-and-white—a marked contrast to the colorful figure who inhabited the room. Drawing board, workbench, desk, open-faced supply cabinet, three chairs—all were white with black trim, or vice versa. The tilted drawing board held a sketch of a brooch, with the exact dimensions carefully written in. The walls displayed colored photographs of finished jewelry. Toomey started off by complimenting her on her designs.

Nicole murmured an automatic thank-you. "I try for a realistic look in my designs," she said, "something more in touch with life as it is lived today. A piece of jewelry must make a statement, or else it's failed in its primary function."

Realistic jewelry? Toomey thought. He asked for her home address and led the talk to the meeting at Vincent Farwell's house. Nicole told the same story as Dorrie, but added that she thought the fire had gone out by the time they left.

"What were you and Mr. Knox and Mrs. Murdoch working on so late here?"

She hesitated a second and then said, "We wanted to bring our gem inventory up to date. In case Uncle Vincent decided not to renew the loan and we might have to sell, you understand."

"Did he give you some reason to think he wouldn't renew?"

"Oh, not really," she said in an overcasual manner. "But with Uncle Vincent, you never could tell what he might do next. We expected an answer last night, you see. When he didn't give us one—well, I guess we started worrying a little."

The story she told was plausible enough, but Toomey felt certain he still didn't have the full dope on the loan. He asked Nicole if she thought she'd leave Ellandy's if Dorrie and Lionel failed to make her a partner.

"How did you know about that?" she asked in surprise. "I honestly don't know whether I'd leave or not, Lieutenant. This is a good place to work. I have complete freedom to do what I want, good facilities—but when I see how much my designs sell for and how much money *I* take home . . . I just don't know. It's complicated by the fact that I've grown fond of Dorrie and Lionel."

"Speaking of, when do you expect Lionel Knox in?"

"I can't say—I thought he'd be here by now."

Toomey asked to use her phone and called Rizzuto with instructions to meet him at the station house. Then he thanked Nicole for her help and left, stopping off at Dorrie's office on the way out—ostensibly to tell her he was leaving but in fact to get a look at the office itself. Like Nicole's office, the walls were covered with colored photographs of finished pieces. But there the similarity ended. Dorrie's office was all soft pastels and flowering plants, an extension of the woman who worked there rather than a contrasting background to play against.

"I'll be on my way," Toomey told Dorrie. "Excuse me—may I look at that necklace?"

Dorrie dimpled prettily. "It's a belt." She held up a length of delicate gold filigree with pearl pendants attached along the bottom edge. "What do you think?"

"I think it's beautiful!"

"Thank you! But I'm wondering now if the pendants aren't too close together. The balance isn't right."

Toomey left her to her problem and decided to take one more look at Nicole's "realistic" jewelry. In the showroom he examined her display of gold rings, each set with a different single gem and designed to be worn in groups. In the next case was a pin in the shape of a stylized cornucopia that spilled out emeralds of various sizes.

Toomey was particularly taken with a—well, it couldn't be called a necklace; it was too oversized. A collar, then. Nicole's collar somehow managed to combine high tech with a hint of paganism. It was made of sapphires set in geometrically shaped silver mountings and trimmed with . . . snakeskin? Unusual, to say the least.

A clerk approached, although he probably wasn't called a clerk, Toomey thought—an assistant or some such, a silver-haired man who looked like a Supreme Court judge. Toomey asked the price of the collar.

"One sixty," was the answer.

Toomey did a double take. "Thousand?"

"One hundred sixty thousand," the assistant nodded.

Toomey fled.

"It'll be a couple of weeks before Uncle Vincent's will goes into probate," Malcolm told the others. "All that means is that the will must be proved valid and all possible heirs notified. Since Gretchen is the only heir, that part will be automatic."

They were in Lionel's office at Ellandy Jewels. Lionel, Dorrie, and Nicole were waiting to find out the legal status of their debt to Uncle Vincent.

"Uncle Vincent appointed Richard Dann his executor," Malcolm went on. "Dann was his attorney, as you may or may not know. Once the will is probated, Dann will place notices in the newspapers for all claims against the estate to come to him. He'll also collect any money owed the estate—and that's the time your loan will be called in."

Lionel groaned. "So we haven't gained much time after all."

"Not a whole lot. But Dann might be willing to accept a partial payment. He has no personal grievance to settle the way Uncle Vincent did—or claimed he did."

"That's up to the executor?" Nicole asked. "Not the heir?"

"Technically, yes—since the loan will come due during the period Dann is going to be settling the estate. But executors generally defer to an heir's wishes in such matters, unless there is some legal reason why they should not. If Gretchen insists on the full amount being paid, I'm afraid Dann will honor her decision."

"Be nice to Gretchen," Dorrie cooed.

Lionel groaned again.

Malcolm cleared his throat. "How big a partial payment did you have in mind?"

"Four hundred thousand," Lionel said.

"A goodly sum," Malcolm nodded. "If we can deal exclusively with Dann, I think we'll be all right. He's not going to turn down four hundred thousand dollars."

"Lionel," said Dorrie, "wouldn't this be a good time to take Gretchen on a nice long trip somewhere? Like to China?"

"Don't you think she might be just a touch suspicious?" Lionel said sarcastically. "Right during the time the estate is being settled? Bad idea, Dorrie."

"The less said to Gretchen at this point the better," Nicole agreed. "She'll more than likely leave everything up to Mr. Dann. Gretchen doesn't go in for making big decisions—not her thing."

"That goddamned loan!" Lionel exploded. "We should never, never, *never* have borrowed from Uncle Vincent!"

"Nobody else would let us have that much money," Dorrie said pragmatically. "Malcolm, if the promissory note doesn't turn up among Uncle Vincent's papers, are you going to blow the whistle on us?"

"Ah . . . why shouldn't the note turn up?" Malcolm temporized.

Dorrie fluttered her hands in the air. "Stranger things have happened. Maybe the burglar took it."

"If there was a burglar," Malcolm said. The atmosphere instantly grew tense; they were on shaky ground. There was no need for anyone to put words to the obvious: that if there were no burglar, then Uncle Vincent had been murdered for the promissory note. Dorrie found herself looking suspiciously at Lionel, but he didn't notice because he was busy looking at Nicole the same way. Nicole, oddly, was looking at Dorrie. Nobody looked at Malcolm.

Then Lionel gave himself a little shake and said, "We're imagining things. Gretchen just told me Uncle Vincent had a wall safe in his bedroom. The promissory note's probably right there."

"A wall safe!" the other three exclaimed.

"In his bedroom," Lionel nodded.

The office door opened. "Ah, there you are!" said Simon Murdoch, striding into the room. "Huddled together like conspirators—I'm interrupting something, I hope? What nefarious intrigue are you plotting? Hello, darling," kissing Dorrie, "I was hoping we could lunch."

"Oh, what a lovely idea," Dorrie beamed. "Malcolm, are we finished?"

"We are," he said, standing up. "I have to be getting back to my office anyway."

"How is everyone holding up?" Simon asked the room at large. "Terrible about Uncle Vincent."

Lionel muttered something unintelligible and bent down to rub his ankle; it was still hurting from the off-balance landing he'd made in his flying leap from Uncle Vincent's terrace wall. Nicole said, "The police were here. *Was* here—one man, a rotund, droopy-eyed little fellow named Toomey."

"No one has been to see me yet," Simon remarked. "I'm feeling slighted."

"Give them time," Lionel said. "Wait until they take your fingerprints. That's loads of fun."

"Darling," Dorrie said to Simon, "just give me a minute to freshen up. Oh—and I have to return some diamonds to the vault."

"Aw, hell, Dorrie!" Lionel said testily. "You didn't leave stones in your office again, did you?"

"Calm yourself, O worrier," Dorrie smiled, dangling a key under his nose. "I locked the door."

"Why don't I return the diamonds for you," Simon asked, "while you do whatever it is you think you have to do to improve your appearance? As if it needed improving."

Dorrie pantomimed a kiss. "You're sweet. Come along, then."

They all left to go their various ways. Preoccupied, Lionel was halfway through the door before he remembered it was his office they were in.

Sal Rizzuto brought in two Styrofoam cups of black coffee and put one on Lieutenant Toomey's desk. Toomey took a swallow and marveled over the variety of tastes that passed as coffee. "Tell me about the test firing first," he said to the Sergeant.

"Okay," said Rizzuto, sitting down. "I *could* hear the shot in Mrs. Polk's room. But to tell the truth, Lieutenant, it was so faint I don't think I'da noticed if I hadn't been listenin' for it. If Mrs. Polk was watchin' television or sleepin' when the gun got fired last night, she wouldna heard it. By the way, that's a whole suite she's got up there, not just a bedroom. Sittin' room, bath."

Toomey nodded. "All right, she's telling the truth about the gunshot. What else?"

"Well, I looked for the rest of that insurance letter like you told me, but Lieutenant, it's the damnedest thing. Nothin' in that file cabinet is where it's supposed to be! *Nothin'*. IBM quarterly report in his medical expenses file, like that. Tax returns scattered through half a dozen different files, none of 'em marked 'Taxes'. And the papers themselves is all messed up—folded and wrinkled and just shoved in any which way."

Toomey tasted his tasteless coffee. "As if someone gathered them all up in a hurry to get them out of sight?"

"Yeah! That's just what it looked like."

"And Lionel Knox took it for granted this morning that Mrs. Polk had cleaned the study."

Rizzuto grinned. "Y'think that's what he was lookin' for? Papers scattered around?"

"Could be. Did you find the insurance letter?"

"Naw, I was still lookin' when you called."

Toomey picked up a yellow pencil from his desk top and played with it. "If Lionel Knox expected to see papers on the floor, that means he was in the library and knew Vincent Farwell was dead before his wife called him. It also means he didn't pick the papers up."

"Gretchen?"

"Must have been. But she missed one page of the insurance letter, under the sofa. And the Infralux—the desk drawers must have been emptied too. Mrs. Polk said the appliance belonged in the desk, didn't she? That looks as if the Knoxes were acting independently—remember they'd had a spat the night before. But by now they've had time to talk it over and get their stories straight." He pointed his yellow pencil at the other man. "What else, Rizzuto?"

The Sergeant looked blank.

"The lawyer," Toomey sighed.

"Oh yeah—Richard Dann. I called him and he does have the combination to the safe."

"Good. Now maybe we can—"

The phone rang; it was Dr. Oringer of the medical examiner's office. "Autopsy report won't be ready until later," he said, "but I thought you'd like to hear this. Post-mortem lividity indicates the body was moved."

"*What?*" Toomey shouted.

Dr. Oringer enjoyed surprising people. "I'd say six or seven hours after death."

"Six or . . . you mean the murderer didn't move him?"

"Not unless he waited six hours to do it."

Toomey tossed his yellow pencil up in the air in exasperation. "*What* is going on?"

"You find out. That's your job. The broken statuette was the murder weapon, by the way—blood and tissue on it were the victim's. The deceased had a paper-thin skull—one of the thinnest I've seen. A blow with that little alabaster statuette would just give you or me a bad headache, but it was enough to kill the old man."

"Whoo. Doc, what about the time of death?"

"Right now I'd say between ten-thirty and midnight—depending on the temperature of the room. Did you find out what time that fire in the fireplace went out?"

"Not definitely," Toomey growled. "Anything else?"

"Nothing out of the ordinary so far. There's a small scratch on the back of his left hand. Fresh, not very deep."

"Godfrey Daniel," Toomey muttered.

"What?"

"Could it be a cat scratch?"

"Could be."

"Okay, Doc, thanks." He hung up. "The body was moved."

Rizzuto nodded. "And both the Knoxes were surprised to learn Vincent Farwell was found at his desk."

Toomey thought a moment and then said, "How does this sound? Lionel Knox killed Vincent Farwell, someplace in the library other than at his desk. Then Lionel went through the file cabinet looking for something, throwing papers every which way in the process. He must not have found what he was looking for—why else make such a mess? Anyway, he leaves, *she* comes in and cleans up the mess. Why?"

"To make it look like nobody *wasn't* lookin' for nothin'."

"Congratulations, Rizzuto, a triple negative. Then she leaves, and somebody else comes in and moves the body over to the desk. Who and why?"

"*Who*, the manservant, Barney Peterson. Mrs. Polk ain't strong enough. *Why* . . . uh."

"Damn—that won't work!" Toomey said. "Farwell was killed before midnight and Lionel Knox was at Ellandy Jewels until *after* midnight, both the women say so."

"Maybe he slipped out for a while?"

Toomey reached for the phone. "What's the number?" Rizzuto read Ellandy's phone number from his notebook and Toomey started pressing buttons. Dorrie Murdoch was still out to lunch, but Nicole Lattimer swore all three of them had been there together from about ten to well after midnight.

"Unless those three are in collusion," Toomey said, hanging up, "we've just eliminated half our suspects."

"What about Mrs. Polk and Barney? And the burglar?"

"Okay, a third of them. But it's damned clear this was no simple burglary—there's more involved than a few knick-knacks picked up at random from Vincent Farwell's library." He told Rizzuto what an upscale place Ellandy's was. "They're nervous there—about the loan. That Nicole Lattimer's a strange one. Nothing extravagant about her speech or her personal mannerisms—but her appearance, and the jewelry she designs? *Very* dramatic, extreme even. Still waters there."

"So what do we do now?" Rizzuto asked. "Go after the Knoxes?"

"First we grab some lunch, and then we go talk to the other two who were at that meeting in the library last night. *Then* we go after the Knoxes."

Paul Bernstein had the look and manner of a funeral director—which, considering the circumstances, wasn't all that inappropriate, Gretchen felt.

"I'm not sure I can help you, Mrs. Knox," Bernstein said. "There might be a conflict of interest—you know I'm working for your uncle."

"Uncle Vincent is dead," Gretchen said bluntly. "Someone killed him last night."

Bernstein was shocked. "How did it happen?"

"A burglar. The manservant forgot to turn on the alarm system."

The private investigator shook his head disbelievingly. "I hope you gave him the sack this morning." He let a small silence develop as he mourned the loss of a lucrative source of income. "Do the police have any leads? Who's in charge of the case?"

"A Lieutenant Toomey—spherical and droopy-eyed, do you know him? And some sergeant who tries to act like a television cop. I don't know whether they've got any leads or not."

"I know Toomey," Bernstein nodded. "The sergeant could be anybody." Bernstein Investigative Services had recently moved to larger quarters and wasn't settled in yet. Bernstein had apologized mournfully as he led Gretchen past packing crates and huge spools of computer cable into his partially furnished office. He'd managed to come up with a cup of coffee for the niece of one of his most valued clients, but now he let his own coffee grow cold as he digested the news she'd brought him.

"Mrs. Knox," he said, "what is it you want me to do? If the police are still investigating your uncle's death—"

"Oh no, it's not that," Gretchen said. "It's just that I'd like you to consider me your client now instead of Uncle Vincent. That's no conflict of interest, is it?"

"No, it's not," he said, still wondering what she wanted.

She told him. "I'd like you to go on doing for me what you were doing for my uncle." When he nodded but said nothing, she asked, "Exactly what were you doing for my uncle?"

Bernstein regarded her somberly and tried to explain. "It's a matter of client confidentiality, Mrs. Knox—"

Gretchen lowered her eyes and raised the pitch of her voice. "But *I'm* youh client now, Mistuh Buhnstein," she said softly. "I know you were watchin' mah husband, and I want you to go raht on doin' that."

"Very well. Your uncle wanted weekly reports—would that be satisfactory?"

"Puhfectly. But I don't know what else you were doin'."

Bernstein considered. "Since you're taking your uncle's place, I suppose you're entitled to know. At the moment I was waiting for instructions. Mr. Farwell had me run checks on the people at Ellandy Jewels, and on Malcolm Conner and Simon Murdoch as well. My instructions were to continue having Mr. Knox followed until your uncle decided what to do next."

"I see. And I suppose you sent him written reports on those othuhs? I'd like copies, Mistuh Buhnstein."

"Certainly. The computer isn't connected yet, but I can get them to you tomorrow." Bernstein made a note to himself and asked pleasantly, "What part of the South are you from, Mrs. Knox?"

Gretchen ignored the question. "Then I'll hear from you tomorrow?"

"Before noon," Bernstein promised, now completely recovered from his grief over Vincent Farwell's unexpected but nevertheless timely demise.

8

Dorrie Murdoch was working desultorily on a sketch, doing a somewhat less than satisfactory job of keeping her mind on her work, when her office door opened.

"Where's Lionel?" Nicole Lattimer asked.

"Gone home. He didn't want to leave Gretchen alone right now. And he said something about going back to Uncle Vincent's house. Mrs. Polk and Barney are probably wondering what's going to happen to them."

Nicole grinned wryly. "I can't work either."

Dorrie tossed her pencil away. "I'm about ready to give up."

"I think I'll go home too. It's impossible to concentrate. I keep thinking of Uncle Vincent slumped over his desk with his head bashed in."

Dorrie nodded. "It's an ugly picture. And so unnecessary! Uncle Vincent was sure to keep his valuables upstairs in that safe—the burglar couldn't have gotten anything of real value."

"Ah yes, the bedroom safe," Nicole remarked grimly. "It's just as well none of us tried to steal the promissory note after all." She was watching Dorrie carefully.

"I suppose," Dorrie said faintly.

"A safe!" Nicole tossed her head in disgust. "You know, we should have thought of that."

"Yes, we should have," Dorrie said more firmly. "None of us was thinking straight last night. We should have known Uncle Vincent wouldn't just leave the note lying about where anyone could get it." Her face darkened. "You'd think he didn't trust us! *He* was the one who was always pulling tricks. *He*—"

"Dorrie," Nicole said quickly, "don't get angry. It won't help."

Dorrie inhaled deeply, let it out. "I'm not angry—just exasperated. To think that note's probably up in his bedroom right now!"

"I wonder," Nicole said carefully, "whether he had the combination written down somewhere. Do you think he'd depend on his memory for something as important as a safe combination?"

"No-o-o-o, I don't think he would," Dorrie said just as carefully. "I wonder where he kept it."

"Right there in the bedroom with him, I should think."

"Like maybe taped to the inside of a drawer or like that?"

"Or something fancier. Circles around dates on a calendar, perhaps?"

"Do you think Gretchen knows?"

"The combination? I doubt it."

After that, they seemed to have no more to say on the subject. Both women agreed there was no hope of getting any work done that day and they might as well go home.

The law offices of Buhl, Fenning, and Conner had the look of a British gentlemen's club—hushed, discreet, and solid as Gibraltar. It had to be a cultivated look instead of an evolved one, since the firm had been in existence only ten years. Lieutenant Toomey wondered idly if a lawyer might find it a disadvantage to have a name like "Conner." A secretary wearing a no-nonsense gray suit ushered him and Sergeant Rizzuto into Malcolm's office.

Malcolm Conner was also wearing a gray suit, and a conservative haircut as well. His manner was courteous but restrained as he invited the two policemen to sit down. "I suppose you're here about Uncle Vincent. I'm sorry he's dead. What can I do to help?"

Whether he meant it or not, Malcolm had been the first to express regret over the old man's death, and Lieutenant Toomey didn't overlook it. Nor did he miss the fact that the home address and telephone number Malcolm supplied were the same as those of Nicole Lattimer. So that made three ties Malcolm Conner had to Ellandy Jewels—as attorney, as brother, and as lover.

Malcolm the attorney told Lieutenant Toomey the same story

the others had told but in a more precise way. Malcolm the brother expressed concern for Dorrie Murdoch. Malcolm the lover had no comment.

"Was the fire still going when you left?" Toomey asked.

Malcolm frowned. "I think it was. I'm not sure."

"Nicole Lattimer says it was out."

"Then it probably was. I don't really remember."

"Where did you go when you left, Mr. Conner?"

"We all went to a bar—it's called Danny's Tavern, I believe. All of us except Gretchen Knox, that is. I hadn't had dinner and wanted a sandwich."

Rizzuto shot Toomey a glance that the Lieutenant ignored; nobody had said anything about a bar before. "How long were you there?" Toomey asked.

"About an hour. It was shortly after ten when we left."

Just long enough to talk things over, Toomey thought. "Then where did you go?"

"Dorrie, Lionel, and Nicole went in to Ellandy's—in Lionel's car. I went home. I presume Simon Murdoch did the same."

Without changing his tone of voice Toomey asked, "What time did Ms. Lattimer get home?"

Not even a flicker of expression passed over Malcolm's face, but Sergeant Rizzuto looked surprised. "It was sometime after midnight," the attorney said. "I'm sorry I can't be more exact, Lieutenant, but I fell asleep watching television. Now may I ask you something? Why are you questioning *our* movements? Wasn't it a burglar who killed Uncle Vincent?"

"I thought so at first," Toomey said honestly, "but now I'm not so sure. Too many incongruities. For instance, why would a burglar scatter Mr. Farwell's papers all over the place?"

Malcolm shrugged. "Looking for what he could find."

"In the file cabinet? Come now, Mr. Conner, ordinary burglars don't search file cabinets. Only extraordinary ones do, burglars who are looking for something specific. By the way, how did you know there were papers scattered about?"

Malcolm's face gave nothing away. "You just told me."

"But you weren't surprised."

"Should I have been? Lieutenant, a man has been killed— I'm supposed to be surprised because the murder room was in disarray? I don't know what happened there last night. There could be any number of reasons why those papers were scattered about."

"Such as?"

But Malcolm cautiously refused to speculate over the events that had transpired in the library during the night. When pressed to speculate about Vincent Farwell's decision concerning the loan, however, Malcolm expressed full confidence that Uncle Vincent would have renewed once he'd had time to study the figures more thoroughly.

When Toomey was convinced he was going to learn nothing more, he and Rizzuto left. In the elevator on the way down, Rizzuto asked, "Howja know Conner and the Lattimer woman was livin' together?"

"Same address and phone number. An odd pairing—they're nothing alike. He's so conservative and she's so . . . not. But maybe he has a Bohemian streak in him that appeals to Nicole Lattimer, who knows?"

"The bar," Rizzuto said just as the elevator reached the ground floor. "None of 'em said nothin' about a bar."

Toomey waited until they were in the car to answer. "It does help fill in the timetable, though. They all left Farwell's house around nine, all except Gretchen Knox. They spent about an hour in Danny's Tavern—plotting their next move? Rizzuto, I want you to check at that bar tonight. See if you can find their waitress and confirm the times."

"Okay," said Rizzuto.

"Then shortly after ten," Toomey went on, "according to Conner, the three Ellandy people left together, Lionel driving. Those three stayed together until after midnight, past the time Farwell was killed. Conner and Simon Murdoch left separately, meaning—"

"Meanin' no alibi," Rizzuto said.

"Meaning no alibi," Toomey agreed. "Let's hear what Mr. Simon Murdoch has to say for himself."

Simon's place of business was about a twenty-minute drive from Malcolm Conner's law offices. Simon Murdoch and two other diamond merchants shared quarters and facilities, and a guard at the door would not let them in until both Toomey and Rizzuto had shown their badges. The guard directed them to a cubicle containing several unfamiliar instruments resting on tables. Simon Murdoch was seated at another table with a small pile of diamonds on it, one of which he was examining through a loupe.

Toomey was amused to see that Simon's hair was the same off-shade of blond as his wife's. And the tie he was wearing was the same soft green as Dorrie's pantsuit. A *color-coordinated marriage*, Toomey thought. *My, my*. He cleared his throat. "Mr. Murdoch?"

Simon removed the loupe from his eye, put down the diamond, looked straight at Lieutenant Toomey, and said, "Fisheye."

"I beg your pardon?"

Simon gestured toward the diamond he'd been examining. "Dead in the center. No fire. From your air of quiet authority, I would say you must be Lieutenant Toomey. And you are . . . ?"

"Sergeant Rizzuto."

"I've been expecting you," Simon nodded, brushing the diamonds into a small paper packet that he folded and slipped into a pocket. "Unfortunately, there's only one extra chair in here. We can go to my office—"

"I'll stand," Rizzuto said, and leaned in the doorway as Toomey took the chair. The Lieutenant remarked on the absence of display cases.

"We're all wholesale merchants here," Simon explained. "We buy rough diamonds and sell them to retailers, so there's no need for display cases and all that foofaraw. Actually, I do deal in polished stones on occasion—it depends on what comes my way."

Toomey said, "I see. You go to that place in London to buy diamonds and then bring them back—"

"No, I'm not a sightholder," Simon interrupted. At Toomey's puzzled look, he went on, "There are about three hundred diamond merchants in the world who are invited to London for periodic 'sights', as they're called. The London operation is run by the De Beers Corporation, which decides who can buy and who can't. If you're a sightholder, you go to London and you're shown a packet of rough and told the price, which can range anywhere from eight hundred thousand to five million. There is no dickering. You are not permitted to buy some of the diamonds in the packet and leave the others—you have to take the lesser goods to get the premium stones. Your only choice is to accept the whole packet or refuse. No one refuses.

After all, De Beers controls about eighty percent of the world market. I'm part of the other twenty."

"Ah. So where do you get your diamonds?"

"Antwerp, Brazil, from other dealers—anyplace I can. I don't know a dealer anywhere who wouldn't give his right arm to find a good, steady source of diamonds that would make him independent of the De Beers people. The world will eventually run out of diamonds, you know. Some say soon."

Toomey turned the conversation toward Vincent Farwell's murder, and listened one more time to the same story of the preceding night's activities. Simon said he thought the fire had gone out by the time they'd left.

"You went directly home from Danny's Tavern?" Toomey asked.

"Directly."

"What time did Mrs. Murdoch get home?"

"Around twelve-thirty or one. Excuse me, Lieutenant, but this sounds suspiciously as if you are investigating Dorrie or me. Or both of us—heaven forbid! I understood from Lionel Knox that a burglar was responsible for Uncle Vincent's death."

"That's Mr. Knox's conclusion and not necessarily mine. Right now I'm trying to pin down everyone's movements. Exactly why were you at that meeting, Mr. Murdoch? You have no connection with Ellandy's other than being married to one of the partners, do you?"

"As a matter of fact, I do," Simon murmured. "Ellandy's buys their diamonds through me—they're one of my regular clients. But last night had nothing to do with that. It was a courtesy invitation, Lieutenant. I was there not as a diamond merchant but as Dorrie's husband."

"Vincent Farwell was given to extending courtesies, then?"

Simon smiled thinly. "I don't think Uncle Vincent knew the meaning of the word. I should have said he knew I'd come with Dorrie whether I was invited or not, so he just went ahead and included me in the invitation."

"I see. Then you must know a lot about the inner workings of Ellandy Jewels."

"Fairly much. Dorrie talks freely about the business."

"What about Nicole Lattimer and Lionel Knox?" Toomey asked, meaning did they talk freely too.

"Oh, you know about that, do you?" Simon answered with

raised eyebrow. "You have been busy, Lieutenant. It's my understanding that it was more a fling than a real affair, and it was over long ago. Of course, Gretchen didn't quite see it like that."

Rizzuto dropped his notebook. Toomey waited until he'd recovered it and then said, "She was upset?"

"She was furious," Simon laughed shortly.

Toomey nodded. "So she decided to stay the night at her uncle's house instead of going home."

"I suppose she needed some time to think things over," Simon nodded back. "It may have been old news, but it was new to her."

Toomey couldn't let it end there. "How did Vincent Farwell find out about the, uh, fling?"

"He'd hired a detective." Simon Murdoch seemed to find the thought vastly amusing. "Usually it's a suspicious spouse who hires the detective, isn't it? Not a suspicious *uncle*."

Toomey waited until Rizzuto had picked up his notebook a second time and asked, "What was the detective's name?"

"Bernstein," Simon said promptly. "I don't remember his first name."

Paul Bernstein, Toomey thought. "I thought the meeting was to discuss the loan. How did this other business come up?"

"You have to understand about Uncle Vincent, Lieutenant," Simon drawled, his half-smile firmly in place. "He enjoyed playing with people. He liked the feeling of power it gave him. Holding that loan over Ellandy's collective head—well, that was Uncle Vincent's idea of good clean fun. He reveled in the role of decision-maker, judge. But it was all warped, the way he did it."

"How so?"

"Well, look at the way he treated Gretchen. He was supposed to be her benefactor, but he hurt and humiliated her by revealing before a roomful of people that her husband had cheated on her. He made her feel like a fool and reinforced his own authority at the same time. Uncle Vincent was not," Simon said dryly, "a nice man."

Rizzuto spoke up. "Is that why nobody seems to care he's dead?"

"He was not what you would call 'beloved'," Simon answered indifferently.

Toomey asked if he thought Vincent Farwell would have renewed the loan.

"Probably. Once he'd gotten all the fun out of it he could."

"There must have been a penalty clause for late payment, wasn't there?"

"That I don't know. Lionel Knox could tell you—or Malcolm Conner. Malcolm drew up the contract or promissory note or whatever you want to call it. You might want to ask him about the loan when you talk to him."

"I've already talked to him, and he didn't have much to say. A very tight-lipped man, Mr. Conner."

"Tight-lipped? Malcolm?" Simon's half-smile spread into a full-blown grin. "You must have intimidated him, Lieutenant. Usually he takes ninety words to say what could be said in seventeen."

Toomey had no comment on that; and after a few more questions that revealed nothing more, he and Rizzuto left. "I'm thinkin' about drawin' up one of those family trees," Rizzuto muttered as soon as they were alone.

"Why?"

"They're all so damned interconnected," Rizzuto complained. "It's hard to keep 'em straight! Ellandy's borrowed money from Vincent Farwell, who was the uncle of the wife of one of Ellandy's owners. The other owner's husband sells them diamonds and her brother is also Ellandy's lawyer as well as the lover of one of Ellandy's employees, who wants to be an owner her own self and who once had a fling-a-ding with Owner Number One. Sheesh. D'you think Malcolm Conner knew about Nicole and Lionel before Uncle Vincent sprung it on 'em last night?"

"You're doing it too," Toomey laughed. "Calling him 'Uncle Vincent'. Farwell had them all crying *Uncle*!—in more ways than one. I'm finding it harder and harder to believe in our anonymous burglars who just happened along on the one night Barney Peterson got so roaring drunk he forgot to set the burglar alarm."

"The Knoxes next?"

"I want to talk to Paul Bernstein first, and I think we'd better get Farwell's attorney to open that bedroom safe before we do any confronting of anybody. I wonder why Farwell hired Bernstein in the first place? Just because he suspected some extra-marital hanky-panky? I can't see him being that concerned about Gretchen's happiness."

Rizzuto said, "Well, if Simon's right, he coulda done it to embarrass Gretchen. D'you think he was really that mean? Gretchen dint like him much, and Lionel sure wasn't grievin' none. What about the other two women?"

"Nicole and Dorrie? Politely startled, I'd say. More interested in getting on with business than in mourning. Malcolm was the only one even to express any regret."

"Simon sure dint give a damn."

"What names these people have!" Toomey exclaimed out of the blue. "Simon and Lionel and Malcolm! Whatever happened to plain, simple names like Ed or Henry or Ralph? And Gretchen and Nicole—both foreign names, aren't they? And what about the oh-so-fancy Dorothea/Dorrie Murdoch?" Toomey suddenly smiled. "Ah, but we musn't forget Dorothy/Dot Polk! That's more like it. And Barney Peterson—now there's a good honest American name for you!"

"So what's so great about that?" muttered Sergeant Salvatore Rizzuto.

Mrs. Polk had been no problem. She'd calmed visibly under Lionel's reassurances that she'd always have a place with the Knoxes, regardless of whether Uncle Vincent's house was sold or not. Lionel felt a brief flash of resentment at having to do the job alone; after all, the housekeeper was not *his* "Polka Dot." Gretchen should have been there.

But Gretchen had been out when he reached home, so Lionel had first made a visit to a mortuary to arrange for Uncle Vincent's burial and had then gone back to the old man's house. *Carry on for now* was his message to Mrs. Polk. But Barney Peterson was another matter.

Lionel was of two minds about Barney. Barney should be fired; no question of that. But Lionel found himself reluctant to give the manservant the gate. He'd always liked Barney; the man was the one person in Uncle Vincent's house he'd felt comfortable talking to. And Barney had done them all a favor, in a shameful sort of way; it seemed a pity to punish him for that. Lionel climbed the stairs, the habit of not using Uncle Vincent's elevator still with him, and knocked on Barney's door.

"It's open," came a muffled voice.

Lionel went in. The manservant was standing looking out the window, his back to the door. Godfrey Daniel lay sprawled out on the bed, lazily washing his face; when he saw the visitor was the one who'd stepped on his tail the night before, he ceased his ablutions and gave Lionel his full attention.

Lionel cleared his throat. "Barney, we have to talk."

Bjarne Pedersen turned from the window, his face a perfect tragic mask. "Nine years," he said. "The first time in nine years I failed to turn on the alarm. And look what happened."

Lionel made up his mind right then. "It may not have been a burglar, you know. It may have been . . . someone who knew him."

Bjarne was puzzled. "Not a burglar?"

Lionel sat down on the side of the bed, trying to think of the best way to put it. Godfrey decided that to forgive was divine and draped himself gracefully over one of Lionel's thighs. "It makes a difference," Lionel said cautiously, stroking the cat. "If someone was determined to kill Uncle Vincent, then the alarm wouldn't have stopped him. Or her. The killer would have broken in anyway. And if not last night, then some other time."

"Someone who knew him?" Bjarne repeated, dumbfounded.

Lionel took a deep breath, let it out. "I think the police suspect one of us, one of the six who were here last night."

"Oh, Mr. Lionel!" Bjarne cried. "They couldn't think that!"

Lionel ran his free hand through his hair. "To tell you the truth, I don't really know what the police think. But they've started investigating us. I'm sure Uncle Vincent made a lot of enemies in his younger days, but since he retired . . . well, there just don't seem to be a whole lot of suspects around. Except us."

Bjarne was alarmed. He didn't have too much faith in the police to begin with; that Lieutenant Toomey's investigative techniques weren't anything at all like Basil Rathbone's. No other suspects, Mr. Lionel had said. The manservant thought rapidly. Should he . . . ? "Well, there was that man who came here last week."

"What man?"

"Fat man, gray hair, had a deep voice," Bjarne said, inventing freely. "I didn't get his name. But he and Mr. Vincent had an awful quarrel," he improvised. "I could hear them yelling at each other right through the library door."

"This was last week, you say?"

"Wednesday or Thursday," Bjarne lied. "Mrs. Polk was out."

Lionel fought down the urge to grin; he'd always looked on the manservant as an ally and it seemed he'd not been mistaken. "Have you told the police?"

"No sir, I didn't think of it until now," Bjarne said truthfully. "Do you think I should?"

"Oh, I do, definitely I do, indeed, yes." Lionel gave Godfrey Daniel one final pat and stood up. "And don't worry about your future, Barney. Gretchen and I still have some decisions to make, but you'll have a job with us as long as you want. Don't worry about a thing."

"Thank you, sir," Bjarne said with immense relief.

Lionel felt a lift of the spirits as he went out of Bjarne's room and started back down the stairs. With the manservant's mysterious caller to chase after, the police might ease up on Ellandy's. It had been a fruitful little chat—*and just in time*, Lionel thought, as he saw Mrs. Polk open the door to admit Lieutenant Toomey and his sergeant. And a dignified, brief-case-toting elderly man with thin white hair, a man Lionel didn't know.

"I see you and Godfrey have made up," were the Lieutenant's first words.

Lionel glanced over his shoulder to see Godfrey Daniel bouncing down the stairs behind him. "This afternoon he loves me," Lionel smiled. "He has a mercurial temperament, that cat. What can I do for you, Lieutenant?"

"You might like to witness the opening of Mr. Farwell's safe. Do you and Mr. Dann know each other?" He introduced Richard Dann, Vincent Farwell's attorney. "Mr. Dann has the combination to the safe."

"My condolences on your recent loss," Mr. Dann said—a bit coolly, Lionel thought.

"Thank you. Do you want to go straight up?"

They did. "Rizzuto, you might as well get started," Toomey said. The Sergeant nodded and moved off toward the library. "He's going to try to restore order to Mr. Farwell's files," the Lieutenant explained.

"Restore order?" Mr. Dann frowned. "I don't understand."

"His papers were all misfiled," Toomey said. "And not very neatly at that. As if the file cabinet had been emptied and then everything just shoved back in any old way."

"Dear me," said Mr. Dann, while Lionel concentrated on looking amazed.

"Well, we might as well get to it." Toomey started up the stairs.

"Do you suppose we might use the elevator?" Mr. Dann asked. "I'm not supposed to climb stairs."

Godfrey Daniel watched Sergeant Rizzuto go into the library and leave the door open. Then he watched Mrs. Polk disappear in the direction of the kitchen. Then at the last second he darted into the elevator with the three men who were going upstairs.

They passed Bjarne Pedersen's room on the way to the master bedroom, which was almost twice the size of the manservant's. "I've been in this room only once," Mr. Dann told the others, "but as I recall, the safe should be right over . . . oh, good heavens!"

They all saw it at the same time: the framed picture that normally covered the safe had been removed and was on the floor, leaning against the wall. The safe door gaped open.

"Damnation!" Lionel muttered.

"The same burglars who were here before, no doubt," Toomey said dryly. "Don't touch anything," he cautioned Mr. Dann, who was hurrying toward the safe. The Lieutenant trotted to the head of the stairs and bellowed, "Rizzuto!" He went back to the bedroom.

"There are papers still in there, Lieutenant," Mr. Dann said anxiously. "I'll need to check to see if anything's missing."

Toomey went over to the safe and, using his handkerchief, carefully lifted the papers out of the safe and spread them out on the bed. "Don't touch them," he warned Mr. Dann.

"No," the elderly lawyer agreed. "I'll just get my list—shoo, kitty." Godfrey Daniel had jumped up on the bed and was trying to help. Lionel lifted him off the bed and dropped him on a chair as Mr. Dann opened his briefcase and took out a file folder.

"Well?" Toomey asked impatiently.

"Just a moment, please." Mr. Dann wouldn't be rushed.

Sergeant Rizzuto appeared in the bedroom doorway. "Yeah, Lieutenant?"

"We've had a break-in," Toomey told him. "And a burglary?" He looked at Mr. Dann.

"Everything seems to be here except a promissory note for one and a half million dollars," Mr. Dann said, studying his list. "For a loan to Ellandy Jewels."

"Uh-*huh*," Toomey grunted. "Call in a burglary, Rizzuto. And get a fingerprint man over here. That safe, the picture leaning against the wall, and those papers on the bed."

"Right." Rizzuto turned and was gone.

"Jeez," Lionel breathed heavily. "Our note! Lieutenant, before you say anything—I didn't take it. I don't know anything about this."

"What were you doing upstairs?" Toomey asked.

"Talking to Barney! Right next door! Ask him!"

"I'll do that. How long have you been here?"

"Not more than twenty minutes, half an hour. I stopped in to tell Mrs. Polk and Barney not to worry about their jobs."

"You're not discharging the manservant?" Mr. Dann asked in tones of disapproval.

"Lieutenant, this could have been done last night," Lionel said, ignoring Mr. Dann. "I didn't even know Uncle Vincent had a safe until Gretchen told me this morning. And she doesn't know the combination—I *couldn't* have opened it!"

"Could the safe have been forced open?" Mr. Dann murmured.

"No signs of it," Toomey said. "Whoever opened it either had the combination or the right instruments for activating the combination. Mr. Knox, I can't search you without your permission until I get a warrant, but—"

"Oh, for crying out loud!" Lionel growled, jerking his suit jacket open. "Go ahead! Search!"

Toomey quickly assured himself that Lionel was not carrying the purloined promissory note. "I'm going to have to ask you not to leave until we've had time to search the house." He stepped briskly to the adjoining bedroom and told a startled Bjarne Pedersen not to leave his room until further notice. When Toomey got back to the master bedroom, he found

Lionel down on his knees peering under the bed, Mr. Dann watching him with bemusement.

Lionel got back to his feet. "Lieutenant," he said excitedly, "what if the note wasn't taken last night? There were police in this house all morning, and—"

"And so it must have been taken this afternoon?" Toomey smiled. "Recently, in fact?"

"Yes! Maybe just now—maybe we interrupted the burglar!" Lionel pulled back a heavy window drape and looked behind it. "He could be anywhere!" He strode into a small dressing alcove and pulled open the closet door.

And found Dorrie Murdoch standing there. Her eyes were enormous, her lips stretched back over clenched teeth, the palms of her hands pressed together in a gesture of supplication.

Lionel quickly closed the door. "He could be in any room on this floor!" he said to Toomey. "Why don't we look before—"

"Mr. Knox," Toomey sighed, "just leave the searching to us, will you? But until Sergeant Rizzuto gets back, I think we'll stay right where we are."

"Lieutenant Toomey," Mr. Dann said, "I'm going to want to take those papers as soon as you've finished checking for fingerprints."

At that moment Godfrey Daniel jumped down from his chair and trotted into the dressing alcove. He sniffed at the door and started pushing at it tentatively with one paw.

"Find a mouse, did you, Godfrey?" Toomey asked.

Lionel scooped up the cat and started talking rapidly. "Mr. Dann, who else knew the combination to the safe besides you? Somebody had to know it, or else the safe would have to be blown open and obviously it wasn't and—"

"No one else had the combination, so far as I know," Mr. Dann said.

"Nobody blows safes that size anyway," Toomey commented. "Not any more."

Godfrey wriggled free from Lionel's grasp and thumped to the floor. He went straight to the closet and this time tried hooking a paw under the bottom of the door.

"Must be a pretty big mouse," Toomey remarked. He shoved

past Lionel, gently pushed Godfrey Daniel out of the way with his foot, and pulled the door open. "Well, well, as I live and breathe—Mrs. Murdoch! Aren't you getting tired of standing in that stuffy closet? Come out here and sit down, why don't you? And then you can tell us why you were hiding in the closet of a room that's just been burglarized."

9

A thorough search of Vincent Farwell's house failed to turn up
the missing promissory note. The police had concentrated their
efforts on Bjarne Pedersen's room, because that seemed to
Lieutenant Toomey the logical place for Lionel Knox to have
hidden the note—if he had in fact taken it. But no, nothing
was found there except a confused-looking manservant and his
belongings.

Dorrie Murdoch had come up with one of the flimsiest excuses Lieutenant Toomey had listened to in all his years on
the force. She'd lost an earring, she'd said, the night before;
and she came back to look for it. While she was there, she
said, she thought she'd go up and take a look at Uncle Vincent's
bedroom—which she'd never seen, she said. The first thing
she noticed was the wall safe open and then she heard the
elevator and she was afraid she'd be accused of trying to steal
something from the safe and so she hid in the closet and she
didn't really do anything *wrong*, Lieutenant. She said.

Toomey put on a show of reluctance when he told her she
was free to go; she'd insisted on being searched and he didn't
have anything to hold her on. Inwardly Toomey was exulting,
for now he thought he knew the reason behind all that extraordinary activity in the murder room the night before. Both
the Knoxes had been in the library after Vincent Farwell was
murdered, Dorrie Murdoch had unexpectedly hidden herself
in Vincent Farwell's closet, and the promissory note Vincent
Farwell held from Ellandy Jewels had disappeared. Lieutenant
Toomey was not a believer in coincidence.

Dorrie left with Lionel Knox, the fingerprint man left with
several sets of prints, and Mr. Dann left with the papers they'd
found in the safe. Toomey and Sergeant Rizzuto settled down
in the kitchen with Mrs. Polk, who'd fixed them a big pot of

coffee. The housekeeper poured some cream into a bowl for Godfrey Daniel and then sat down in the breakfast nook with the two policemen. She was obviously still worried, but she seemed calmer than she'd been earlier in the day.

Toomey almost hated to do it to her. "Mrs. Polk, you moved Mr. Farwell's body, didn't you?" he charged abruptly. "You and Barney."

She turned white, but tried to bluff it out. "What do you mean? I didn't touch him!"

"Barney must have done the actual moving, but you knew about it. Maybe it was even your idea. You moved him before you called the police."

"That's not true!"

"Mrs. Polk, we know the body was moved after Mr. Farwell had already been dead a while. There's medical evidence that says so—*medical* evidence. If you and Barney didn't move him, then it had to be Gretchen Knox who did."

The housekeeper looked stricken. "Oh, no! You can't think Miss Gretchen . . . you're wrong, Lieutenant! Miss Gretchen didn't—wouldn't . . ."

"Nobody else was in the house."

"But she—"

"Either you or Gretchen," Toomey said mildly.

She lowered her head, and for a moment Toomey was afraid she was going to cry. She didn't. After a minute or two she admitted in a voice even higher than usual that she had indeed moved the body, from the middle of the floor back to the desk.

"You and Barney together," Rizzuto put in. "You ain't big enough by yourself, Mrs. Polk."

"I'm stronger than I look," she said defiantly.

Toomey waved Rizzuto to silence; she obviously felt guilty for involving Barney and was trying to protect him. That could wait. "Why did you move him, Mrs. Polk?"

"Because he looked terrible, sprawled out like that. It was indecent. He shouldn't have been left that way. It was a matter of respect, Lieutenant."

Toomey asked the housekeeper if she'd cleaned up the study before she called the police. "Like gathering up papers from the floor, for instance?"

"Papers? There were no papers on the floor. I didn't touch—oh. I did move the gun. I put it on the desk."

"Where was it?"

"On the floor, underneath Mr. Vincent. I'm sorry if I've caused trouble, Lieutenant. I honestly thought it wouldn't make any difference. I still don't see that it matters."

"So after you moved him," Toomey plowed on, "you called the police—and then woke up Gretchen and told her?"

"Yes."

"How did you know she was in the house? You told Sergeant Rizzuto you didn't speak to her again last night after you'd served the drinks and left the library. Come on, Mrs. Polk, you might as well tell us the whole story."

That one took a little longer, but Mrs. Polk finally admitted she'd been listening outside the library door. "It was hard not to hear them. I was just starting up the stairs to my room when they all began shouting."

"What were they shouting about?"

"At first, the loan. Then Mr. Vincent told Miss Gretchen about what that detective found out, about Mr. Lionel and that Nicole, and I knew Miss Gretchen would be staying here. She always does, whenever she and Mr. Lionel quarrel."

"Wait a minute—back up a bit. They were shouting about the loan? Why?"

"Well, they were all angry because Mr. Vincent had told them he wasn't renewing it. Mr. Lionel was especially upset."

Toomey and Rizzuto exchanged a satisfied smile. *Motive.* "Just one more question for now, Mrs. Polk," the Lieutenant said. "Did you happen to notice the jewelry Mrs. Murdoch was wearing last night?"

"Yes, indeed. She was wearing a lovely new gold pendant. It had rubies in it."

"Was she wearing earrings?"

"Oh no—earrings would have distracted from the pendant."

Rizzuto snorted. "Searching for a lost earring, huh?"

Mrs. Polk looked puzzled, but Toomey reassured her they'd just have a word with Barney and then be on their way.

"Where's your car?" Lionel Knox asked.

"In the garage," Dorrie Murdoch answered. "I took a cab."

"I'm parked around the corner." Lionel waited until they were in the car and then blurted out: "Did you get it?"

"No!" Dorrie cried in frustration. "The safe really was open when I got there! I looked through the papers, but the note wasn't there. I was just trying to decide what to do next when I heard the elevator and . . . well."

They looked at each other and pronounced one word: "Nicole." Lionel started the car.

"She's not at Ellandy's," Dorrie said. "She might be at home."

"Right," said Lionel, and pulled away from the curb.

"The computer's not hooked up yet," Paul Bernstein said.

Toomey took his time answering, looking around Bernstein's new office. More space, higher rent district—the detective was moving up in the world. "But your memory's still hooked up, isn't it? I can wait for the details. Just give me a rough outline. This is a homicide investigation, remember. And don't say anything about client confidentiality—your client's dead."

Bernstein saw no reason to volunteer the information that Gretchen Knox was now his client. "There's not much to tell," he shrugged. "Except for that one fling Lionel Knox had with Nicole Lattimer, he's been hewing to the straight and narrow. Doesn't even cheat on his income tax more than most."

"What about the rest of them?"

The detective shrugged again. "Dorrie Murdoch spends a lot of time buying clothes and getting her hair done. So does Simon. Nicole seems to have settled in nicely with Malcolm Conner. Conner himself is squeaky clean. They're all doing well financially—except Simon Murdoch may be in for a rough time."

"Oh? How's that?"

"He made a killing on a diamond deal several years ago, and he put his profit into real estate—which is unusual for a diamond merchant, I'm told. Most of them just buy more diamonds. Anyway, Murdoch started buying condos and shorefront properties, and he got in over his head. He's been buying diamonds on extended credit, and he *has* managed to come up with enough cash to keep both the real estate and the diamond business going. But he's doing a juggling act."

Toomey mulled that over. "What does that have to do with Ellandy Jewels?"

"Not a damned thing, far as I can see. But the old man wanted reports on all of them, and that's what I turned up on Simon."

"Anything illegal in what Simon's doing?"

"I couldn't find anything. It's just a high-risk business he's in and he's running close to the edge. He's a pretty shrewd dealer, though. He'll probably pull out of it."

Toomey asked, "If he were a corporation, would you invest money in him?"

Bernstein grinned. "I'm a conservative investor, Lieutenant. The only one of that gang I'd put money in is the old man himself, and he's gone now."

"How'd he make his money?"

"Smart investments, most of them in the late thirties right before the war broke out. His U.S. Gypsum shares, for instance—they'd doubled in value by the time the war was over. And his Colgate-Palmolive shares had *tripled*." Bernstein shook his head. "Whoever'd think of *toothpaste* as a wartime investment? Everything he bought didn't pay off that big, of course, but he never really took a bath on anything. Money makes money."

"So I've heard," Toomey said dryly. "Well, thanks, Bernstein. Those reports you gave Farwell—you'll send me copies when your computer's clicking again?"

"Tomorrow," Bernstein nodded. "This means you owe me one, Lieutenant."

"I know," Toomey sighed.

Dorrie and Simon Murdoch sat propped up side by side on the big bed, looking at themselves in the mirror that surrounded them on three sides.

"Tell me I misunderstood," Simon drawled. "Tell me you didn't really say you went back to Uncle Vincent's to rob the safe."

"Well, we didn't know about the safe last night, did we?" Dorrie asked a mite testily. "I thought if the note was there, I ought at least to make a try for it."

"Tell me, did you come home first and put on your black housebreaking outfit?"

"Don't be silly, darling—black's no protection in the daytime."

"And so Lieutenant Toomey found you hiding in Uncle Vincent's closet. However did you explain that?"

"I told him I was looking for an earring I'd lost."

"In Uncle Vincent's closet?"

"Oh, Simon, you're not even *trying* to understand!" Dorrie cried. "You're so smart—what would you have done?"

Simon raised an eyebrow. "I wouldn't have allowed myself to be caught, for one thing. For another, I wouldn't have been there in the first place. All you've done is direct suspicion toward yourself, my love."

"Thanks a lot. Whatever would I do without you?"

"Now, darling, don't be sarcastic—that won't help. We have to think what to do next. You and Lionel are sure Nicole took the note?"

"Who else would want it? She and I had been talking about it, and about where Uncle Vincent was likely to keep the combination. She just beat me to it."

"You think she beat you to it."

"Where *is* she?" Dorrie screamed, making Simon wince. "She's not at Ellandy's and she's not at home. Malcolm's off consulting with a client somewhere and I couldn't get hold of him either. I've left messages everywhere for both of them."

"What's Lionel doing?"

"Trying to decide how much to tell Gretchen."

They sat in silence for a few minutes, staring at their reflections in the mirror. Then Simon got up. "There's one thing we've got to do, and we've got to do it *now*. We have to get rid of our 'loot'. Where'd you put it?"

"In the linen closet. In a blue airline bag."

Simon found the bag, brought it into the bedroom. "You know, this is just heavy enough to sink nicely if it were tossed into a body of water. A large body of water. Like an ocean."

"You want to drive down to the shore?" Dorrie unzipped the airline bag and started looking through the things they'd taken from Uncle Vincent's library. "Why not just drop the bag into the river? That's closer."

"They drag rivers, darling. I've never heard of anyone dragging an ocean, have you?"

Dorrie held up the jade horse and examined it closely. "You know, Simon, some of these things are really quite nice."

"Now, dear, you know we can't keep them. That's all we need—Lieutenant Toomey to come charging in here with a search warrant and find incriminating evidence all over the place."

"Oh, he wouldn't do that!" She was half laughing, half scoffing. "Why should he? Just because he found me in Uncle Vincent's closet? That's not reason enough to get a search warrant for our *home*, surely."

Simon raised an eyebrow at her. "Oh, you're certain of that, are you? I suppose we could call Malcolm and find out the law's position on searching and the issuance of warrants pertaining thereunto, but somehow I don't believe that would be a wise thing to do."

"Now who's being sarcastic? Look at this jade horse, Simon—it's a lovely little thing. Do we have to get rid of it?"

Simon took the horse and examined it. "You're right, it is lovely." He sighed. "But we must be strong, darling. Into the water it goes. Along with the rest of Uncle Vincent's playthings." He gave the horse back to her.

"What a pity. Darling, I really don't want to drive all the way to the shore. Suppose someone did fish the airline bag out of the river. How would they ever know who put it there?"

"Fingerprints, my love."

"Oh, well, if that's all . . ." Dorrie jumped up and fetched a linen handkerchief from one of the bureaus. She started polishing the jade horse furiously.

Simon watched her a moment and then said, "That *is* a long drive to the shore. Be sure you don't miss a spot."

"I'm being very careful." She put the jade horse aside and started working on Uncle Vincent's wristwatch.

"I'll get the car out," Simon said. "You bring the bag."

Fifteen minutes later Dorrie slid into the passenger seat of Simon's Mercedes, the airline bag on her lap. "Where would be a good place?"

"The middle of the river would be safest," Simon mused. "We'll have to drop it off a bridge."

"Pick an unimportant bridge, darling. One without many people."

"With the whole world on its way home from work? That may take some doing." Simon started the engine. "However, let us see what we can find." He pulled away from the curb to start their search for an unimportant bridge.

Half a block away, Sergeant Rizzuto also pulled away from the curb, concentrating on keeping a discreet distance behind them.

* * *

Malcolm Conner dipped his pita bread into the chick-pea sauce, took a bite, and chewed thoughtfully. "We ought to think about going to the police."

"No, that is the one thing we ought *not* to think about." Nicole Lattimer ate a stuffed grape leaf and said, "We're out of that free and clear, Malcolm—let's leave well enough alone."

Malcolm shook his head. "I haven't been able to think of anything else all day. If it were just the gun—you should never have fired that gun, Nicole, and you most certainly should not have removed the statuette from the scene of the crime."

"So you've told me. A hundred times you've told me."

"If it were just the matter of my returning the statuette, I could live with that. But the condition that room was in— papers all over the place, a real mess. Somebody was there after you left, Nicole. After you left and before I got there. We can help the police pinpoint the time. If we don't tell them, we're guilty of withholding information in a criminal investigation. That's two to five years, and I could be disbarred. I *would* be disbarred."

Nicole signaled the waiter and asked for iced tea. When he inquired unbelievingly whether anything was wrong with the wine, she told him everything was wrong with the wine and to bring some tea, please. When he left muttering to himself, Nicole said to Malcolm, "So somebody else was in Uncle Vincent's library between the times you and I were there. So what? It wasn't the murderer—Uncle Vincent was already dead. It must have been Lionel or Dorrie, looking for the same thing I was looking for."

Malcolm was scandalized. "Dorrie wouldn't do something like that!"

That struck Nicole as so funny that she was laughing out loud when the waiter came back with her iced tea. She waited until he was gone and said, "Of *course* Dorrie would do something like that, and Lionel too. Dorrie isn't the little girl you grew up with, Malcolm, not any more. Suppose we do go to the police and tell them Uncle Vincent's library was searched by someone between the time I left and the time you got there—and that someone turns out to be your sister? Do you really want to take that chance, Malcolm?"

He sat staring at her until his food grew cold. "It couldn't have been Dorrie," he said finally.

"You know perfectly well it could," Nicole answered in her most practical voice. "And what happens to you when the police find out you diddled with the evidence? Not as much as I did, but you didn't call the police and you smuggled the statuette back in."

"I *returned* the murder weapon . . . ," he started, but then trailed off.

"You know what I think, Malcolm? I think you have no intention of going to the police. But you feel you ought to make noises about going just to square things with your conscience. And I think my role is to talk you out of it. Well, consider it done. We are *not* going to the police. There, it's settled."

Malcolm was hurt. "That was unkind, Nicole."

She sighed. "Yes, it was—and I'm sorry. But we're both in the clear so long as we *keep quiet*. And I know you don't want to run the risk of implicating Dorrie."

"Not Dorrie," Malcolm frowned. "Lionel. You might have interrupted him, you know. Have you thought of that?"

Now it was Nicole's turn to stare. "Are you saying you think *Lionel* killed Uncle Vincent?"

Malcolm leaned back in his chair and tried to consider the matter from the viewpoint of a prosecuting attorney. "Look at what we know. Uncle Vincent was murdered and the library was searched. I think we can assume that what the killer was looking for was the promissory note. Say he dispatched Uncle Vincent and was just starting his search when you showed up. He hid somewhere, in another part of the house. When you left, he went back into the library, and—not knowing that you had already looked for the note—proceeded to go through Uncle Vincent's desk and file cabinet, tossing the papers away when he'd finished looking at them. Since you'd already looked in the same places, that would mean the killer didn't find what he was looking for."

"I think that's a safe conclusion," Nicole murmured.

"You still don't think it was Lionel? We know it wasn't you or Dorrie. Gretchen's too ineffectual to pull off a murder, or even to think of pulling one off. Simon might have done it to protect Dorrie—but frankly I don't believe my doting brother-in-law is all *that* doting. As far as that goes, I could have done it myself—to protect you *and* Dorrie. But I didn't. So who's left? Lionel Knox, I'm sorry to say. Process of elimination."

"Aren't you eliminating a name or two rather easily? Malcolm—be honest. Who of the six of us gets mad the quickest? Who flares up without any warning and then cools off a minute later? Who scares everybody with the intensity of her anger—and might even strike in the heat of that anger?"

Malcolm looked as if she'd just dropped a pair of dirty socks in his dinner plate. "You can't be serious! You think *Dorrie* killed him?"

"That little scenario you wrote starring Lionel as the killer —try it on Dorrie. It fits."

Malcolm stared at her open-mouthed for a while and then recollected himself. "This is far too public a place to be talking about this. Are you finished? Good." He signaled the waiter for the bill.

Outside the restaurant, Malcolm told the parking lot attendant, "Silver BMW." As soon as the young man was out of hearing, he said, "You amaze me, Nicole, you really do. I cannot understand why you are so determined to blame Dorrie for Uncle Vincent's death."

"I'm not trying to *blame* her, Malcolm, I'm trying to cover for her. Don't you understand? That's why I fired Uncle Vincent's gun in the first place."

"That makes no sense whatsoever."

"Yes, it does," she said impatiently. "When I found him dead like that, the only thing I could think of was that Dorrie had lost her temper and let him have it. So I fired the gun so it would look like more of a struggle—you know, so she could plead self-defense if she got caught?"

"Then why remove the statuette? Why not leave it there?"

"Because I was afraid I couldn't wipe it clean enough! You saw the condition it was in—broken and covered with blood. All those little *crevices*. The police have all sorts of sophisticated detection instruments nowadays, and it just seemed better not to give them anything to work with. Dorrie or whoever *should* have taken the statuette."

The attendant was back with Malcolm's car. Nicole walked around to the passenger side.

"I think I see," Malcolm mused. "Even if the murder was

a spur-of-the-moment thing, the killer should know not to leave the murder weapon behind to aid the police in making a possible identification. The blood could be covering latent fingerprints—that sort of thing?"

"That's the idea," Nicole said, getting into the car. "Unless the killer was wearing gloves, of course."

"Gloves—yes," Malcolm said, sliding in under the wheel. "That would explain why the statuette was left lying out there in full view."

The parking lot attendant closed the door after Nicole and bent down until his face was level with hers. "You guys mystery writers?"

"That's right," Nicole smiled tightly. "This one's called *Who Killed Uncle Vincent?*"

"Great, I love mysteries! I'll watch for it."

"You do that," Malcolm said, reaching across Nicole to hand the attendant his tip. He pressed down on the accelerator and drove away. "Why didn't you tell me all this last night?"

"Because nobody could tell you *anything* last night," Nicole said in exasperation. "When you found me trying to hide the statuette in the laundry, you came as close to blowing up as I've ever seen you! Such outrage, such indignation! You started lecturing me about responsibility and legal evidence and the penalties for interfering with the investigation of a crime—so I let you take the statuette back just to get you to stop *talking* at me!"

"Well, you have to realize you gave me a considerable shock. First you tell me Uncle Vincent has been murdered, and then you calmly inform me the broken statuette you're holding is the murder weapon. How did you expect me to react? Have you forgotten I'm an officer of the court? I don't just casually step into a murder case and start rearranging evidence to suit myself—I don't think you appreciate what it cost me to sneak into Uncle Vincent's house and put the statuette back. By the way, did you know Barney got drunk last night and forgot to set the alarm system? That's why the dining room window was left unlocked—he didn't check any of the windows or doors."

"Did you remember to return the neighbor's ladder?"

"Of course I remembered," Malcolm said testily. "I cannot believe that *both* of us borrowed a ladder without permission, climbed over Uncle Vincent's wall—that's trespass—and then crawled in through a ground-floor window. *That's* illegal entry. We broke a lot of laws last night, Nicole."

She waved a hand dismissively. "Piddling stuff. The real lawbreaker was the one who clobbered Uncle Vincent."

"And you think it was Dorrie. Nicole, you couldn't be more wrong. Dorrie has had these little flare-ups all her life, but they're never violent. They're certainly not violent enough to let her kill a man. I know my sister, and she'd never run the risk of striking out at Uncle Vincent if he caught her going through his files. Her natural inclination would be to try to talk her way out of it."

"She's not the same little girl you grew up with," Nicole repeated darkly.

Lieutenant Toomey sat at his desk at the police station and chewed away at a roast beef sandwich made exactly the way he liked it—mustard on one side, butter on the other, not too much lettuce. He'd called his wife and said not to wait dinner.

Spread out on the desk were a series of photographs and the crime lab reports. The fingerprints found in the library had all been accounted for: Vincent Farwell's, the two servants', the six guests'. He read the medical examiner's report. There'd been no powder residue on Vincent Farwell's gun hand, but that was to be expected; too much time had elapsed between the firing of the gun and the application of the test.

Dr. Oringer had at last narrowed down the time of death. Rigor mortis usually set in between three and five hours after death, and lasted anywhere from eight to ten hours. It started in the face and spread downward, the body cooling at a rate of one and a half degrees an hour for twelve hours. Dr. Oringer had tentatively set the time of death between ten-thirty and eleven, since Farwell's rigor had stopped around noon. But he'd cautioned that the time of death could be an hour or two later, depending on when the fire went out in the library fireplace. Did the fire burn late and delay the onset of rigor? It was the variable they couldn't pin down.

Toomey wiped a glob of mustard off the medical examiner's report. He'd sent a legman to talk to the nightwatchman at Ellandy Jewels; he'd come back with confirmation that Lionel Knox, Dorrie Murdoch, and Nicole Lattimer were indeed at Ellandy's during the time they said they were. The same legman had also interviewed the waitress at Danny's Tavern, since Toomey decided he wanted Sergeant Rizzuto tailing Dorrie Murdoch instead of asking questions. The waitress had also confirmed the time five of Toomey's suspects had spent in the bar.

So from eight to nine they were all in Uncle Vincent's library. From a little after nine to around ten all but Gretchen Knox were in the bar. And from then until after midnight, Lionel, Dorrie, and Nicole were together at Ellandy's—it did look as if those three were out of it. That meant the killer was either Simon Murdoch or Malcolm Conner. Or Gretchen Knox.

Or that unknown visitor who—Barney Peterson miraculously happened to remember—had threatened Uncle Vincent only last Thursday. Just what the case had been needing—a Mysterious Stranger! Barney had claimed with a perfectly straight face that he'd heard this man (name unknown, detailed description willingly supplied) tell Mr. Vincent that he'd never let him get away with it, that he'd kill Mr. Vincent first. What the "it" was that Vincent Farwell was supposed to be trying to get away with, Barney didn't know. But he'd heard the threat, oh yes sir, indeed he had, sir. *Why didn't you mention this before?* Toomey had asked. *I didn't think of it, sir,* Barney had replied.

That part Toomey believed.

Well, a Mysterious Stranger would certainly get everybody else off the hook—which was undoubtedly why Barney Peterson had come up with him in the first place. Had the man-servant worked out some sort of deal with one of the others? Lionel Knox had been there talking to Barney that afternoon right before Toomey arrived. (And Dorrie Murdoch had been there hiding in a closet.) But on the slim chance that Barney might be telling the truth, Toomey had put out an APB on a silver-haired fat man with a deep voice. Rumpled white suit, expensive rings on both hands, imperious manner. Sydney Greenstreet?

Toomey looked at the photographs of the murder scene. Vincent Farwell lay spread out on his desk, the gun just beyond his fingertips. The photos showed the drinking glasses from the night before, the fingerprints from each telling Toomey where everyone had been sitting. No fingerprints on the murder weapon, the broken alabaster Hermes. But the fingerprint report did have one interesting tidbit: Dorrie Murdoch's prints had been found on the papers in Uncle Vincent's safe—there, he was doing it too! *Uncle* Vincent. But Dorrie hadn't taken the missing promissory note with her when she left, Toomey was sure of that. Was it still hidden in Uncle Vincent's house, somewhere his men hadn't been able to find it? The men *had* found the combination to the safe, taped under the narrow overhang of a window sill in the bedroom.

"Lieutenant!" A grinning Sal Rizzuto stood in the doorway of Toomey's office. "Look what I've got!" He stepped aside to let Dorrie and Simon Murdoch in. "I caught 'em throwin' somethin' into the river. Evidence, maybe? Twenty-second Street Bridge, right in the middle of rush hour."

Both Murdochs looked more than a little put out. "If it is a crime, Lieutenant," Simon drawled, "to dispose of old tax records by tossing them into a body of water, then we are indeed guilty and should be locked away where we will wreak no further havoc on the human race. But if it is not a crime, however, will you kindly instruct your minion here to *let us go*?"

Toomey pointed to a couple of chairs. "Have a seat, folks. Now what's this all about?"

"Minion?" said Rizzuto.

The Murdochs sat down. "As I said," Simon went on, "we were merely disposing of some old tax records. Every year at about this time we get rid of those records that are seven years old."

"By puttin' them in an airline bag?" Rizzuto snorted. "And throwin' the bag into the river?"

"We always make a little ceremony of it, you see," Dorrie said helpfully. "We go out and have dinner at a nice restaurant afterward." She laughed charmingly. "It's just an excuse for celebrating, but it's fun. *Did* we break a law, Lieutenant?"

"A light bag containing nothing but paper," Toomey mused. "It sank all right, did it?"

"Like a stone," Rizzuto said. "Whatever's in that bag, it ain't no buncha papers."

"Oh, come now, Sergeant." Simon raised an eyebrow at the man who'd brought them in. "Surely you know how heavy paper can be. Besides, we weighted it down."

"With what?"

"A rock," the Murdochs said simultaneously, and then glanced at each other with what looked suspiciously like relief.

Toomey got up and walked around his desk where he stood facing the Murdochs. "Vincent Farwell was murdered last night. A promissory note that most likely was the motive for the murder has been stolen. Both Ellandy Jewels and Simon Murdoch are having financial troubles." He paused. "And this is the time you pick to clean out old tax records?"

Simon let loose a great sigh of exasperation. "The cleaning-out was already done, Lieutenant. We'd packed the bag several days ago—we just didn't get around to throwing it away until now."

"Darling, are you having financial troubles?" Dorrie asked with concern.

"No, I am not. Wherever did you get an idea like that, Lieutenant Toomey?"

"From Paul Bernstein, as a matter of fact."

"Ah, the detective. Yes. Remind me never to hire Mr. Bernstein. The man's obviously incompetent."

"No, he ain't," Rizzuto objected. "He usta be a cop."

"And all police, whether former or present," Simon remarked with a half-smile, "are infallible, of course."

"Hey, don't get smart," Rizzuto bristled.

"Take it easy, Rizzuto," Toomey said. The Lieutenant started back to his chair but brushed against the side of the desk and was surprised to hear a metallic *clunk* sound. What the . . . ? He put a hand into his jacket pocket—oh yes, it was that blasted can of Redi-Whip; he'd been carrying it around all day. Annoyed, he set the can down sharply on the desk top.

And heard Dorrie Murdoch gasp.

Quickly she rearranged her startled features into the nearest thing to a poker face she could manage. But it was too late; she'd given herself away.

Toomey leaned across the desk toward her. "What's the matter, Mrs. Murdoch? Frightened by Redi-Whip, are you? Whippingcreamphobia?"

"Why, I, ah, I was just surprised, that's all. I didn't expect a police lieutenant to carry something like that in his coat pocket."

"That's your can of Redi-Whip, isn't it? You left it on the terrace outside the library, and you left it there last night."

"Don't be absurd, Lieutenant," Simon interrupted sharply. "Why would Dorrie take a can of Redi-Whip to a business meeting?"

"Not to the meeting. Later. When she went back."

"Went back!" Dorrie cried. "Why would I go back?"

"Suppose you tell me."

"You're making a mistake, Lieutenant," she protested. "I didn't go . . . why would I . . . and the Redi-Whip . . ."

Simon stood up. "Lieutenant, this has gone far enough. Either charge us with, ah, littering, or let us go. Well, Lieutenant?"

"What was in the airline bag?" Toomey asked softly.

Simon threw up his hands. "Tee, ay, ex, pea, ay, pea, ee, are, ess. Tax papers!"

Dorrie stood up quickly and took his arm. "Darling, don't let him upset you. That's what he wants."

Simon smiled at her reassuringly. "Don't worry, love, I'm not upset." His smile disappeared as he turned to Lieutenant Toomey. "Are we under arrest?"

"No," Toomey said blandly. "You're free to go."

"Ah!" Dorrie beamed her pleasure at all three men.

"There, darling," Simon said smoothly. "I told you there was nothing to worry about."

"Yes, I know. You were right, dear."

"Then let us linger no longer in this bastion of law enforcement. Goodbye, Lieutenant . . . Sergeant. Come along, Dorrie-love."

"Yes, darling, let's go." She waved goodbye and the two of them left.

Rizzuto grunted. "I bet they don't talk like that when they're alone."

"I'll bet they do." Toomey sat down at his desk. "What do you think was in that bag?"

The Sergeant took the chair just vacated by Dorrie Murdoch. "The stuff that's missin' from Uncle Vincent's study? Maybe they *both* went back. Could be they're our burglars."

Toomey picked up the can of Redi-Whip. "I wonder what this was for? Well, what've we got? Mrs. Murdoch snuck back into Uncle Vincent's house this afternoon and either opened the safe or found it open. She looked through the papers and then hid in the closet when she heard us coming. She lied about looking for a lost earring. Then she and her matching blond husband claim to be in such a rush to get rid of some useless papers that they can't wait until rush hour is over to go throw them off a bridge. And last but not least, the lovely Mrs. Murdoch all but claims ownership of a can of Redi-Whip that places her at the murder scene."

"So what does it add up to?"

"What it adds up to," Toomey smiled grimly, "is grounds for a search warrant. First thing tomorrow."

10

The Knoxes' house, Lieutenant Toomey thought as he looked about him, was oddly impersonal. A blank-faced maid had let him in and left him standing in the entryway while she went to tell the Knoxes he was there.

Toomey wandered into the living room. It was modern and expensive-looking and in apple-pie order, a layout for a fancy-living magazine. But there was nothing of Lionel or Gretchen in it he could see at all; they'd probably just called in a decorator and said go to it. His and hers facing sofas, covered with some sort of butternut-colored leather. Toomey ran his hand across the back of one of them; soft as a baby's bottom. He was looking at some sort of Aztec plaque hanging over the surrealistic fireplace when the maid came back and led him to a cheerful, sunny breakfast room.

Lionel and Gretchen had just finished eating and were lingering over coffee and newspapers. Toomey turned down their offer of breakfast but accepted a cup of coffee. "Sorry to barge in on you so early," he said, sitting down at the table, "but I have a full day ahead of me and I need to get going."

Gretchen handed him his coffee. Lionel said, "Where's your shadow, Lieutenant?"

"Sergeant Rizzuto? He's got something to take care of this morning." Rizzuto was, in fact, walking through the procedure needed to obtain a warrant to search the Murdochs' apartment.

Gretchen asked, "How is your investigation coming along, Lieutenant? Any, um, clues to Uncle Vincent's killer?"

Toomey wasted no time. "One or two interesting things have turned up. For instance, the housekeeper and the manservant moved your uncle's body before they called the police. Mrs. Polk admitted it."

Two pairs of eyes blinked at him but both Knoxes managed

to keep their faces straight. "How extraordinary," Gretchen murmured. "Why did they do that?"

Instead of answering her, Toomey said: "That must be a relief to you two. Knowing how the body got over to the desk, I mean. You both expected him to be found in the middle of the floor."

They both started protesting vociferously. "Why would we expect him to be found *anywhere*?" Lionel demanded. "We didn't know he was dead!"

"Yes, you did," Toomey answered mildly. "You knew he was dead, and you knew he'd been murdered. You both went into the library long after that meeting was over and you found him there. You found him in the middle of the floor. Now I want you to tell me why you went back—although I think I know the answer to that one—and what you did when you got there."

They both glared at him, said nothing.

Toomey sighed. "Look, you gave yourselves away yesterday morning. You were both surprised when I told you Uncle Vincent's body was found at his desk. You," pointing to Lionel, "expected to find papers strewn all over the floor. Sergeant Rizzuto discovered that all the papers in the file had been jammed in every which way, without regard to what papers went in what folders." He looked at Gretchen. "You did that? Mrs. Polk swears there were no papers on the floor when she found your uncle, and I believe her. So that sounds to me as if you two went into the library separately, Mr. Knox first and then Mrs. Knox. You both lied about that."

Still they said nothing, but they'd stopped glaring at him. Lionel was concentrating on his coffee cup while Gretchen's eyes were taking on a glazed look.

"Also," Toomey went on, "I know that Uncle Vincent refused to renew the Ellandy loan. He didn't just put you off, the way you said he did. He told you no. Unequivocally. That's something else you lied about."

Gretchen's eyes were closed. Lionel had slumped down until his nose was only a few inches above his coffee cup.

Toomey played his last card. "There's still a question about the exact time of death, but it's pretty clear Uncle Vincent was killed sometime during the period you were taking inventory at Ellandy Jewels, Mr. Knox. That means you're in the clear. And if Mrs. Knox went into the study *after* you did, then she's in the clear too. Do you want me to find the killer? Then help me."

Lionel lifted his eyes from the coffee cup. "Are you playing straight, Lieutenant? Or is this a trick?"

Toomey smiled. "Tricks can't substitute for evidence in the courts, Mr. Knox. That's straight."

Lionel looked at Gretchen; she nodded. "I did go back, Lieutenant," Lionel said, "and you must have guessed it, I was looking for that promissory note."

"What time was this?"

"Oh, I got there around five, a little after. It was close to one-thirty when I went to bed, and I spent three hours tearing up the sheets. I couldn't sleep, thinking about that goddamned note. So I got to the point where I had to get up and *do* something."

"So you went back to Uncle Vincent's house. And what did you find?"

"I didn't find the note, obviously. Uncle Vincent was sprawled out at his desk, and the room was a mess. I spent a lot of time looking at every piece of paper I could find."

"Wait a minute—Uncle Vincent was at his *desk*?"

Lionel looked uncomfortable. "I moved him. I put him in the middle of the floor."

The body was moved *twice*? "For god's sake *why*, man?"

"Well, it seemed to me as if someone had deliberately tried to make the place look as if there'd been a burglary. All those papers everywhere, the desk drawers emptied and turned upside down, the broken glass from the terrace doors—it looked *staged*, Lieutenant."

"That's what I thought too," Gretchen said. "A real burglar wouldn't take that much time—to make such a mess, I mean. Real burglars like to get in and out fast, don't they?"

"So why did you move him?" Toomey asked, a bit dazed.

"To help," Lionel said frankly. "To make it look like more of a struggle. Well, look, Lieutenant—I was there to find the note. The only thing I could think of was that somebody else had had the same idea but got there before I did. I thought that whoever'd killed Uncle Vincent had the note—which was good news for me, in a gruesome sort of way."

Toomey smiled wryly. "Which one did you suspect? Dorrie or Nicole?"

"Now that is something I'm *not* going to tell you, Lieutenant," Lionel said with determination. "So okay, I'm guilty of attempted burglary and maybe meddling with evidence, but I didn't kill Uncle Vincent. I didn't even take anything out of the room—I meant to take that broken statuette, but I stepped on Godfrey Daniel's tail and he let out a howl to wake the dead. I got spooked and ran."

Toomey remembered the cat's brief hostility toward Lionel the previous day. "Ran where? How'd you get in in the first place?"

"I used Gretchen's extra key to get in. But I went out over the terrace wall. There was a table—"

"I saw it," Toomey said. "So that's your scuff mark on the surface. And that's how you got your limp? Jumping off the wall?"

Lionel shrugged. "It seemed quickest."

Toomey thought a moment. "When you moved the body, was there a blotter on the desk?"

"Oh yeah, the desk blotter—I burned it in the fireplace. It had blood all over it."

"Ugh," said Gretchen.

"Anything else?" Toomey sighed.

"Yeah—I tucked the gun under Uncle Vincent's body. Let's see," said Lionel, thinking back and enumerating, "I turned on the lights, saw the mess, looked at each of the papers, moved Uncle Vincent, moved the gun, burned the blotter, stepped on Godfrey, and ran. That's all." That wasn't quite all, but Lionel was not going to mention burning the private investigator's report unless he had to.

Interfering with evidence and withholding evidence—both felonies, Toomey thought. "The lights were off when you got there? You're sure?"

Lionel nodded. "I remember looking to see if there was any light showing under the library door before I went in. That's an old house, Lieutenant, and some of the doors don't fit tight against the floor. The lights were off."

"Now this next question isn't going to be pleasant, but I have to ask it. When you moved Uncle Vincent, what condition was the body in? I mean—"

"He was stiff as a board," Lionel said bluntly.

"Ugh," Gretchen said again.

So by five-thirty or so, rigor was well advanced. "All right, Mrs. Knox," Toomey said, "it's your turn. What time did you go into the study?"

"I guess right after Lionel left," Gretchen said. "I heard Godfrey scream and went down to see what was the matter. It must have been around six."

"And?"

She shrugged with one shoulder. "It was the way Lionel said. The library was a mess and Uncle Vincent was lying on the floor. So I straightened up—"

"Why? Why did you do that?"

Gretchen bit her bottom lip. "I was mad at my husband, Lieutenant. I wanted to cause trouble for him. It was stupid and I shouldn't have done it, but I thought if I could make the room look as if a robbery had *not* taken place—well, I thought the police would give Lionel a hard time. I didn't think he'd be *arrested* or anything like that. But I just wanted him to, you know, suffer a little?"

Nice, thought Toomey. "So tell me what you did."

"Well, I picked up the papers and put them back in the file—it took me the *longest* time. Then I gathered up the stuff from the desk drawers."

"Missing a couple of things along the way," Toomey told her. "There was one page of a letter still under the sofa, and your uncle's Infralux was over in a corner."

"Oh dear." Gretchen smiled tentatively and said in a soft voice, "I don't have much experience with murder scenes, Lieutenant."

Toomey waited for her to bat her eyes but she didn't. "What about the ivory owl and the other things? Did you put them around the room?"

"Yes, I did. I thought the jade horse and the rest had been taken just to make it look like robbery. A real burglar would have taken the Degas, or at least the mantle clock. So I fetched a few knick-knacks to fill in the empty spaces."

"Anything else before you left—no? Did you turn off the lights?"

Gretchen thought back. "Yes. I turned off the lights, closed the door, and went back up to my room."

"How?"

"How what?"

"How did you go back up to your room? By the stairs?"

"Oh—no, I took the elevator. I mean, Uncle Vincent wouldn't be using it, would he?"

Toomey grunted; one more loose end tied up. "What time was it when you got to your room?"

"About six-thirty."

"And Mrs. Polk called us at seven forty-five. Yes, that works out. Now. Have you two told me everything?"

"Oh, absolutely!" Lionel exclaimed.

"Uh-*huh*," Gretchen nodded vigorously.

"Because if I find you haven't, I can still charge you with interfering at the scene of a crime. The courts don't take that offense lightly, let me tell you."

"We've told you everything, Lieutenant," Lionel said in his most earnest manner.

"I hope so. I want you both to come into the station sometime today and dictate your statements to one of our stenographers." They nodded reluctantly and Toomey got up from the table. "Thanks for the coffee. By the way, what are you going to do with Uncle Vincent's house? Sell it?"

Lionel just shrugged but Gretchen said, "No, I thought we'd keep it and live in it. We'll sell this one instead."

Lionel's eyebrows shot up. "We will? Well, that's a nice surprise! Thanks for talking it over with me first, Gretchen."

"The house *is* in my name, Lionel."

"As you never tire of reminding me."

Toomey beat a hasty retreat.

Dorrie Murdoch reached out her racquet—but not far enough and not fast enough. The ball thudded against the wall behind her and fell to the floor. Furious, Dorrie hurled her racquet after the ball.

Malcolm Conner picked up his sister's broken racquet. "I'd say that ends the game for now. What's the matter with you today, Dorrie? You can't keep your mind on what you're doing."

"Nothing!" she screeched. "Nothing's the matter!"

Malcolm knew his sister better than that. "Let's have some orange juice," he suggested.

They went out and sat at a small table on the club's glassed-in terrace. When the waiter had brought their juice, Malcolm said, "All right, Dorrie—let's have it. What's wrong?"

Dorrie stared into her orange juice a moment as if looking for an answer there and then blurted out, "Simon and I almost got arrested last night!"

"Arrested! What happened?"

Dorrie had been thinking about it ever since she woke up that morning, and she could see no way to explain last night's episode without telling him everything; Malcolm would no more believe that airline bag had contained tax records than Lieutenant Toomey had done. So she took a deep breath and plunged in. She told about the way she and Simon had redecorated the murder scene, about how Toomey had found her hiding in Uncle Vincent's closet during her second frustrated attempt to steal the promissory note, and about how she and Simon had thrown the incriminating evidence from the library into the river—only to discover that that police sergeant had been *following* them! She looked at her brother's horrified face and finished limply, "I think I need a lawyer."

"What you need is to have your head examined!" Malcolm snapped, as soon as he'd recovered enough to speak. "What on earth possessed you, Dorrie? Just about everything it was possible to do wrong, you've done! Of all the irresponsible, feather-headed—"

"Now you stop that, Malcolm Conner!" Dorrie exclaimed, just as she'd done a hundred times as a child. "Don't you think I'd *undo* it all if I could? My hindsight is just as clear as yours! Don't fuss at me, Malcolm, please."

He gave her hand a little squeeze. "All right. No point in crying over spilled milk," he said, heartily wishing she'd not confided in him. "Fortunately, we can consider what you told me as privileged information—I'd hate to have to take *that* story to the police. You actually interfered with the evidence at a murder scene? And Simon too? I thought he had better sense."

"Don't blame Simon, it was my idea. He didn't even want to go back to look for the note. Oh, he was marvelous last night, Malcolm! Even when that wretched sergeant dragged us into the police station, Simon never lost his cool. The Lieutenant tried to rattle him, but you know Simon—he just won't rattle. *I* would probably have spilled out the whole story, if I'd been there alone. Simon says that was the whole idea, to prod one of us into letting something slip. He says they'll try it again. Simon says they're not finished with us."

Simon says hands on hips; Simon says hop on one foot. "He's probably right," said Malcolm. "They didn't have anything solid."

"But the police suspect us now, especially me. Now I want you to tell me—is there something *legal* I can do to protect myself?"

Malcolm thought a moment. "It depends on what the police do next. They'll probably send divers into the river to look for that airline bag—"

"Oh dear!"

"And if they find it, you're in trouble. But until then, just sit tight—do nothing, say nothing. Don't talk to the police. If they ask you more questions, simply don't answer. Have you got that, Dorrie? *Do not answer.*"

"I got it."

"Tell Simon to keep quiet too. And from now on, you are going to be the very model of law-abiding decorum. Go to work, go home, do absolutely nothing to attract further attention to yourself. Become a *mouse.* Don't spend any large sums of money, don't even go shopping. Don't go away for the weekend. Be open and obvious in all your actions. Don't—"

"Malcolm," Dorrie interrupted. "I get the picture."

"And for god's sake, forget about finding that promissory note. Don't you see, whoever has that note is going to be the police's number one suspect? Now that they know about the note, they're not going to keep on looking for nonexistent burglars. They have to know that the killer was one of the six of us there at the meeting. The last thing in the world you want is to be found with that note, Dorrie."

She agreed. "I guess that lets out Lionel, too. He doesn't have the note." She hesitated, and then went on, "We think Nicole has it. Somebody took it out of Uncle Vincent's safe, and it wasn't either Lionel or I."

Malcolm was shocked. "Dorrie, you don't know what you're saying! Nicole might talk about stealing the note, but she'd never actually do it. She doesn't share your larcenous impulses." *Like hell she doesn't,* he thought to himself. Malcolm didn't like lying to his sister, but he couldn't see any way around it. "Besides, she would have told me if she had it."

"Are you sure about that?"

"Of course I'm sure! You know what you're saying, don't you? You're saying Nicole is the killer! That's absurd. Personally, I'd be more inclined to suspect Lionel."

"He was my first choice, too," Dorrie said, "but now I'm not so sure. If the person who has the note is also the killer—"

"Now wait a minute—I said that's what the *police* would think. It doesn't necessarily follow that whoever took the promissory note also killed Uncle Vincent. There could have been any number of people looking for that note. That doesn't make them murderers." He was beginning to get upset; Nicole suspected Dorrie, and had in fact tampered with the evidence to protect her. And now Dorrie was shifting her suspicions from Lionel to Nicole. Malcolm was as sure as he could be that neither woman was guilty. It had to be Lionel. He attempted a laugh. "The only happy solution I can see is for one of the servants to turn out to be guilty."

"Or Gretchen," Dorrie smiled wickedly. "None of us would mind that, particularly. I'm going to ask Nicole straight out if she has the note. I tried to get hold of her yesterday—and you too. But you both seemed to have vanished off the face of the earth."

"We were out all last evening. Dinner and theater—we both felt in need of distraction. But you are *not* going to ask her about the note, Dorrie. You are going to do *nothing* out of the ordinary, remember?"

"But who would know—"

"*Nothing whatsoever*, is that understood? I don't think you realize how much you have to live down, Dorrie. You broke into somebody else's house, you discovered a dead body, you failed to notify the police, you tampered with the evidence—"

"I know, I know," she said with irritation. "*You* would never do anything that dumb—do you have to rub it in?"

Malcolm shifted his weight uneasily. "Well, what's done is done. Just forget about the note. Be completely passive. Don't even get a traffic ticket."

She sighed. "All right."

He glanced at his watch. "I'm meeting a client in an hour and I still have to shower. Shall I drop you off at Ellandy's?"

"Make it the BMW garage. They said my car is ready."

"Drive *very* carefully," Malcolm cautioned.

* * *

Lieutenant Toomey sat in his office reading the copies of Paul Bernstein's reports while he waited for Rizzuto to get back with the search warrant. Bernstein had sent over the reports early that morning, just as he'd promised.

They bore out the detective's brief summary the day before. Vincent Farwell had not requested twenty-four-hour surveillance on anyone, not even Lionel Knox. Lionel had been watched during the day, and only once in a while all night as an occasional spot test. Toomey read about Lionel's first marriage, the failure of his nationwide chain of flower shops, his present indebtedness. He read about his brief fling with Nicole Lattimer, which ended as abruptly as it started and evidently had never resumed.

The report did offer one interesting new bit of information about Lionel. Four months earlier he'd flown to England; he'd told his wife and his partner he had an elderly relative living in Somerset he wanted to check up on. But Lionel had never gone near Somerset; he'd stayed in London the whole time. The English private investigator Bernstein had hired to shadow Lionel—called an "inquiry agent" over there—reported that his subject had had two meetings with representatives of the De Beers organization and then had flown back home. What they'd talked about in the meetings was unknown; the English investigator reported the De Beers people were more tight-lipped than MI5.

Toomey thought back to what Simon Murdoch had told him earlier. Simon had said the De Beers Corporation controlled eighty percent of the world's diamonds; and they would sell to only a certain number of approved merchants—what were they called? *Sightholders*, that was it. Lionel Knox was not a sightholder; he wasn't any kind of diamond merchant— Ellandy's *bought* from merchants, like Simon Murdoch. So what was Lionel doing talking to the De Beers people, and behind his partner's back? Did he have aspirations toward being his own merchant? Toomey couldn't see what it meant, and filed the information away in his mind to be mulled over later.

For the other four—Nicole, the Murdochs, Malcolm Conner—Uncle Vincent had wanted only background reports.

Three of the four came out smelling like a rose; only Simon Murdoch and his finances had a faint taint to them. Simon owed enormous amounts of money, but he *was owed* a number of large sums as well. Bernstein had added a note that in the diamond business, the constant granting and getting of credit were part and parcel of the industry and essential for the survival of all participants.

Simon. He had the opportunity to commit the murder; there was a gap of about three hours between the time Simon said goodbye to the others when they left the bar and the time Dorrie got home from Ellandy's. But how would killing Uncle Vincent and stealing the promissory note solve Simon's particular financial problems? Perhaps he was counting on his wife to bail him out in a pinch and was taking steps to protect her money?

Toomey's other main suspect was Malcolm Conner—an honest, upright, conscientious type, according to Bernstein. An earnest sort who belonged to another era. Too good to be true, Toomey suspected. Conservative as all get-out, with one glaring exception: he was living in glorious sin with the very nonconservative Nicole Lattimer. Toomey wondered again whether Malcolm had a well-hidden wild streak in him that Nicole found attractive; he still had trouble reconciling those two. Malcolm had had the same opportunity to commit the murder as Simon, that three-hour gap when both men were alone. Motive? Both his sister and his lover were being threatened by the same man, mean old Uncle Vincent. Could Malcolm's hypothetical wild streak have broken through long enough to make the lawyer take the law into his own hands?

Uncle Vincent had not asked Bernstein to investigate his niece.

Toomey paused; perhaps they'd all been taking Gretchen Knox too lightly. True, she presented a helpless-little-girl persona to the world, but that could be just an act. She had more opportunity than any of them, since she was right there in the house with Uncle Vincent all night long. And lord knows she had the best motive, Toomey thought; she benefited more from Vincent Farwell's death than all the other five put together. So why was it so hard to take her seriously as a suspect?

Mrs. Polk and Barney Peterson? Possible, but unlikely. And where did Dorrie Murdoch fit into this mess? At that very moment divers were poking through the murky river bottom in search of the airline bag that Simon Murdoch had so glibly announced contained tax records. Toomey had the use of only two divers, and for only four hours; that was all the strain the budget could take, his captain had told him. So if they didn't find anything by noon. . . .

Toomey had put out an APB on Barney Peterson's Mysterious Stranger, but so far no police patrol had spotted a Sydney Greenstreet type wandering about looking suspicious. *What a surprise*, Toomey smiled to himself, wondering if Barney watched a lot of television. What liars these people were! Barney, Mrs. Polk, the two Knoxes, the Murdochs—they'd all lied to the police without a second thought. Even Malcolm and Nicole, come to think of it; they'd told the same lie about the loan as the others, saying Uncle Vincent was thinking it over when he'd already said no. Toomey wondered if they all lied to one another as easily as they lied to him.

He made a note for Rizzuto. Finish straightening up Uncle Vincent's files and keep an eye peeled for the original report Paul Bernstein had submitted to the old man. There was always the chance that the detective might have thought it prudent to hold something back from the police.

He was reading through the report on Lionel Knox a second time when Sal Rizzuto came in, waving the search warrant over his head. "I hadda little trouble trackin' Judge Humphries down," said the Sergeant, "but it's all set now. Which one do we pick up—Dorrie or Simon?"

"Neither," said Toomey. "We get the apartment manager to let us in. Let's go."

When Nicole Lattimer got in to Ellandy Jewels that morning, she found Lionel Knox and Dorrie Murdoch waiting in her office—arms folded, grim looks on their faces. Nicole posed dramatically, using the doorway as a frame. "Close the door," Lionel said.

Nicole closed the door and stood looking at them.

Dorrie couldn't stand it. "Well?" she burst out. "Do you have it?"

Nicole took her time. She walked over to her desk and put her purse in the bottom drawer. Then her face broke into a big smile. "I've got it."

The craftsmen and the sales personnel wondered what the outburst of cheering from the offices was all about.

"Oh, Nicole—you're *wonderful*!" Dorrie burbled. "*I* tried to get it and nearly got myself arrested instead! How did you manage it?"

"I was lucky—I found the combination to the safe right off."

Lionel said, "Lieutenant Toomey's men found it too. What made you look under the window sill?"

"Oh," Nicole waved a hand vaguely, "I thought in a drawer or behind a picture was too obvious. But it had to be somewhere that Uncle Vincent could get to easily—so I looked under the *edges* of things. The window sill seemed likely."

Dorrie gave her a big hug. "Well, I'm glad one of us is an efficient burglar. God, what a *relief*! It's over at last!"

"Where's the note now?" Lionel asked.

"In a safe place," Nicole smiled.

"You didn't destroy it?"

Nicole's smile grew brighter. "I think," she said slowly, "that now would be a good time to talk about my partnership. Don't you?"

Dead silence.

The two partners stared open-mouthed at Nicole, then glanced at each other, then went back to staring at Nicole. Finally Lionel burst out, "For Pete's sake, Nicole—you don't have to *blackmail* your way into the business!"

"Not blackmail. Buy."

"Oh, Nicole!" Dorrie said in the tone of a parent reproving a naughty child. "You wouldn't really hold that over our heads, would you? We told you we were going to take you in as soon as we could."

"Yeah," Lionel added, sounding hurt. "You know it was just a question of money. We were going to make you a partner just as soon as . . . as soon as . . ."

"As soon as Uncle Vincent's loan was paid off?" Nicole was still smiling. "But that's no longer a problem, is it? Lionel, you told me you and Dorrie would have made me a partner long ago if I'd had enough capital to buy in. Well, now I've got a piece of paper that's worth one and a half million dollars to Ellandy Jewels. To my way of thinking, that's more than enough capital. So now I'm ready to buy. Are you ready to sell?"

"Aw, hell, Nicole!" Lionel protested. "You didn't have to do it this way! You—"

"Lionel." Nicole's smile was suddenly gone. "Put yourself in my place. If *you* were the one on the outside, would you meekly hand over the promissory note and then just stand back and hope to be noticed? Would you?"

That brought a wry grin. "No, I guess not," he said.

"And another thing," Nicole went on. "Without that loan to repay, Ellandy's is going to have a greater profit margin. Even that four hundred thousand you earmarked for a partial payment—that can go straight back into the business. I think you'll find your third of the profits will total as much or more than the half you're each getting now—if not this year, then next, at least."

"Gee, thanks for explaining my business to me, Nicole," Lionel said, feeling understandably tetchy. "I can add and subtract too, you know. You don't—"

"Lionel." This time it was Dorrie who interrupted him. "You're not going to argue with her, are you? *She has the note*, Lionel."

"She has the note," he nodded. "That says it all, doesn't it?" He and Dorrie looked at each other ruefully for a moment; then they both shrugged and smiled. "Welcome to Ellandy Jewels," Lionel said heartily to Nicole, extending a hand in congratulations and trying to sound sincerely pleased rather than the way good losers usually sounded.

"I have to say this, Nicole," Dorrie laughed, "you have nerves of steel. Maybe we need you more than we realized."

"Oh, I'm so glad you're taking it this way," Nicole sighed in relief. "I would have been furious if either of you had pulled that on me. Thanks for being so nice."

"Well, maybe we're a little bit furious," Lionel grinned, without rancor. "Shall we make a ceremony of destroying the note?"

"Oh, yes!" Dorrie liked that idea. "With champagne and music! How shall we do it? Burn it? Pour acid on it?"

"*When* shall we do it?" Lionel asked Nicole.

"As soon as the new partnership papers are signed."

"I'll call Malcolm," he said, and did.

At first, the apartment manager had flatly refused to let the police into the Murdochs' apartment. It was only when Lieutenant Toomey explained in detail the penalties for defying a search warrant that the man gave in. He was afraid of losing his job, he said; it turned out the Murdochs owned the building and paid his salary.

More real estate, Toomey mused. Simon's idea, no doubt, not Dorrie's. Toomey and Rizzuto and the two men they'd brought with them rode up in the elevator with the worried-looking apartment manager. No one spoke.

The manager unlocked the Murdochs' door and left without a word. *Going to call Simon*, thought Toomey. The two extra men had been armed with copies of Mrs. Polk's list of the items missing from Uncle Vincent's study. If the airline bag the Murdochs had tossed into the river the night before did indeed contain those items, then it was all so much wasted effort. But it had to be done. Toomey and Rizzuto would concentrate on looking for the promissory note.

Toomey had expected to find an opulent apartment and he was not disappointed. The Georgian-paneled walls of the north-facing living room had been painted a soft rust tinted with blue so that natural light cast a dusky haze around the room. Tall, curved windows clad in patterned balloon shades. A variety of furniture spanning centuries, from Regency chairs to Victorian needlepoint to a modern upholstered sofa. In the bedroom, the Murdochs had turned three walls into one big mirror, a little bit of interior decorating that didn't surprise Toomey at all. Sheepishly he leaned over their bed and looked up at the underside of the canopy. No mirror.

The Murdochs used the smallest room of the apartment as a home office. Two desks, a computer, shelves of storage boxes, a file cabinet. Toomey took the file cabinet while Rizzuto started opening the storage boxes. Cancelled checks, receipts for household expenses, insurance policies, warranties, maps of Paris and Vienna, correspondence, catalogues, airline flight schedules, papers, papers, papers. No stock certificates or bonds, but a receipt for a bank safe deposit box.

Four bank accounts—his, hers, theirs, and savings. The "theirs" was the most active, paying out all the Murdochs' living expenses. All Simon's ventures in real estate were handled through his own account. The savings account was surprisingly small; the Murdochs preferred to invest their money whenever they got a little ahead.

They live well, our Dorrie and our Simon, Toomey thought with a touch of envy. They spent more on clothing than the Lieutenant earned. "Any luck?" he asked Rizzuto.

"Old tax records," the Sergeant said. "Goin' back fifteen years for him, eleven for her. Back to before they was married."

"Every year accounted for?"

"Ever' one. They weren't no tax records in that airline bag."

Toomey picked a floppy disc at random and slipped it into the computer. He was staring at the Murdochs' budget when Simon walked in. The apartment manager had wasted no time.

"Well, Lieutenant, I see you've made yourself at home," Simon said archly. "Do you need anything? Shall I send out for pizza?"

Toomey held out the search warrant without taking his eyes off the computer screen.

Simon glanced at the warrant and drawled, "How very official-looking. Whatever do you expect to find? A signed confession tucked away amidst old telephone bills? Ah, I have it! You're looking for the Ellandy promissory note! Look as much as you like, Lieutenant. You won't find it here."

"You have a safe deposit box."

"Doesn't everybody? Ours contains stock certificates and some of Dorrie's jewelry. And deeds to some property. But I don't think your search warrant covers safe deposit boxes."

"I can get another one."

"I'm sure you can," Simon half-smiled. "Very well, I'll open the box for you if you insist." He peered over Toomey's shoulder at the computer screen. "Tell me, Lieutenant—how is knowing how much we anticipate spending on dry-cleaning this year going to help you catch Uncle Vincent's killer?"

Just then one of the men searching the rest of the apartment came in. "Lieutenant, I got something that looks like one of the items on the list. I found it in Mrs. Murdoch's bureau—wrapped in a nightgown." Using his handkerchief, he placed a small jade horse on the desk nearest Toomey.

Toomey thought he heard Simon groan. The Lieutenant examined the little horse without picking it up; it was a lovely piece of workmanship. He turned toward Simon and cocked an eyebrow at him.

Simon cocked his own eyebrow back.

"It's only a matter of getting Mrs. Polk to identify it," Toomey said mildly.

"Yes, I suppose it is," Simon sighed. "Oh Dorrie, Dorrie! Well, Lieutenant? What happens now?"

"Now we go downtown for a nice, long chat. We're going to talk and talk and talk until I can no longer think of anything to ask you, and then we'll talk some more. Rizzuto, pick up Mrs. Murdoch at Ellandy Jewels and bring her in. Come on, Murdoch—let's go."

11

Gretchen Knox sat in her breakfast room with Paul Bernstein's report spread out on the table in front of her and wondered what it all meant.

The private investigator had phoned earlier in the day to say the report would be delivered shortly by his secretary. Then he'd told her the police had also requested a copy. However, Bernstein had pointed out smoothly, the report he'd provided Lieutenant Toomey was missing several pages that were included in her own copy. He told her which pages.

They were the ones that detailed her earlier short-lived affair with Malcolm Conner. Uncle Vincent had had Malcolm investigated, not her; but the investigation had been carried out at the time Gretchen was making secret visits to Malcolm's pre-Nicole apartment and once or twice to a hotel, just for variety. Everything was there—dates, places, even the few lunches they'd had together.

But the police didn't know anything about the affair—how fortunate she'd gone to Bernstein when she did! But of course that was what she was supposed to think; Bernstein was no fool. The police didn't know about the affair—but *Uncle Vincent had known.* He'd known, and he'd not said a word. By now Gretchen knew better than to think Uncle Vincent had been trying to protect her; it was just that acknowledging her own marital infidelity would have weakened his attack on Lionel.

It was the report on Lionel's visit to London that was causing her trouble. He'd lied to her about having to check on an elderly relative. Gretchen hated being lied to, but what puzzled her was that he'd apparently lied to Dorrie Murdoch as well. Gretchen remembered the trip; Lionel had been gone only a week and Dorrie too had thought it was a personal matter that took Lionel to England. Or at least she'd said she did.

The English investigator who'd followed Lionel around London reported the "subject" had made two visits to the De Beers Corporation offices. Gretchen frowned. She was vaguely aware that De Beers had something to do with diamonds. A business trip? The real purpose of which Lionel was concealing from his partner?

The phone rang; it was her uncle's manservant. "Miss Gretchen, I don't like bothering you," said Bjarne Pedersen, "but may I have permission to use Mr. Vincent's Rolls tomorrow? To drive Mrs. Polk and me to the funeral?"

"Of course, Barney. You know the time and place?"

"Yes, ma'am, Mr. Lionel told us. Is there anything we can do to help?"

She thought a moment. "Ask Mrs. Polk to have some light refreshments prepared—some of us will be going to the house afterwards. She'll know the sort of thing."

"Yessum. Anything else?"

She told him no and hung up. Uncle Vincent's lawyer wanted to have a reading of the will after the funeral. It seemed to her Uncle Vincent's house was the proper setting for such a scene.

Gretchen sat and thought about that will for a few minutes. She'd known for years she was Uncle Vincent's heir, but it was only now sinking in on her that she was a very rich woman. She could do whatever she wanted, without having to talk it over with a husband or an uncle. *Whatever she wanted!* An unfamiliar feeling began to creep over her—was it *power?*

Money *was* power—she'd never really understood that before. Now she had the control of a great deal of money, and she didn't have to spend it the way other people told her to. She must be strong about that; it was her money now. The money was her strength. She would make her own decisions.

Strong—Gretchen liked that word. *Sensitive* was all right as far as it went, but people sort of took that quality for granted. She'd been sensitive all her life, and where had it gotten her? Nobody paid any attention to her when she talked, and Lionel made fun of her and called her Lou Ann Poovey. Well, there'd be no more of that; from now on she was going to be *strong.*

And she could, too. *Because I believe in me!* she thought with a sudden, self-congratulatory surge of exuberance. She tried pumping her fist the way she'd seen the Wimbledon players do, but it just made her feel silly.

Gretchen looked through the pages of Bernstein's report until she found those relating to Lionel's London trip. She read them again. De Beers, diamonds. There was one person she knew who could tell her about diamonds.

Decision number one. Go see Simon Murdoch.

At that very moment Simon Murdoch was sitting in a police interrogation room trying hard to look amused.

He was not amused. He was furious, and it was his lovely and ever-loving wife who was the cause of his fury. It was Dorrie who had dragged him back to Uncle Vincent's on the murder night, it was Dorrie's idea to muss up the library to confuse matters, it was Dorrie who'd been caught hiding in the closet, it was Dorrie who had gasped when she saw the can of Redi-Whip and aroused Lieutenant Toomey's suspicions even more, and it was self-coddling Dorrie who hadn't been able to bring herself to give up the little jade horse. It was a good thing they were so much in love, Simon thought; otherwise he might *kill* her.

"The lights were still on when you left," Lieutenant Toomey said. "You're sure about that?"

"Positive," said Simon. "We talked about whether a burglar would bother turning them off or not, and we decided not."

Simon had called Malcolm Conner before leaving the apartment, and the lawyer had been waiting for them at the police station when they got there. Malcolm's advice was to make a clean breast of everything, hold back nothing. *They've got the goods on you now*, he'd said. The police were looking for a killer, he'd said, not a couple of misguided meddlers. If they cooperated fully, the police might not be too hard on them. Simon had been surprised and irritated to learn that Malcolm knew all about their illicit nocturnal visit to Uncle Vincent's library; Dorrie had confided in him and asked his advice. Simon wondered what else dear little Dorrie had done that he didn't know about.

"You touched the body, didn't you?" Toomey wanted to know. "Had it started stiffening yet?"

"Oh dear." Simon pulled at the lobe of his ear. "I'd say it was tending slightly toward rigidity."

"How did you leave the house? Back over the wall?"

"No, we simply opened the terrace gate and walked out. We were loaded down with things like *little jade horses*, if you'll recall."

Toomey smiled and wondered how long it would take the lovebirds to make up. "All right, let's go over it again. You got to Uncle Vincent's at what time?"

"Lieutenant, we've already been over the whole thing twice. You've got my wife shut away in another charming room like this one where she is undoubtedly saying exactly the same things I've been saying. Why do I have to keep repeating myself?"

"To make sure you didn't forget anything. Once more now. What time did you get there?"

Simon sighed wearily. "Around two-thirty," he said, and started all over again.

Forty minutes later Toomey took a break. He summoned Rizzuto out of the interrogation room where Dorrie had been put, and the two compared notes. The Murdochs were telling the same story.

"Do you believe 'em, Lieutenant?" Rizzuto asked. "I gotta feelin' she's tellin' the truth."

Toomey agreed. "I think we're hearing the true story. Thank god Dorrie coveted that jade horse—we'd never know any of this otherwise." The divers had not found the airline bag in the muck at the bottom of the river, but that no longer mattered. Now they had the jade horse.

"You can't charge 'em," Rizzuto said, "not without arrestin' the Knoxes too. They did the same thing, messin' with the evidence."

"I don't want to arrest them—any of them. I want them all running loose. For a while, at least. Have you noticed, Rizzuto? This crowd just can't sit still. They always have to be doing something. Let's see what they do next."

"Turn 'em loose?"

"In a bit. What say we swap? I'll take Dorrie for a while and you give Simon a try."

Malcolm Conner was in the interrogation room with his sister, his face pinched and disapproving. Dorrie herself was beginning to wilt. Malcolm said, "How much longer is this going on, Lieutenant? We've been here—"

"Just a little longer, Mr. Conner. I want to hear Mrs. Murdoch's story myself."

"I already told that sergeant umpty-three times," Dorrie complained tiredly.

"Once more," Toomey said, not unkindly. "What time did you and your husband get back to Uncle Vincent's?"

"After two," she said lethargically. "Maybe two-thirty, around there." She went on to repeat the story.

Toomey interrupted her frequently, to keep her from just repeating a tale that was beginning to sound memorized. But the basic facts never varied; she and Simon told the same story. In reply to a question from Toomey, Dorrie had described the condition of Uncle Vincent's body as "a mite inflexible". When he asked her who she thought killed Uncle Vincent, she replied that at first she'd suspected Lionel but now she was pretty sure he was innocent. When Toomey asked her if she thought Nicole could have done it, she became flustered and refused to answer.

"Mrs. Murdoch, what made you decide Lionel Knox was not the killer?"

"Oh, things," she said vaguely.

"What things?"

"I don't know, just things!" she snapped. "It was silly of me to suspect him in the first place. I changed my mind, that's all."

That wasn't all, Toomey knew, but it was all he was going to get out of her today. She really looked done in. "Okay, I want you to sign a statement and then you can go," he said abruptly, and watched both their heads jerk up in surprise. "Don't leave town. You may still be charged with interfering at the scene of a crime. Keep yourself available, Mrs. Murdoch."

After they'd all gone, Toomey called Rizzuto into his office. "Notice a little problem their story left us with? About the lights?" Rizzuto hadn't caught it. "They both swear they left the library lights on. Yet Lionel Knox says they were out when he got there. He said he looked for a line of light under the library door before he went in, to make sure nobody was in there."

Rizzuto's eyes bugged. "You mean somebody *else* went into the library—between the Murdochs and Lionel?"

"Looks like it. Let's see, the Murdochs stayed the better part of an hour, so that means they left around three-thirty. Lionel went in at five. Sometime during that hour-and-a-half gap Uncle Vincent had at least one more visitor. Well, there are only two left—it had to be Malcolm or Nicole."

"Assumin' nobody went in more'n once."

Toomey's eyebrows rose. "Good point, Rizzuto. Just for kicks—who's your candidate for Uncle Vincent's killer?"

"Gretchen," the Sergeant said without hesitation. "All that stuff about the loan and Ellandy Jewels and Simon's diamond business and Lionel's affair with Nicole—that's all just a buncha red herrings. Gretchen stood to inherit and she dint like her uncle anyways, so—*pow*! She lets him have it."

"That simple, huh?"

"Could be," the Sergeant replied with a knowing air.

Toomey suddenly felt as tired as Dorrie Murdoch had looked. Rizzuto might be right; it could be just as simple as that. An heir who didn't want to wait any longer to inherit. A passive, soft-voiced woman who said *Ugh* whenever anyone mentioned blood.

Sure.

The day of Vincent Farwell's funeral dawned as bright and cheerful as any spring morn that e'er gladdened the soul of a poet. Bjarne Pedersen disapproved; violent death and bright spring days didn't go together. He wanted a gloomy day, with wisps of graveyard mist rising from the ground. It should at least be raining; but there wasn't even one cloud in the sky. Bjarne tried to put himself in the proper mood by imagining Boris Karloff to be among the mourners.

Mrs. Polk had surprised him by getting into the front seat of the Rolls looking as if she'd been crying. She'd actually liked the old man? They'd both gotten along with him all right, but as for actually *liking* him . . . Bjarne thought it must have been the somberness of the occasion that made her cry. Some people cried at even the thought of a funeral.

Not that it was a real funeral. There was no religious service scheduled; they were just going to poke him in the ground and be done with it. Well, not quite; Mr. Malcolm was going to say a few words at the graveside. Except that Mr. Malcolm never stopped with just a *few* words.

Bjarne drove into the cemetery and eventually found the gravesite. They were the first ones there, other than the undertaker's hearse. The manservant parked the Rolls and waited. The coffin was already in place, on an apparatus for lowering it into the grave when the time came. Standing by the hearse was a dark-suited man Bjarne took to be the undertaker, a plump, rosy-cheeked man who offended Bjarne's sense of decorum. Undertakers should be John Carradine—thin.

The Murdochs drove up; they too parked and stayed in their car. Then came Mr. Malcolm and Miss Nicole, followed soon after by the two police investigators who'd been sticking their noses into everybody's business ever since Mr. Vincent died. At last Miss Gretchen and Mr. Lionel arrived. They all started getting out of their cars.

"She's wearing white!" Mrs. Polk gasped, scandalized.

Everyone there was dressed in muted colors except Nicole Lattimer, who was wearing a shimmering white . . . pantsuit? No, Bjarne decided, pants*dress*. Her dark hair was pulled behind her ears and tied into a single thick braid that hung down the middle of her back. Bjarne smothered a smile. Her walk was as duck-waddly as ever, but she looked terrific. She also stood out like a sore thumb—which was undoubtedly the idea.

Mr. Vincent's lawyer had come with Mr. Lionel and Miss Gretchen. Everyone stood around feeling awkward while the undertaker murmured words of condolence to Gretchen. The Murdochs made a point of not speaking to the two policemen who'd put them through that embarrassing scene at the police station the night before. Now and then Dorrie would shoot a bellicose look in their direction; both men pretended not to notice.

Nicole saw Lieutenant Toomey looking at her outfit. "White is the color of mourning in some cultures," she explained.

Bjarne nudged Mrs. Polk with his elbow.

"I heard," she muttered.

Malcolm cleared his throat. "I suppose we can begin." He stepped over to the head of the grave. "We are here to mourn the passing of a remarkable man," he began, "a man who occupied a significant place in all our lives."

Ain't that the truth, Lieutenant Toomey thought as he and Rizzuto edged back away from the group around the grave. Did any of them really mourn Uncle Vincent's passing? They were all wearing the appropriate expressions, but only Mrs. Polk looked truly grieved.

Malcolm Conner was leadenly extolling the virtues of a man nobody really liked. Then Toomey caught sight of someone new: a woman in her forties, immaculately groomed, the brim of her black hat shading her face. She stood apart from the others, none of whom seemed aware of her presence. She was absolutely motionless, in stark contrast to the others who were all beginning to fidget as Malcolm droned on and on.

"Know her?" Toomey whispered. Rizzuto shook his head. "Find out who she is."

Rizzuto started inching his way around the others toward the mystery lady in the black hat. Malcolm was praising the courage of a man who'd had to face life from a wheelchair, with about as much conviction in his voice as a ten-year-old reciting Shakespeare. Lionel Knox was heavily shifting his weight from one foot to the other, Dorrie Murdoch's hands kept patting her blond curls and smoothing her dress, Simon Murdoch's left eyebrow had climbed almost to his hairline, Nicole Lattimer shimmered whitely, and Gretchen Knox startled everyone by saying in an overloud voice, "That was very nice— thank you, Malcolm."

There was a brief moment of awkward embarrassment, and then Malcolm acknowledged the command in Gretchen's voice by winding up his eulogy with a few hasty sentences and stepping back from the grave. The undertaker took over, assuring Gretchen the burial itself did not require her attendance and he would see to everything himself. The "funeral" was over.

Mrs. Polk headed straight for Gretchen. "Miss Gretchen, I need to talk to you. Soon."

"Well, we're going to read the will as soon as we get back." She looked at her uncle's lawyer. "Aren't we, Mr. Dann?"

Mr. Dann said they were. "It won't take long."

"Right after," Gretchen promised Mrs. Polk.

Nicole buttonholed Lionel and Dorrie. "Are you two going into Ellandy's today?" she asked in a low voice. "Malcolm has the new partnership agreement drawn up."

"Already?" Dorrie asked in surprise. "That was fast."

"He just used the same form he used for the original partnership—only this one's made out for three partners instead of two."

"I'm going in now," Dorrie said.

"I'll be in later," Lionel told them. "As soon as this will thing is over."

"Suppose I tell Malcolm one-thirty," Nicole offered. "Is that all right?"

Lionel agreed. Dorrie said, "I'll have to miss my aerobic mime class—but yes, one-thirty's fine."

Lieutenant Toomey raised an eyebrow and passed on by.

A few steps away, Simon was congratulating Malcolm on the eulogy. "I'm amazed you found so many positive things to say about the old boy," he remarked dryly. "It must have taken you a while."

"All night, as a matter of fact," Malcolm muttered. "That and the new Articles of Partnership."

"Ah, yes, the new partnership—Nicole's not wasting any time, is she?"

"You don't approve?"

"Frankly, no. It seems to me Dorrie and Lionel ought to wait until Ellandy's financial picture is clearer before making a change as significant as that. But Dorrie is determined, and I suppose Lionel must be too."

"Nicole's waited a long time, Simon," Malcolm said with a hint of reprimand in his voice.

"So she has," Simon smiled, and changed the subject.

Lieutenant Toomey nodded vacantly at no one in particular. Bjarne and Mrs. Polk left in the Rolls. Then everyone was piling into cars, engines were started, the exodus was under way. Sal Rizzuto slid into the passenger seat next to Toomey.

"Well?" Toomey asked. "Who is she—the lady in the hat?"

"The undertaker's wife," Rizzuto said in annoyance. "She goes to alla funerals of their 'more important clients', she says."

Toomey laughed, glad not to have another Mysterious Stranger to worry about. He told Rizzuto that as of one-thirty that afternoon, Nicole Lattimer would be a partner in Ellandy Jewels.

Rizzuto whistled. "A full partner?"

"Sounded like it, from what I was able to hear."

"Why now?" the Sergeant puzzled. "How was she able to

convince 'em to take her in now, with that loan business still hangin' over their heads?"

"That is something we're going to have to find out," Toomey said, and started the car.

The Knoxes, Mr. Dann, and the two servants were already at Uncle Vincent's house by the time the policemen got there. Bjarne let them in. Mrs. Polk had set up a buffet in the dining room, but no one was in there. Mr. Dann was in the living room with Lionel; Gretchen had thought using the library for reading the will would have verged on the ghoulish. The heiress herself was nowhere in sight. Godfrey Daniel came over and greeted Lieutenant Toomey, the only one in the house who seemed glad to see him.

Gretchen kept them all waiting while she changed her clothes. She came into the living room wearing white trousers and a bright yellow top. Short mourning period. "Did he make one of those video wills?" she asked Mr. Dann. The lawyer looked pained and said no.

The two Knoxes, the two servants, and the two policemen settled down to hear Mr. Dann read the will. The reading took all of two minutes. Two hefty bequests to Bjarne Pedersen and Dorothy Polk, slightly more to the latter because she'd been with the old man longer. A small legacy for the ASPCA— *Godfrey Daniel's influence, no doubt*, Toomey thought. The rest of the estate went to Gretchen Knox, as expected. Total amount for Gretchen estimated in the neighborhood of twenty-two million, dependent upon a final accounting. Not sufficient to take over an airline, but enough to render the saving of grocery coupons unnecessary.

Toomey was eyeing the manservant curiously. "Bjarne Pedersen?" he asked, stumbling over the pronunciation.

"Too hard for most people," Bjarne explained. "Just call me Barney."

Rizzuto sniggered. "Good honest American name, huh?"

"Do I have to sign anything, Mr. Dann?" Gretchen asked. "No? Well, in that case, I have something I need to do." And without even saying goodbye, she hurried out of the house. They heard her car start and drive away.

"Oh dear," said Mrs. Polk. "I wanted to talk to her."

Toomey said, "Mrs. Polk, does she always keep a change of clothing here?"

But it was Lionel who answered. "She's started bringing her clothes over. Since we'll be living here."

"I'm glad to hear that," Mr. Dann said. "I'd hate to think of this good old house being sold and divided into apartments. Now I must go. Barney, if you would call me a cab . . . ?"

The lawyer and the manservant went out. Mrs. Polk invited the others to help themselves from the buffet and led the way into the dining room. Sergeant Rizzuto piled a plate high with cold cuts and retired to the library. Toomey had given him two instructions. First, don't come out until those files have been restored to order; and second, find the original report Paul Bernstein had given to Uncle Vincent.

Toomey nibbled a bit of cheese. "Are you going to mind living here?" he asked Lionel.

"No, I like the place. It's much grander than the house we're living in now. I simply didn't like the way Gretchen decided we were moving without asking me what I wanted. I just got the new satellite dish up, for crying out loud."

"Maybe that's what inheriting twenty-two million dollars does to you. It won't bother you, living in the house where Uncle Vincent was murdered?"

"I'm *hoping* it won't bother me," Lionel said.

Toomey picked up another wedge of cheese from the dining table. "This is good stuff—lots of bite. Let's go out on the terrace. There's something I want to ask you about."

"Oh-oh," Lionel grinned wryly, opening the dining room door that led to the terrace. "Mind the cat."

Toomey glanced down to see Godfrey Daniel winding around his legs. Stepping carefully, the Lieutenant led the way outdoors and chose a chair for himself in the sunlight. Godfrey jumped up on his lap and started sniffing at the wedge of cheese Toomey still carried in his hand.

"He loves cheese," Lionel said, sitting down opposite the Lieutenant. "Cheese and goose liver and fresh salmon. Hates cat food."

"I've got one at home like that." Toomey took a bite of his cheese and put the rest down on the terrace floor; Godfrey Daniel jumped down to enjoy his snack. The Lieutenant said to Lionel, "Well, now. Tell me about your visit to the De Beers people in London."

Lionel's mouth dropped open. "How in the *hell* did you know about that?"

"Uncle Vincent knew. His detective hired a London detective and you were followed. It was all in Bernstein's report, of which I now have a copy."

Lionel looked dazed. "Jesus. You can't keep anything secret any more."

"You didn't know you were followed in London?"

"I found out about it later—I meant I couldn't keep anything secret from *you*. Look, Lieutenant, I'd appreciate it if you didn't spread this around. That trip to London wasn't one of my more shining moments."

"What happened?"

Lionel thought a moment, trying to come up with the best way of putting it. "Do you know anything about the buying and selling of diamonds?"

"Simon Murdoch told me about De Beers' control of the market, and how only the relatively few 'chosen' become sightholders."

"Ah, that makes things easier, then," Lionel said. "I was trying to persuade De Beers to make me a sightholder. I've *been* trying for almost two years now. It was Simon Murdoch's idea. You see, Simon was never made a sightholder because he doesn't process his own diamonds. The idea was for Ellandy Jewels to buy the necessary equipment and prove to the De Beers people we were serious about diamond-processing. Once I was made a sightholder, Simon would act as my representative and buy the rough diamonds, I'd finish the stones, and we'd both make a nice profit."

"What about Dorrie Murdoch? Were you planning to squeeze her out?"

"Hell, no! When I say 'I', I mean Ellandy's."

"But you lied to her about your reason for going to England, Bernstein's report says."

Lionel made a face. "Hedging my bets, Lieutenant. It was a gamble, investing all that money in diamond-finishing equipment in the hopes that De Beers would smile on us. Frankly, I didn't want Dorrie to know what I was up to. I'd already had one business failure, and I was afraid she might start having second thoughts. So it just seemed better to keep her in the dark. Simon went along—he agreed not to tell her either."

"But when you started buying the new equipment, didn't she—"

"She was all for it. Designers love seeing their work all the way through the process, Lieutenant, and that includes finishing the stones as well as constructing the mountings. Both my 'creative' partners were in favor of buying the equipment." Lionel grinned wryly. "We're making Nicole a partner."

Toomey nodded. "Why now?"

"Oh, she threatened to leave if we didn't."

Toomey was sure Nicole had threatened something. Godfrey Daniel finished his cheese and leaped back up to the Lieutenant's lap, sniffing for more. "That's all there is, kitty." Godfrey lay down, stretching out the length of Toomey's thighs to stare at Lionel. "So what happened in London?"

Lionel groaned. "It was a fiasco. They said Ellandy's wasn't financially stable enough. And the *way* they said it—they made it painfully clear I was out of my league. Hell, I felt like a country singer auditioning at the Metropolitan Opera. The whole thing was a mistake—we should never have done it."

"So is this a setback for Simon Murdoch as well as for you?"

"It's not really a setback for Ellandy's—more like a failed opportunity. We still have the equipment and that's worth a lot, whether we sell it or use it. As for Simon—I can't tell about Simon. He's hard to figure sometimes."

"In what way?"

"Well, he's not like most of the men in the business I've met. Diamond merchants are a queer breed, Lieutenant. They're all intense, competitive men whose whole life is made up of the buying and selling of diamonds. They're not interested in anything at all except trading those stones . . . and maybe sex. But they don't do anything else—they don't read, they don't go to the theater, nothing. The only thing in life that matters to them is diamonds. But Simon's not like that. He's not obsessed the way the rest of them are; his life is more balanced. He has other interests."

"Like buying real estate."

"Yeah, like that. And like leaving himself time to have some fun. He and Dorrie play a lot. But the successful men in the business are diamond merchants twenty-four hours a day. No time off, for anything."

"Do you think that could be part of the reason De Beers

turned you down?" Toomey asked. "Maybe they sensed that same lack of obsession in you."

"Oh, I'm sure of it," Lionel grinned wryly. "They know I'm not one of the clan."

Just then Mrs. Polk appeared at the terrace door. "Mr. Lionel—telephone. It's Miss Dorrie."

"Probably wants to know when I'm going to get back to work," Lionel sighed. "Excuse me, Lieutenant."

Toomey watched him go indoors. According to what the Murdochs told him yesterday about Uncle Vincent's body, rigor mortis had already started by the time they returned to the library. By five o'clock, when Lionel got there, it was well advanced. That put the time of death back to ten-thirty or eleven, just as the medical examiner had estimated. That meant Lionel Knox had to be innocent.

Toomey was glad. All six of his suspects were attractive people who were very much products of their times: they were overkempt, they drove BMWs or Saabs or Mercedeses (what an awkward word in the plural) and they had the kind of energy successful people of the eighties were supposed to have. Too, they were all narcissistic to some degree. But Lionel . . . Lionel was a little less beautiful than the other five. He worked harder, he worried more. And he sweat. Not fashionable workout sweat, but *sweat* sweat. Lionel was the one Toomey could feel a kinship to.

Godfrey Daniel was purring contentedly in his lap. Toomey closed his eyes and tilted his head back, enjoying the warm sun on his face. Lionel and Nicole and Dorrie had alibis. Mrs. Polk and Barney had no motive. The field was definitely down to three. Sergeant Rizzuto still suspected Gretchen, but Toomey thought it had to be one of the two men.

"There you are, Lieutenant—I been lookin' ever'where for you." Toomey opened his eyes to see Rizzuto looming over him. "I finished puttin' the file back in order, like you said," the Sergeant told him, "but there ain't there no private investigator's report in those papers. Not a sign of it."

Toomey sat up straight, unbalancing Godfrey Daniel, who dropped complaining to the terrace floor. "Are you sure?"

"Absolutely. I checked twice. There's a letter from Paul Bernstein confirmin' financial details of their arrangement, but no report on what he found out."

"Hm. Since Uncle Vincent had it earlier in the evening—"

"That means one of 'em took it. One of the Knoxes or the Murdochs, when they went back and messed things up."

"Or Mrs. Polk," Toomey sighed, "who doesn't seem to balk at tampering with evidence either."

"Naw, not Mrs. Polk. There wasn't nothin' about her in that report. And ever'body knew about Nicole and Lionel's affair, 'cause Uncle Vincent told 'em about it. So why would anybody bother stealin' Bernstein's report? What was in there that they didn't all know about anyway?"

Lionel's surreptitious visit to De Beers, Toomey thought immediately. Only Simon Murdoch had known about that, and he and Lionel had agreed to keep quiet about it.

And Simon was the one who didn't have an alibi.

12

Oh gawd, Simon Murdoch moaned inwardly when he saw Gretchen Knox standing in the doorway. He'd thought he was safe in his own office.

But it seemed Gretchen hadn't come to flirt or suggest lunch or anything potentially awkward like that. She had a sporty look, white trousers and yellow top, but somehow she didn't seem out of place in Simon's rather formal office. "I want to know," she said, sitting down in the chair Simon offered her, "whether Ellandy's buys diamonds from De Beers in London."

Simon wondered why she hadn't asked her husband. "Not directly, no. I sometimes buy De Beers diamonds from other merchants and resell them to Ellandy's. The stones may have changed hands a dozen times before they get to me."

Gretchen thought a minute. "And every time the diamonds change hands, the price goes up?"

Simon smiled at her sudden interest in business. "That's the way it works."

"Then wouldn't it make more sense to buy directly from De Beers?"

"A great deal more sense." Simon explained to her why that wasn't possible, why only sightholders were permitted to buy directly from De Beers. "That's why I make so many trips to Antwerp," he finished. "To get hold of as many diamonds as I can that De Beers doesn't control."

"I see." Gretchen asked a few more questions, until she had at least a good surface understanding of how the traffic in diamonds flowed.

All the time he was answering her, Simon kept thinking there was something different about Gretchen, something he couldn't quite put his finger on. She'd never shown any concern for business affairs before, so her visit caught him by surprise.

"Why this extraordinary interest in diamonds, Gretchen?" he asked.

"Lionel went to the De Beers place in London," she said. "That time he told everybody he wanted to check on some relative or other. Now why would he do that if he's not a sightholder?"

Simon's face darkened. After a moment, he said, "Because he has aspirations toward *becoming* a sightholder, obviously. Well, well . . . isn't this an interesting development? Our Lionel, a De Beers sightholder. Who'd have thought an ex-florist would set his sights so high?"

There was no missing the sarcasm in his voice. "It would be good for Ellandy's, though, wouldn't it?" Gretchen asked.

"It would be a *disaster* for Ellandy's, and almost a disaster for me. Lionel doesn't know doodleysquat about diamonds— I always deal directly with Dorrie or Nicole. Lionel's forte is juggling debits and credits and getting loans and finding tax write-offs and other undoubtedly fascinating endeavors in a similar vein. But he's no expert in diamonds."

"Why would it be almost a disaster for you?"

"Ellandy's is one of my biggest customers, remember. Your dearly beloved husband is doing his damnedest to cut me out."

"Well, that answers one question," Gretchen said matter-of-factly. "Why he lied to everybody about his reason for going to England."

"Just a moment—how do you know Lionel visited De Beers? Did he tell you?"

"No, Paul Bernstein told me." She explained about the private investigator's report and how he'd provided her with a copy—at her request. "He'll be reporting to me from now on."

Simon suddenly realized what it was about Gretchen that seemed different; she was sounding more and more like dear dead Uncle Vincent. "Have you confronted Lionel with it yet?" he asked.

"Not yet."

"Don't, then—not for a while. Let me ask around first, see if my contacts know anything."

"Why? What good will that do?"

Simon spread his hands. "All we know for certain is that Lionel called on De Beers. We don't know whether De Beers said yes or no."

"It must have been no. It's been four months—"

"Means nothing, Gretchen. De Beers thrives on keeping its supplicants waiting. They may still be considering his application. Let me see what I can find out."

Gretchen thought about it a minute, and then agreed. She stood up. "I don't know what all this means, but the underhanded way Lionel's gone about it makes me suspect he's up to no good. I'll leave it in your hands for the time being. Right now, you may take me to lunch." She walked out of the office.

Startled, Simon had no choice but to follow.

Malcolm Conner was placing papers neatly across Lionel Knox's desk. "These are the same Articles of Partnership I drew up the first time," Malcolm explained, "except that now three partners are listed instead of two. Concomitant changes have been implemented throughout, such as three-way liability and tax responsibility, and of course the division of profits into thirds. Everything else remains the same," he glanced at Nicole, "including the fictitious name of the business."

"*One* letter," Nicole grumbled.

"One letter or a dozen, the cost of changing the name is the same," Malcolm said, "and it's exorbitant. I advised Nicole and I advise you two," looking at Dorrie and Lionel, "to wait until you are free of debt before indulging in luxuries such as name-changing. Also, I question the wisdom of changing an established name at all. Besides which, the consent of all three partners is—"

"What *is* all this?" Lionel complained. "Who said anything about changing the name?"

"I just wanted to change one letter," Nicole sighed heavily. "I didn't know it would be such a big deal."

"Which letter?" Dorrie asked, curious. "What do you want the name to be?"

"Ellendy Jewels, instead of Ellandy—*e* in place of the *a*. That way instead of standing for L and D, Lionel and Dorrie, it would be L, N, D—the *N* for Nicole."

Lionel rolled his eyes heavenward. "Jeez."

But Dorrie inclined to agree with Nicole. "It seems only fair, Lionel. There are three of us now—"

"I do not agree to a name change," Lionel said flatly. "Especially not if it's going to cost us more money."

"And it would," Malcolm nodded. "In addition to being a questionable business practice, you'd have to change all your legal papers—your lease, your insurance, your tax reports. . . ."

"All right, all right!" Nicole said testily. "You said all that last night, at extraordinary length and in excruciating detail! Let's just drop it, shall we?"

"Perhaps it would be better to wait," Dorrie said in a conciliatory tone.

"For god's sake, let's get on with it!" Lionel snapped, not in the best of moods for the legal forming of a new partnership.

Malcolm showed them where to sign, and the three new partners sat at Lionel's desk in turn and affixed their signatures. Nicole was the last. "That's it?" she asked. "It's legal now?"

"I have to file an amendment to the original registry statement," Malcolm said, "but we don't have to go through Common Pleas court again—that's the slow part. The amendment will take care of everything."

"This amendment," Nicole said, "what does it involve?"

Malcolm slipped one set of the papers they'd signed into a mailing envelope and held it up. "It involves my dropping this envelope into the mail. Approval is virtually automatic. Don't worry, Nicole," he smiled, "you are a legal partner, as of this moment."

Nicole smiled back, decided that wasn't enough, and gave him a kiss. "Thank you, Malcolm."

"Hey—how about the rest of us?" Lionel grinned, belatedly determining to be a good sport about the sword's-point partnership.

Nicole kissed him lightly, exchanged hugs with Dorrie, and turned back to Malcolm. "Now it's time to celebrate! Didn't somebody say something about champagne?"

"I wish I could join you," Malcolm said, "but I have an appointment I can't break. Have a good time."

Nicole's face fell. "You aren't staying? I thought you'd be staying."

"Sorry, I can't. I have a case going to court tomorrow morning, and this is my last chance to consult with my client. He's suing his insurance company and I have to be sure he understands our strategy. You three celebrate."

"But—"

Dorrie laid a hand on Nicole's arm. "If he can't stay, he can't stay. Thanks for your help, Malcolm, and for getting it done so fast."

"Yeah, we appreciate it, Malcolm," Lionel said, opening the office door for him. Malcolm waved goodbye and left.

The minute Malcolm was gone, Dorrie and Lionel pounced on their new partner. "Where is it? Do you have it with you?"

"Whoa, wait a minute," Nicole laughed artificially, "what's the rush?"

"Nicole," Dorrie said in a no-nonsense voice, "*where is the note for the loan?*"

Nicole licked her lips and swallowed. "I—I don't have it." The other two stared at her. "I never had it. I lied." The others kept on staring at her, open-mouthed. "Somebody say something," she finished nervously.

"You don't have the note," Lionel repeated dully. He looked at Dorrie, then back at Nicole, and then roared: "*You don't have the goddamned promissory note!*"

"Let's make sure we've got this right," Dorrie said. "Nicole, are you saying you *didn't* take the note from Uncle Vincent's bedroom safe?"

"I've never even been in Uncle Vincent's bedroom," she said apologetically. "I have no idea where the note is. I just made that story up."

Dorrie smiled absently, patted her curls once or twice—and blew up. She started screaming at Nicole until Ellandy's new partner was cringing against the wall. Lionel made no move to quell the outburst, thinking Nicole deserved every word of it. Eventually Dorrie ran out of steam and stopped yelling. She paused to get her breath and asked the world at large, "Then who did take the note?"

Nicole lifted her shoulders. "I can't see why anyone would need to steal it, other than the three of us. All I know is *I* didn't take it."

Lionel was frowning. "But . . . but you knew where the combination was kept," he objected. "When we were talking about it, right after the safe had been opened, you knew the combination was written on a piece of tape stuck under the window sill. If you've never been in Uncle Vincent's bedroom, how did you know that?"

"I knew because you *told* me, Lionel," Nicole explained

patiently. "You and Dorrie both jumped to the conclusion that *I* had taken the note from the safe—and I thought I'd never see another opportunity like that one. When you asked me, all I said was that I got lucky and found the combination fast. And then you mentioned it had been under the window sill, so I just embroidered on that a little. I took my cues from you."

Lionel sank slowly into his desk chair and buried his head in his hands. "My god. God, god, god! We still owe that million and a half. One and a half million dollars!"

"About that," Nicole said uncomfortably. "Malcolm told me we're still liable whether the note turns up or not. Too many people know about the loan. Gretchen can take some sort of legal action, if she thinks of it. It all depends on Gretchen."

Lionel lifted his head and stared at Nicole, blood in his eye. "Strangling. Poison. *Evisceration.*"

"Oh, I know how you feel," Nicole cried. "What I did was wrong, and I feel terrible about it! But I'll make it up to you —you'll see! It'll take a while, but I am *determined* to convince you you aren't making a mistake taking me in." When neither of them answered her, Nicole's lower lip began to tremble. "Do you hate me?"

"Yes," said Dorrie and Lionel in unison.

Nicole sighed. "Well, I can't really blame you."

"That's understanding of you," Dorrie said sarcastically. "Nicole, I was *sure* you were going to try to get into Uncle Vincent's safe."

"And I was! But you got there first, Dorrie. I drove over to Uncle Vincent's house, but I spotted Lionel's car parked around the corner. And right in front was another car—I guess it was Lieutenant Toomey's. So I was sitting there in my own car wondering what to do when all these other people drove up—"

"What other people?" Lionel asked.

"I think they were more police."

Dorrie said, "They were. Toomey sent for help to search the house, to look for the note—remember?" Lionel nodded.

"Anyway," Nicole finished, "I got out of there as fast as I could, and the next thing I knew you two were asking me if I had the note."

"So of course you said yes," Lionel growled. "It didn't occur to you simply to tell the truth."

But Nicole had had enough of being meek and apologetic. "I do think you're overreacting, both of you. It's done. I'm a partner. Now we ought to be thinking about what we do next."

"But is it done?" The beginnings of a smile appeared on Lionel's face. "That amendment or whatever it was. Until that's filed—"

"Malcolm's already mailed it by now," Nicole said quickly.

Dorrie sighed. "She's right. Malcolm never puts things off. It's one of his more annoying habits." She walked over to her new partner. "Nicole, I was always in favor of taking you into the partnership—but I don't know if I can ever forgive you for the *way* you made it happen. You're right about one thing, though. We ought to be thinking of our next move. Lionel, do you suppose you could sound Gretchen out? Find out what she plans to do about the loan?"

"That might be a mistake," Nicole interjected before Lionel could answer. "Why plant the idea? Gretchen would never think of it on her own—she's never shown the least interest in the business. I think our best bet is just to keep our mouths shut."

In the end, that's what they agreed to do.

At 9:15 the following morning, the defense in the case of *Morrow vs. Springfield Mutual Life Insurance* was granted a continuance, much to Malcolm Conner's irritation. The plaintiff's case was ready, and so, Malcolm suspected, was the defense. Just one more stall. He spent a few minutes reassuring his client before leaving the courthouse.

Back at his law offices, he was surprised to find Bjarne Pedersen waiting in the reception area. Since Malcolm now had some unexpected free time, he told Bjarne to come on into his private office.

The manservant had never been in a lawyer's office before and was feeling a little intimidated. Malcolm noticed and tried to put him at ease by offering him a drink. "No, thank you, sir," Bjarne said. "I don't drink any more. Not after . . . not after that night."

Malcolm understood. "A bit early in the day anyway." Bjarne turned down coffee too; Malcolm poured himself a cup. "Now. What can I do for you, Barney?"

Bjarne hesitated, wishing Malcolm looked more like Raymond Burr. "I'm sorry to take up your time, Mr. Malcolm, but I can't go to that Mr. Dann. He thinks I should be fired, because I . . . you know."

Malcolm decided Bjarne needed a good talking-to. "You mustn't let yourself dwell on that night, Barney. It's not healthy. What's done is done. Vincent Farwell is dead because someone wanted him dead. All you did—"

"But he wouldn't be dead now if I'd stayed sober and done my job!"

"You don't know that. A man desperate enough to kill isn't going to be stopped by a burglar alarm. If Uncle Vincent hadn't died that night, he would have the next. Or the day after. You were negligent, that's true. But you couldn't have kept the old man alive if someone was determined to kill him. And someone was, obviously. The most you did was make the killer's entrance easy for him that particular night. Don't dwell on it, Barney. I want you to put the whole thing out of your mind."

"But that's just what I can't do!" the manservant wailed. "That's why I'm here, Mr. Malcolm. It's the inheritance. I don't want that money Mr. Vincent left me. It's like getting a reward for letting him be killed! It's not right."

"Oh Barney, I'm sure nobody thinks of it that way," Malcolm sighed. "You're overwrought—understandable, given the circumstances. My own experience has been it's better never to make any decisions at all when one is caught up in emotional turmoil of any kind. It's *always* better to wait, no matter how urgent you think the matter might be. We're all upset right now, not knowing who killed Uncle Vincent or why. And seeing the police casting a suspicious eye on us all doesn't precisely help matters. It's difficult to make a reasoned judgment under such conditions, and—"

"It doesn't make any difference," Bjarne interrupted as soon as Malcolm paused for breath. "I don't deserve that money and I can't take it. It keeps me awake at night, worrying about it."

Malcolm frowned. "Barney, I'm not going to do anything about this right now. I refuse to. At least wait until the police catch the killer. We'll all have cooler heads then."

"Do you think they will? Catch him?"

"I think they'd better. Things are getting a bit tense. But wait before you make any decision. I *insist* you wait."

Bjarne looked dubious. "Well, I suppose a little longer wouldn't make any difference."

"Good. Things will look different once the police have made an arrest—you'll see. Then the pressure will be off all of us. Remember, Uncle Vincent wouldn't have left you that money if he didn't want you to have it—"

"But he didn't know I was going to—"

"—and I think you should honor his wishes," Malcolm went on, interrupting the interruption. "Don't do anything right now."

At that moment Malcolm's secretary buzzed to say Mr. So-and-So had just arrived and insisted on seeing Mr. Conner immediately, and Bjarne found himself being ushered out of the office with a friendly clap on the shoulder.

Right across the street from Ellandy Jewels was a minipark carved out of one city block, part of the neighborhood reju-venation process then in full swing. The park was equipped with benches and a small fountain that worked, and had be-come a favorite lunchtime basking place once the weather had turned warm. The pigeons had moved in long ago.

One of the birds pecked suspiciously at the sandwich crust Lieutenant Toomey had put down for it. "Pigeons don't like mustard," Sal Rizzuto said knowingly.

Toomey turned his attention back to the entrance of Ellan-dy's. The clientele coming and going were all well-heeled, self-confident people; you could tell that just from the way they walked. "Who turned off the lights in Uncle Vincent's library?" he mused out loud. "The lights were on when the meddling Murdochs left at three-thirty, and Lionel Knox didn't get there until five, at which time they were off. An hour and a half."

"A long time," Rizzuto said unhelpfully.

"Who was in there during that hour and a half? What did he do?"

"Or she."

"Or she," Toomey acknowledged. "The Murdochs messed the place up, Lionel moved the body, Gretchen cleaned the place up, and the servants moved the body back. What's left?"

"Maybe the Murdochs went back a second time. Maybe they remembered somethin' they shoulda done the first time."

"Then why didn't they say so? They admitted everything else. No, I think we've got the truth about the Murdochs' felonious little expedition. Somebody else went into that library, and I think we can safely discount Barney Peterson's mythical Mysterious Stranger." He paused. "Malcolm or Nicole. Malcolm *and* Nicole? Those who prey together stay together? What were they, she, he, after?"

"Nicole coulda gone lookin' for the promissory note," Rizzuto said. "Malcolm coulda too, I s'pose."

"Or Paul Bernstein's report?"

"Naw, Lionel took that," Rizzuto said with a certainty that made Toomey raise an eyebrow. "He was the only one still hidin' somethin'—ever'thin' else was out in the open. He was still keepin' that visit to the diamond people in London a secret, right? Lionel took Bernstein's report—or burned it, mebbe, the same time he burned that desk blotter. There warn't no reason for those others to take it."

Rizzuto's laboriously fractured English was getting to Toomey again. "Nobody says *warn't*," he snapped. " 'Warn't' is just a funny sound invented by Charles Dickens. Nobody *says* it!"

"Well, excuse *me*," Rizzuto huffed.

I'll try, Toomey thought, and felt his irritation pass. Rizzuto was right about one thing: Lionel was the only one with a reason to take the private investigator's report. "So it must have been the note they were looking for," Toomey murmured. "Nicole and Malcolm."

They sat staring at the entrance to Ellandy Jewels a little longer. People were beginning to leave the small park; the lunch hour was over. The pigeons stayed.

Finally Rizzuto stirred. "Bring 'er in?" he asked.

Toomey nodded. "Bring her in."

Gretchen Knox had stopped in at Paul Bernstein's office on her way home from lunch with Simon. Simon had been charming and attentive and obviously puzzled. Gretchen grinned; he probably didn't know what to make of the new Gretchen.

Bernstein had been consulting with a client when Gretchen arrived, a client he speedily abandoned once he was told Mrs. Moneybags Knox was waiting to see him. Gretchen's newfound power was still enough of a novelty for her to gloat a little over

Bernstein's kowtowing. Gretchen said she wanted the London detective to try again to find out what happened between Lionel and De Beers. Bernstein expressed the opinion that it would be a waste of money but agreed to make the arrangements when she insisted.

So that was two people she had digging into Lionel's little trip to London—Bernstein with his overseas colleague and Simon Murdoch with his contacts. One way or the other, she was determined to find out what Lionel was up to.

She left her Saab in the driveway and hurried into the house. Once she'd made up her mind to move into Uncle Vincent's house, Gretchen wanted it done fast. So she'd put the maid to packing. Most of her clothes were already over at the other house, but there were always a million things that couldn't be left to the movers.

She'd just thrown out six pink lipsticks she was sure she'd never want to wear again when the doorbell rang. The maid was busy placing perfume bottles in a box filled with Styrofoam packing material, so Gretchen ran downstairs to see who it was. "Polka Dot!" she exclaimed to the familiar figure at the door. "What are you doing here?"

"I need to talk to you, Miss Gretchen," Mrs. Polk said apologetically. "I thought we'd have time after Mr. Dann finished reading the will, but you left right away and . . ."

Gretchen slapped a hand lightly against her cheek. "Oh, that's right! I'm sorry, Polka Dot—I just plain forgot. Come on in. We can talk now." She led the housekeeper into the living room where they sat on one of the lambskin-covered sofas.

Mrs. Polk opened the huge black purse she was carrying and took out a paper, which she promptly handed over to Gretchen. "I wanted to be sure you had that."

"What is it?" Gretchen asked, unfolding the paper.

"It's the promissory note for that loan everybody was arguing about the night Mr. Vincent got killed," Mrs. Polk said complacently. "I was afraid somebody would try to steal it. And I was right—Miss Dorrie *did* try," she finished disapprovingly.

Gretchen was speechless. She read the paper through quickly once, then more carefully a second time. It was indeed the missing note Lionel and Dorrie had signed for Ellandy Jewels. "I don't understand. How did you happen to have this? Did Uncle Vincent give it to you for safekeeping?"

Mrs. Polk laughed at the thought of that. "Lord no, Miss Gretchen—Mr. Vincent didn't trust anybody. Not even me. No, I took it out of the safe. Not right away, mind you. I was too upset at first, finding him in the library like that, you know."

"Poor Polka Dot," Gretchen murmured. "But then . . . ?"

"I didn't even think of it until after the police had questioned me. Then it hit me how important that note must be, and I got to thinking you might lose a lot of money if any of those *others* got their hands on it first. So I opened the safe and took it out. I didn't touch another thing, Miss Gretchen, only the note. And just in time! That police lieutenant and Mr. Dann came in and they found Miss Dorrie hiding in Mr. Vincent's closet—imagine! You'd never see the note again if *that* one ever got her hands on it! Then they were all making such a fuss I thought it best just to keep quiet until I could tell you about it."

By then Gretchen was laughing hard, tears running down her cheeks. "All those people running around like chickens with their heads off—and all the time *you* had the note! Oh, that's wonderful, Polka Dot! But how were you able to get into the safe? Did you know the combination—well, obviously you did. But *how* did you know?"

Mrs. Polk gave a big sigh. "Miss Gretchen, I always cleaned your uncle's room myself. How could I dust that window sill once a week and *not* find the combination? It was just written on a piece of adhesive tape and stuck underneath." She gave a smug little smile. "I've known how to open that safe ever since the week it was put in."

Gretchen threw back her head and laughed again, pleased to learn that Uncle Vincent's little secret hadn't been so secret after all. "It's a good thing you're an honest woman, Polka Dot!"

"I always try to be," the housekeeper said primly. "What are you going to do now?"

Gretchen became serious. "I'll need to think. This note may be the very thing I need to . . . to bring about some changes

I've been wanting. But I think you've just given me the weapon I need." Her face brightened. "In fact, I know you have! This will make all the difference!"

"I'm so glad," Mrs. Polk cooed.

"Polka Dot, if ever you feel like retiring to the South of France, just say the word," Gretchen said rapidly in a gush of enthusiasm. "Whatever you want, just tell me!"

"I'll let you know," the housekeeper smiled sweetly.

13

Nicole Lattimer's eyes were large and frightened; she'd never been "picked up" by the police before. But she was determined to appear in control of the situation; she set her mouth firmly, raised her head, and attempted to look down her nose at Sal Rizzuto—not easy to do, since he was nearly a foot taller than she. "So what happens now? Why am I here?"

"Lieutenant Toomey'll be here in a mint," the Sergeant said casually. "He wantsta askya some questions."

The interrogation room surprised Nicole. She'd expected a claustrophobic cubicle with a two-way mirror in the wall. Instead the room had plain glass panels in two of the walls and in the door; she could see anybody who looked in at her from the adjoining rooms or from the corridor. No one did. Nicole sat at the head of the room's one table and tried to look composed.

Finally Lieutenant Toomey came puffing in, not at his best in warm weather. "Thank you for coming," he said mechanically, and without giving her a chance to protest, he immediately launched his attack. "We know you were in Vincent Farwell's library the night he was murdered, Ms. Lattimer. I want you to tell us why you were there and what you did."

Nicole managed not to let her mouth drop open. "We were all in the library that night," she stalled.

"I don't mean the meeting at eight o'clock, I mean later. Between three-thirty and five in the morning."

This time Nicole's mouth did drop open. "Wherever did you get a crazy idea like that? I certainly was *not* in Uncle Vincent's library between three-thirty and five!"

"Oh? What time were you there, then?"

Whoops. Nicole pressed her lips together, tried to think of something convincing to say.

"Ms. Lattimer," Toomey said patiently, "we know either you or Malcolm Conner went back to the library. If it's not you, we're going to have to bring in Mr. Conner. I think it was you."

"How do you know it was Malcolm or I?" she cried, her voice going from contralto to soprano in one sentence. "It could have been any one of the others—Gretchen or Lionel or Dorrie or Simon . . . it could have been Simon Murdoch!"

"We know Simon Murdoch's movements that night. And Dorrie's. And both the Knoxes'. It wasn't any of them. That leaves you and Malcolm Conner." He paused dramatically, letting it sink in. "Well, Ms. Lattimer? Do we arrest Mr. Conner? It's up to you."

In all their combined years on the force, neither Lieutenant Toomey nor Sergeant Rizzuto had ever seen a suspect *bare his teeth* at them. Or her teeth, in this case. But that's what Nicole did. She clenched her teeth and stretched back her lips and *hissed*. "How *dare* you put me in a position like this?" she demanded.

"Malcolm or you," Toomey repeated expressionlessly.

"It was you, wasn't it?" Rizzuto prompted.

Nicole inclined her head, defeated and angry.

"Were you looking for the promissory note?" Toomey asked.

"Yes," Nicole sighed. "I needn't have bothered, I know now. But I thought it would be in Uncle Vincent's file cabinet, so I went back to look for it. And found somebody had been there before me. Uncle Vincent was sprawled out on his desk, exceedingly dead. It occurred to me the killer might have taken the promissory note, but I went ahead and looked anyway."

"I think we'd better start at the beginning," Toomey said. "What time did you get there?"

"It must have been around one-thirty," she said. "I know the clock on the mantle was striking two when I left." Toomey and Rizzuto exchanged a quick look but didn't interrupt her. Nicole went on to explain how she'd completed her search, and then calmly mentioned how she'd picked up Uncle Vincent's exceedingly dead hand and used it to fire the gun.

"*You* fired the gun?" Rizzuto yelled in surprise. "For Chrissake *why*?"

Nicole was uncomfortable. "Well, at the time I thought I knew who had killed him. So I figured if I could make it look like self-defense, sh . . . that person might not be in so much trouble."

Rizzuto jumped on it. "She! You said *she*! You mean Gretchen!"

"She means Dorrie," Toomey corrected.

"I didn't say that!" Nicole cried.

"Same as. Why would you protect Gretchen?" Toomey said imperturbably. "No, you thought Dorrie Murdoch had been there before you and for the same reason you were there. You were trying to cover for her, because you thought she'd found the promissory note. Well, Dorrie did go back to the library, but she got there *after* you did. And she didn't have any more luck than you did."

"After? Dorrie was there after I left?"

"About half an hour after you left. She and Simon both."

Tears appeared in Nicole's eyes as relief washed over her. "Then she didn't kill Uncle Vincent? Oh, thank god!" She took a moment to assimilate this news. "But if Dorrie didn't . . . who did?"

"Who indeed?" Toomey said tiredly. "When you were so busy falsifying the evidence, what condition was Uncle Vincent's body in? I mean, had his fingers stiffened yet when you used his hand to fire the gun?"

Nicole shuddered at the memory. "They were just starting to turn stiff."

"Was the fire going?"

"No, it had been out for some time. The room was a little chilly."

Toomey exulted. That fit; the murder did take place around ten-thirty or eleven. "All this is very interesting, Ms. Lattimer, but we're still concerned about who was in the library between three-thirty and five. If you left at two—"

Nicole licked her lips. "I went back again," she said nervously. "I had to put the murder weapon back."

Rizzuto stood up abruptly and loomed over her, hands on his hips. "Oh. You hadda put the murder weapon back, didja? Well, thass nice. Thass real considerate of you. Puttin' the weapon back so we could find it. Thanks a heap."

"There's no need to be sarcastic, Sergeant," Nicole said crossly. "I guess I forgot to tell you I took the two pieces of the broken statuette away with me."

"I guess you did. Wanna tell us now?"

"There's nothing more to tell. I was worried about finger-prints and the like, so I wrapped up the two halves of the statuette in my scarf and took them with me. Then later I got to thinking about it and decided that wasn't too smart, so I took them back."

"But going back to a murder scene a second time *was* smart?" Toomey murmured. "Is there anything else you've forgotten to tell us, Ms. Lattimer?"

Nicole thought a moment. "No, that's all."

"Was the cat in the library while you were there?"

She sighed. "Yes, he was. I didn't know you meant that sort of thing."

"I mean every sort of thing. Let's start again and take it step by step. Tell me exactly what you did, and the order in which you did it."

But Nicole decided she'd been quite cooperative enough for one day, thank you. "I want my lawyer," she announced. "I'm not going to say another word unless he's here. I want Malcolm."

Toomey was only glad she hadn't thought of it earlier. "Call him," he said to Rizzuto; the Sergeant left the interrogation room. "You know what you did was wrong," Toomey said reproachfully.

"So I've been told," Nicole answered dryly.

"Oh? Who told you that?" he asked quickly. "Who knew what you'd done?"

Nicole's eyes widened momentarily, but then she thought of an answer. "My priest."

Toomey just stared at her. "What *liars* you people are! All of you, you lie as easily as you breathe. Don't you ever even think about telling the truth?"

Nicole tilted her head back and looked down her nose. "I'm not saying another word until Malcolm gets here."

They waited.

Gretchen Knox sailed through the door of Ellandy Jewels and stopped with a twirl right in the middle of the showroom, trying to look at everything at once. She'd lusted over the jewels Ellandy's sold ever since Lionel and Dorrie first went into business together, but she'd never paid much attention to the *place* before. Now she took in the various levels of display cases, the consulting areas, the discreet gray man who must surely be a security guard.

She stepped up to one of the display levels and examined a graceful ruby brooch in the shape of a rose, a design Gretchen could now quickly identify as Dorrie's. The rose had a gold stem and a sprig of three emerald-encrusted leaves. An impeccably tailored, beautiful young man—no, Beautiful Young Man, in capitals—came up and asked if he could help her.

Gretchen smiled at the Beautiful Young Man. "No, thank you—I'm just on my way back there." She waved a hand vaguely in the direction of the offices.

The B.Y.M. smiled back. "Do you have an appointment?"

Gretchen managed another smile, this one a little smaller. "I'm Gretchen Knox." She started toward the offices.

"Excuse me, but those are private offices and workshops back there." And the vault. "The guard won't let you through unless you have an appointment."

"I'm your *boss's wife*," Gretchen said tightly, not even trying to smile.

The B.Y.M.'s face lit up. "Oh, Mrs. *Lionel* Knox!" Gretchen ground her teeth. "Go right on back, Mrs. Knox."

"Whythankyousoverymuch," she said sarcastically. The B.Y.M. flashed a model's smile, unperturbed.

She found Lionel not in his office but in the workshop, talking to one of the craftsmen. "I think you'd better hold off on it," he was saying. "Wait until you can ask Nicole—I don't know where she's got to. Hello, Gretchen! What are you doing here?"

"We need to talk, Lionel."

"Sure. What's up?"

"Let's go to Dorrie's office. This concerns her as well—and Nicole too, but since she's not here we'll have to go ahead without her."

"Sounds mysterious." Lionel led her back to Dorrie's office, grumbling all the way about Nicole's unexplained absence.

Dorrie wasn't in her office, though. They tracked her down to the vault. One tray of diamonds was out on a small table, and Dorrie was sitting there examining one of the stones through a loupe. When she heard the other two approach, she looked up and said, "Lionel, take a look at this stone!"

He took the rock between thumb and forefinger and squinted at it. "What about it?"

"It's glass! It's a fake!"

Lionel made a strangling sound and pointed to the tray of diamonds.

"No, they're all right," Dorrie assured him. "And they're all accounted for—I checked the inventory list."

"Perhaps it strayed over from a different tray?" Gretchen suggested.

Dorrie shook her head. "I checked the trays on both sides of this one. This fake hasn't been substituted for a real one. We've simply *acquired* a phony diamond!"

Lionel rolled the fake diamond around on the palm of his hand. "That's weird," he said. "Could Nicole know anything about it?"

"I don't know—she's not here."

"I think I'll hold on to this a while." Lionel dropped the fake diamond into his jacket pocket. "We'll ask Nicole about it later. Right now, Gretchen wants to talk to us."

Center stage at last, Gretchen took a paper out of her shoulder bag, unfolded it, and laid it on the small table next to the tray of diamonds. "That's a photocopy," she said in her new loud voice. "The original is in a safe deposit box."

Dorrie picked up the paper. When she saw what it was, she gasped. "The promissory note!" She looked at Gretchen. "*You* have it?"

"Let me see that." Lionel snatched the paper out of Dorrie's hand. As he read, his face first went white and then turned red. "You had it all along? *You?*"

Gretchen shook her head. "I just got it today. Mrs. Polk took it out of Uncle Vincent's safe." She smiled smugly. "For safekeeping. Right before Dorrie made her little attempt at burglary."

Dorrie dropped her head on one hand and groaned. "Mrs. Polk. I didn't even think of Mrs. Polk."

"No one did, fortunately for me." Gretchen took a deep breath. "Now. It's time we talked a little business. That piece of paper is worth one and a half million dollars. I am willing to tear it up, on one condition. And that is that you make me a full partner in Ellandy Jewels. That's all."

"That's *all!*" Lionel exclaimed, horrified.

"That's all. I won't even insist you get rid of Nicole. But from now on I get one-fourth of Ellandy's profits, or I will collect the full amount of the loan, and I'm going to collect it under the same conditions Uncle Vincent laid down. I mean no time extension."

"Gretchen!" Dorrie cried. "How can you—"

"That's your choice," Gretchen plowed on. "Take me in as a partner, or come up with one and a half million dollars right now. Plus interest, of course."

Lionel was looking at her as if he'd never seen her before. "Gretchen—what's happened to you? I don't even know you! You come in here and try to bulldoze us into—"

"Lionel, don't argue with me about this, please. I've made up my mind to be strong and you're not going to talk me out of it."

"Grettttchennnn," Lionel said in exasperation, "*bullying* people isn't the way to be strong! I don't know where you got your notions, but we can't just let you force your way in!"

"Why not? That's what Nicole did, didn't she?"

"Yeah, and that was bad enough, but at least Nicole contributes something to the business. She contributes a hell of a lot."

"What do you call a million and a half dollars?"

"I call it a lot of money," Lionel said earnestly, "but eventually it will be used up, Gretchen. Dorrie and Nicole and I are going to keep on giving to this business until we drop. What can you contribute?"

Gretchen got a gleam in her eye. "I thought I'd concentrate on marketing." She knew that word.

Lionel snorted. "What do you know about marketing?"

"Nothing, so I'll have to learn. That will give the rest of you a grace period of sorts. But I'm going to be involved—and the sooner you make up your minds to that the better."

Lionel threw up his hands. "You talk to her," he said to Dorrie. He was surprised that Dorrie hadn't blown up at Gretchen the way she had at Nicole. But this time Dorrie just looked depressed.

Dorrie played with the diamonds on the table for a moment or two, and then stood up and replaced the tray in its slot in the vault. "Gretchen, running Ellandy's involves more than playing at being a businesswoman. You can't even just sit at home and collect your share of the profits. If something happens and we go into debt, you'd be responsible for a fourth of everything we owe. If somebody sued us, you'd have to—"

"I don't care about any of that," Gretchen said loudly. "I'm tired of being shut out of everything! You all think I'm some kind of softie you can ignore whenever you feel like it. Well, I'm not! Not any more."

Lionel stared at her. "I think I liked Lou Ann Poovey better."

"Well, she's not here any more. *I'm* here. It's time for me to grow and explore my own self and learn about me. I'm going to identify my life goals and focus my energies toward achieving them. I can do it—I believe in *me.*"

Lionel looked positively ill. "Where do you *get* this stuff?"

"Ellandy's is the first step," Gretchen went on, unhearing. "I'm coming in, Lionel, whether you like it or not."

"Gretchen," Dorrie said, her distaste showing on her face, "do you realize what's happening? You're acting just like Uncle Vincent! This is the sort of thing he used to do all the time— he *loved* forcing people to their knees! You don't want to end up like Uncle Vincent, do you?"

"She's even starting to look like him," Lionel muttered.

"Lionel," Dorrie reprimanded, although secretly she half agreed with him. "Gretchen, I want you to take some time and think about what you're doing—"

"No!" Gretchen covered both ears with her hands. "I don't want to hear about it. I'm tired of being told what to do. I've made up my mind, and that's all there is to it." She took her hands down. "I suppose you'll get Malcolm to handle it, but I'm going to want Mr. Dann to look over the papers before I sign anything. But take care of it soon. This week."

Dorrie and Lionel went on arguing with her a while longer, all three of them frequently losing their tempers, but Gretchen wouldn't budge. When Dorrie said Gretchen was mule-headed, the latter retaliated by calling Dorrie "Little Miss Perfect". Lionel told his wife she was unethical, immoral, and envious of other people's ability to do something with their lives. His wife told him he was dishonest, sarcastic, and a leech on the talents of others. In his defense, Dorrie said Lionel was a conscientious, hard-working man while Gretchen had done nothing but sit on her backside all her life. Gretchen said that every time she'd tried to do something, she'd met the same sort of put-down she was getting from them now. Lionel pointed out that people didn't like being coerced and maybe that had something to do with why she kept running into a wall of resistance. Dorrie suggested a cure for that might be locking Gretchen in the vault until a week from next Tuesday.

Gretchen put an end to it by raising her voice and repeating that they had until the end of the week to get the process rolling for making her a partner. "Otherwise I go see Mr. Dann," Gretchen said, "and I start legal proceedings against you."

The other two exchanged a disgusted look and, hating it, gave up; they knew they were licked. "I've lost half my income in two days," Lionel mused in a strange voice.

"Oh, not really," Gretchen said lightly. "You can look at my fourth as still in the family, can't you?"

He didn't answer immediately. Then he said, "I don't think I'll be making the move to Uncle Vincent's house with you, Gretchen—not right away, at least. I need some time to think."

Gretchen smiled at him almost as if she felt sorry for him. "Punishing me?" she asked. "Somehow, dear husband, that fails to surprise me." She walked out of the vault, leaving her new business partners smoldering with resentment and thinking thoughts they didn't dare speak aloud.

Sergeant Sal Rizzuto's phone call had set off all sorts of alarms ringing in Malcolm Conner's head. The police had Nicole—what had given them away? How much had Nicole told them? Malcolm cancelled an appointment and hurried to the police station.

He was ushered into Lieutenant Toomey's office. Before Toomey could say a word, Malcolm demanded, "Has she been charged? Where is she?"

"Sit down, Mr. Conner," Toomey said easily. "No, she hasn't been charged, and she's right down the corridor in an interrogation room with Sergeant Rizzuto. We just wanted to ask her some questions."

"What's the room number? I want to see her."

"In a moment. There's something I have to say to you first. Please sit down." Malcolm sat, not bothering to hide his annoyance. Toomey made a temple of his fingers and said, "She told us what happened the night Uncle Vincent was murdered.

She said she found his body around one-thirty, and then spent another half hour looking for the promissory note. Then she fired Uncle Vincent's gun and wrapped up the two pieces of the broken statuette in her scarf, leaving the premises at exactly two o'clock—she remembers hearing the mantle clock strike. The medical evidence indicates the murderer did his dirty work between ten-thirty and eleven, roughly two and a half to three hours before Ms. Lattimer got there." Toomey paused. "She also told us about the later visit, to return the murder weapon."

Malcolm visibly shrank two sizes as Toomey watched. "So," Malcolm muttered, "she told you about that, did she?"

"She did. There are some details that aren't quite clear yet, such as the matter of the papers on the floor—"

"Oh, they were there, all right," Malcolm said resignedly. "The Murdochs had already come in and turned the place upside down. As you well know. But that was after Nicole left—she never saw the mess Dorrie and Simon had made. It was a complete surprise to me, you can be sure. Lieutenant, I was merely *restoring* evidence to the scene of the crime, not destroying it. I know the penalties for removing evidence."

Lieutenant Toomey was afraid to breathe. "So what time did you get there?"

"About four."

"How did you get inside?"

"Through the dining room window, the same way Nicole got in. That's illegal entry, if Gretchen wants to press charges. But it's not breaking and entering—the window was open."

"And you did what?"

"I replaced the two halves of the statuette where Nicole said they'd been. Then I left immediately. I was very careful not to disturb anything."

"Did you turn the lights off when you left?"

Malcolm frowned. "I think so, I really don't remember. But I probably did—I always turn out the lights when I leave a room." A childhood lesson well learned. Dorrie had *never* turned out the lights when they were children and it had always fallen to him to do so. In spite of the danger of his present circumstances, Malcolm felt a sudden flash of an old resentment never completely outgrown.

Toomey leaned back in his chair and let loose a long-suffering sigh. "Do I need to remind you of your responsibility to notify the police when you come upon evidence of violent death?"

"No, you don't," Malcolm replied grimly. "I made a bad judgment. I've been in crisis situations before, when the ability to make sensible decisions quickly often meant the difference between success and failure. So I have no excuse. I allowed my desire to protect Nicole to override my obligations as an officer of the court. I am guilty of the very thing I'm always warning my clients against—making emotional judgments instead of arriving at coolly reasoned conclusions. I should have notified the police immediately upon learning of Uncle Vincent's murder, and I should have insisted that Nicole tell you everything she knew. I can't tell you how many times since I have fervently wished that I had done just that. But instead I—"

"Yes, yes," Toomey impatiently interrupted Malcolm's *mea culpa* lament, regretting he'd brought the subject up. "I'm going to want signed statements from both of you."

"Of course. I'll need to consult with Nicole—the attorney-client relationship still holds in her case."

"Certainly." Toomey couldn't resist. "I might as well tell you—Ms. Lattimer said *she* was the one who returned the broken statuette to the library. She didn't even mention your name, not while she was recounting her illicit activity in the murder room. She sent for you because she suddenly felt the need of legal counsel."

Malcolm's mouth was hanging open. He recovered quickly, his face turning angry. "You lied to me! That's entrapment! You deliberately misled me—"

"No, sir, I did not," Toomey said emphatically. "I didn't know you'd gone back to the library too until you just now told me you did. I merely mentioned the second visit, to return the murder weapon, and you assumed I was talking about you."

Malcolm groaned. "Another mistake."

And a big one, Toomey thought. He took Malcolm down the corridor to the interrogation room where Nicole was waiting and motioned Sergeant Rizzuto outside. Nicole greeted her lawyer/lover by opening both arms wide in an operatic gesture. Outside in the corridor, Toomey filled Rizzuto in on Malcolm's four o'clock visit to Uncle Vincent's library.

Rizzuto was stunned. "Malcolm was there too?"

"And Nicole and the Murdochs, before the Knoxes."

Rizzuto leaned against the door of the interrogation room, shocked into good grammar. "All of them were there. I find this incredible, frankly. Do you mean to tell me that *six different people* coincidentally discovered the same dead body—not one of whom notified the police? *Six people?*"

"Only five," Toomey corrected. "One of them had been there before."

When the Lieutenant had let them go with a totally unnecessary warning that they were not to leave town, Malcolm and Nicole went separate ways. Nicole said she just wanted to go home and soak in the tub for three hours; Malcolm said he had one more thing to do before he could call it a day. Both were thinking a brief cooling-off period would be helpful. Malcolm was more than a little resentful of the way Nicole had spilled the beans. Nicole could justify herself easily enough by explaining that Lieutenant Toomey had threatened to arrest *him* if she didn't talk, but she didn't like being put on the defensive. Better to wait, for both of them.

So it was in an atmosphere of strained courtesy that Malcolm drove Nicole back to Ellandy Jewels to pick up her car. Then Malcolm drove to a public phone booth; he called Simon Murdoch and asked him to meet for a drink. They agreed on a tavern called Ollie's.

Malcolm got there first. He was just ahead of the after-work crowd; he picked out a booth and ordered a bourbon and water. He was halfway through his drink when Simon came in, paused at the bar to leave his order, and joined Malcolm in the booth.

Neither man said much at first. Simon knew this wasn't a social drink he'd been invited for, and Malcolm was having trouble getting started. Only after the waitress had brought Simon his martini did Malcolm plunge in.

"I came within a gnat's eyelash of being arrested this afternoon," he started out. He told Simon about his and Nicole's separate trips to the library the night Uncle Vincent was killed, and about their recent session with the police concerning those nocturnal visits. "So it seems Nicole was the first to discover Uncle Vincent's body. She left the library shortly before you and Dorrie got there. I arrived sometime after you had gone

—and was a bit overwhelmed by the extraordinary disarray you left behind you, incidentally. I thought . . ." He trailed off when he realized Simon was laughing silently. "What's so funny?"

Simon wiped a tear from one eye. "I was just delighted to hear that you and Nicole had joined the party. Did you know the Knoxes both went back to the library too?"

"No! You mean after Uncle Vincent was killed?"

"That's what I mean. Gretchen told me about it at lunch yesterday. It seems Lionel got it into his head to look for the promissory note too. He ended up moving Uncle Vincent from the desk to the middle of the floor—Gretchen said he thought it would look more as if a struggle had taken place. Then a little later Gretchen went in and picked up all the papers Dorrie and I had so carefully strewn about. So it would *not* look as if a struggle had taken place. She was trying to make trouble for Lionel, I think."

Malcolm was puzzled. "I thought Uncle Vincent was found at his desk."

"Oh, yes—I forgot to mention that. Gretchen said the servants put him back. Mrs. Polk thought the old man looked undignified, sprawled out on the floor like that. I imagine Barney did the actual moving."

"The servants too," Malcolm said in amazement.

"It would have been so much neater if we'd all gotten together ahead of time and coordinated our movements," Simon drawled. "Not that it would have mattered in the long run, since the note everyone was so assiduously searching for was safely locked away upstairs in Uncle Vincent's bedroom all the time. I wonder who got it?"

A sad smile played across Malcolm's lips. "Do you want to hear something? I actually considered stealing the note myself. I can't stand thieves—I mean, I can't *stand* them. But I did give serious and extensive thought to the possibility of becoming one myself. When Nicole first suggested stealing the note—at the bar we went to, right after the meeting in the library ended, remember?"

"I remember."

"When she first suggested it, I was horrified. Then later I got to thinking about it, and it did begin to look like the only solution. But I came to my senses in time, feeling thoroughly ashamed of myself, you can be sure. Then Nicole came home with a little broken statuette which she calmly explained was a murder weapon. And I was horrified all over again—horrified at what had happened to Uncle Vincent, at what Nicole had done, at the decision I was going to have to make. I had a choice of either seeing Nicole accused of murder, it seemed at the time, or of breaking the law myself by returning the murder weapon and not reporting the crime."

"You didn't have any real choice," Simon said sympathetically. "You couldn't let Nicole be accused."

"No, of course I couldn't," Malcolm worried.

Simon examined his brother-in-law thoughtfully. "Malcolm. Why are you telling me all this?"

Malcolm licked suddenly dry lips. "Because of something the Lieutenant mentioned. He said the murder took place between ten-thirty and eleven."

"Oh, they've got it pinned down now, have they? I suppose that's important?"

"Of course it's important. It means Dorrie and Nicole and Lionel couldn't have done it. They were all together at Ellandy's until after midnight." He paused. "That leaves you and me."

Simon didn't like that. "And Gretchen," he was quick to point out. "She had more opportunity than anyone."

"Opportunity, yes, but no real motive. Uncle Vincent hadn't cut her out of his will or even threatened to. All she had to do was wait."

"Perhaps she got tired of waiting."

Malcolm shook his head. "Can you see Gretchen running that big a risk solely to acquire an assured inheritance a little sooner? It doesn't make sense—she was in no desperate need of money. Gretchen isn't the most sophisticated woman in the world, but even she would know better than that."

Simon did not look amused at all. "Then am I to infer that you've asked me here in order to accuse me of murder?"

"*No*," Malcolm said emphatically. "Personally, I am quite willing to go on believing it was a burglar after all. Look, Simon—Lieutenant Toomey is going to be concentrating on the two of us, there's no question of it. But what happens to his case if, say, we alibi each other?"

Both of Simon's eyebrows shot straight up. "Are you suggesting what I think you're suggesting?"

"I'm suggesting we lie."

This time Simon's laughter wasn't silent, and it went on far too long, to Malcolm's way of thinking. At last Simon chortled, "Why, Malcolm Conner, you devious, rascally shyster, you! This is a whole new side of you I've never seen! You're the last person in the world I would have expected to suggest, ah, *perjury*, for starters—"

"All right, all right," Malcolm cut him off, irritated. "We could say that after we all left the bar—around ten, I think it was—you and I decided to go off somewhere, and we remained in each other's company for at least two hours. That would take us through the danger period, between ten-thirty and eleven."

"So where did we betake ourselves in such unseemly haste?"

"I don't know, anywhere that might reasonably be expected to keep us occupied for two hours. Another bar. A movie, perhaps."

"Or a house of ill repute."

Malcolm was shocked. "How could you think of humiliating Dorrie and Nicole by—oh, I see, it's a joke. Simon, *please* don't be facetious. This is far too serious."

"Sorry." Simon avoided looking Malcolm in the eye. "Malcolm, surely you've thought how this must appear—to me, I mean. If you and I are the only real suspects, and you come to me with a plan for a phony alibi . . . well."

"Of course I've thought about it," Malcolm said with anguish. "I'm virtually volunteering myself as the prime suspect. But I can't help that. Simon, the only way we're going to get out of this is if each of us simply *refuses* to suspect the other. I'm counting on your instinct for self-preservation."

"Which is quite strong," Simon drawled. "You got that part right." He thought a moment. "Well, let's see. A bar won't do. You can't spend two hours drinking steadily without some eagle-eyed bartender noticing you. As for a movie—we'd have to find one we've both seen. You know they'll question us about it."

Malcolm scowled. "Damn, that's right. And I haven't been to a movie in months. Well, then, what about a ball game?"

"Malcolm, ball games *end* at ten-thirty, they don't start then."
The noise level in Ollie's Tavern was beginning to rise, as more
and more people stopped in on their way home from work.
Simon leaned forward across the table so he wouldn't have to
shout. "What about one of those revival movie houses? There's
always some place that's holding a Bogart festival or a John
Huston retrospective or the like. We ought to be able to find
something we've both seen."

"That's an idea! What's playing?"

"I haven't the foggiest," Simon murmured. "We'll have to
check the paper." They both looked around as if expecting a
newspaper to materialize nearby, conveniently open to the
entertainment section. "We'll have to wait until we get home."

Malcolm's eyes were glistening. "Then it's agreed? We pro-
vide each other with alibis?"

Simon hesitated. "I don't know, Malcolm—we could just be
buying trouble for ourselves."

"What do you think we've got now? I'm as certain as I am
of my own name that the police are going to arrest one of us
unless we do something to forestall them. Simon, *it's coming*.
If we're going to take steps to protect ourselves, we have to
do it now."

Simon slowly nodded agreement. "I don't like it, but . . .
very well. Let us check the paper and choose a movie that
attracted us so strongly we were able to put Ellandy's im-
pending financial collapse out of our minds for the requisite
two hours. Tomorrow will be plenty of time—nothing more's
going to happen today."

He was wrong.

When Simon got home, he found Dorrie stretched out on
the sofa, listlessly watching *Glen or Glenda?* on the VCR.
"Hello, darling." Simon kissed the top of her head lightly and
said, "Mind if I turn the volume down? I have something to
tell you."

"Turn it off if you like. I have something to tell you too."

Simon settled for turning the sound off, leaving the grainy
black-and-white images flickering silently on the screen. He
sat on the sofa, cradling Dorrie's bare feet in his lap. "You'll
never dream what your brother has been up to." He repeated
everything Malcolm had told him in Ollie's Tavern, including
his proposal for coming up with two-way alibis. Dorrie listened

with an earnest concentration that disconcerted Simon slightly; he'd expected her to be amused. "Doesn't it surprise you, darling? Upright, squeaky-clean Malcolm Conner playing games with the law?"

"After all that preaching he did to *me* about responsible behavior! What a hypocrite," she muttered tiredly. "Do you think they'll believe you went to a movie?"

"Probably not. But so long as Malcolm and I tell the same story, I don't see that there's anything they can do about it."

"Seems pretty chancey to me."

"It is. I agreed only because Malcolm is undoubtedly right about one thing. It does look as if the police have narrowed their suspects down to two people, your beloved brother and your adoring husband. And since I know *I* didn't do it—"

"Don't be silly, Simon." Dorrie dismissed his thinly veiled accusation as not worth discussing. "When Nicole went back to look for the note—why did she fire Uncle Vincent's gun?"

"To protect you, evidently."

"Me!"

"Malcolm says she thought you'd killed him. She was trying to make it look like self-defense."

"She thought *I* killed . . . *how dare she*?" Dorrie flared angrily. "Well, I like that! She took one look at Uncle Vincent's dead body and decided *I* was a murderer? I'll *kill* her!"

"Now, Dorrie," Simon soothed, smiling.

"Of all the *fucking* nerve! Who does she think she is?"

"*Fuckin'*," Simon corrected. "You don't pronounce the *g*. And don't be so hard on Nicole. Her first instinct was to help, remember. She made herself into an accomplice after the fact just to keep you out of trouble. At least, that's what she thought she was doing. Do try to calm down."

Dorrie took a big breath, let it out. "I suppose you're right. I should be grateful instead of angry, shouldn't I? Well, I'll work on it. Later. Right now, I've got something to tell *you*."

"Oh, that's right. Very well—your turn."

Dorrie got up and began to pace nervously back and forth in front of the television. "Three things, actually," Dorrie said. "Number one, Ellandy Jewels now has a fourth partner. Gretchen has the promissory note. She says if we don't make her a partner, she's going to call in the loan."

"*Gretchen?*" Simon was appalled. "Why, that conniving . . . where did she find the note?"

"Mrs. Polk had it. It seems she knew the combination to the safe all along."

"Oh, Dorrie! That is about the *worst* thing that could happen. Can't you—"

"Number two, Lionel and Gretchen are now separated, a direct result of number one."

Simon wasn't interested in the Knoxes' marital problems. "Dorrie, it might be worth going into the hole just to keep Gretchen out. She's not going to pour her own millions into the business—there's too much of Uncle Vincent in her for that. She'll leech you dry. There must be—"

"Number three," Dorrie persisted. "Lieutenant Toomey called just before you came in. He wants to reenact all the events that took place the night Uncle Vincent was murdered. He wants to do it tonight."

Simon's left eyebrow rose. "*All* the events?"

"Everything he knows about. We're going to have to mess up the library again."

"Oh, for the love of heaven," Simon grunted in disgust.

"We might as well go change—he wants us all to wear the same clothing we had on that night. We're going to start as soon as it gets dark. Come on—it's going to be a long night."

"It is indeed," Simon agreed heavily.

14

Sergeant Sal Rizzuto was in disagreement with his superior officer. He couldn't see what was to be gained from acting out everything that happened *after* Uncle Vincent had been done in. Before, maybe, if they knew what had really happened. But now, they were going to have to go through the whole silly rigamarole and Sergeant Rizzuto was going to have to go through it with them, when he could be home watching Great Performances on PBS.

"Why?" he'd complained to Lieutenant Toomey. "Howzit gonna help us?"

"They might tell us something," Toomey had answered. "We'll have them all watch what the others do. Can you imagine this bunch keeping quiet for two or three hours straight? They'll talk, and they might let something slip. Like Malcolm—he's new at double-dealing and hasn't quite got the hang of it yet. Dorrie—Dorrie's a gasper. And Gretchen isn't the most discreet person in the world. They're bound to tell us something."

At eleven o'clock they were ready to start. The front and back doors of Uncle Vincent's house were locked, but the double doors leading from the terrace into the library were not. The alarm system was off, and one window in the dining room was open. Mrs. Polk was in her rooms, Bjarne Pedersen was in the kitchen, and Godfrey Daniel was in the library.

So was Sergeant Rizzuto, seated in a wheelchair and slumped over the desk, playing the role of the corpse. Two things were different from the night Uncle Vincent was murdered. Gretchen would walk through the reenactment with them; they'd just pretend she was upstairs in her room asleep. Also, Toomey had had Bjarne turn on all the terrace lights; there was no need for everyone to go stumbling around in the dark.

Toomey faced his six resentful suspects outside the terrace

wall. Simon and Dorrie were dressed in their black house-breaking outfits, the camouflaging benefits of which were nullified by their blond heads shimmering brightly in the moonlight. Dorrie carried a light pack on her back. Gretchen was wearing every pearl she owned. Lionel and Malcolm had on the same clothes they'd worn all day, but they'd both removed their ties and added gloves—just as they'd done the night Uncle Vincent was killed. Nicole, however, was dressed in an orchid velour running suit with matching Nikes. "Nike was the goddess of *fate*," Toomey grumbled, "not *feet*."

"Beg pardon?" Nicole asked.

"I thought I told you to wear the same outfit you had on the night of the murder. You weren't wearing that, were you?"

"What did he say about the goddess of feet?" Dorrie whispered. Simon shrugged.

"Lieutenant, do you have any idea how difficult it is climbing over a wall in hose and high heels?" Nicole asked. "I didn't see that it would matter if I dressed for the part this time."

Malcolm spoke up. "I thought Nike was the goddess of *victory*."

"You're right," Lionel said, remembering. "Winged Victory? That's Nike."

"*Forget Nike*," Toomey barked, ending the discussion. He glanced at his wrist; he was wearing two watches, one telling the real time and the other set to approximate the time of the murder night. "Let's say it's one-fifteen," Toomey told them. "That gives Ms. Lattimer fifteen minutes to get over the wall and into the library. Is that enough time?"

"It should be," Nicole said.

"All right, then, let's get started. Where was the ladder?"

"It was leaning against the wall of the garage next door. But Lieutenant, it's not there now."

Toomey sighed and went over to ring the neighbor's doorbell. Simon glowered at Dorrie. "There was a *ladder*," he accused.

"You didn't see it either," she answered defensively.

Toomey was showing his identification to the neighbor, who'd answered the door in his pajamas. The man went back in the house, and a minute later the garage door opened from the inside. Toomey brought out the ladder and positioned it against the side of the garage.

At the Lieutenant's signal, Nicole started wrestling the heavy ladder toward the terrace wall. When Malcolm stepped forward to help her, Toomey waved him back. Nicole reached the top of the wall and dropped down out of sight on the other side. The neighbor stood by his garage door, watching with interest.

"All right, everybody up the ladder!" Toomey called out.

"I most certainly am *not* going up that ladder!" Gretchen announced in a voice not to be argued with. "I'd ruin my clothes!"

"Now, Mrs. Knox, don't cause trouble," Toomey remonstrated. "Nobody else is objecting. Why do you have to be different?"

"I gotta be me," she declared defiantly.

"Must you really?" Simon murmured.

"I'm *not* climbing the wall." Gretchen headed toward the terrace gate, calling to Nicole to unlatch it from the inside.

"Why don't we all go in that way, Lieutenant?" Lionel suggested. "We've seen that Nicole *can* get in over the wall, and that was the point, wasn't it?"

Toomey made a show of thinking it over and then conceded, secretly relieved at not having to climb the ladder himself. They all trekked in through the gate, leaving the disappointed neighbor behind. They followed Nicole through the open dining room window and to the library, where the lights were already on.

Rizzuto lay motionless at the desk, Uncle Vincent's automatic near his outstretched right hand. Half of the Hermes statuette lay on the desk, the other half on the floor. Godfrey Daniel darted under the sofa, alarmed at the arrival of so many people at once.

"That's a good place for you, kitty, you stay right there," Toomey said, adjusting his murder watch to read 1:30. "Now, Ms. Lattimer—show us what you did."

"I think I just stood here staring at him a minute or two," she said.

The others moved out of the way as she started her search. But she'd no more than pulled out the top drawer of the file cabinet when Toomey stopped her. "We didn't find your fingerprints there."

"Oh. I used my scarf." She glanced down at her running

suit and smiled sheepishly. "I had a scarf wrapped around my waist."

"You see why I wanted you to wear the same clothing?" Toomey said reprovingly and handed her his handkerchief. "Use this."

Nicole was working her way through the first drawer when Godfrey Daniel overcame his alarm and emerged from under the sofa. He jumped lightly to the top of the file cabinet and watched Nicole as she closed the first drawer and went on to the second. "He did the same thing that night," she remarked. She went on working her way through the files.

"What a fascinating way to spend an evening," Lionel said dryly. "Watching Nicole look in file folders. When she's finished, let's go to an all-night garage and watch them align wheels."

"You just can't pass up a chance to be sarcastic, can you?" Gretchen said sharply.

"She's almost done," Malcolm interposed quickly, ending the quarrel before it could start. Nicole hurried through the last drawer.

"Lieutenant, I'm gettin' a cramp," said the corpse.

"Okay, you can move." Rizzuto sat up and started working a kink out of his shoulder. "Now what, Ms. Lattimer?" Toomey asked.

"The desk."

Rizzuto made a face and resumed his position. Nicole went through the motions of searching the desk. Then she placed the automatic in Rizzuto's hand and fired, putting a bullet squarely into the desk. The noise made everyone jump and sent Godfrey Daniel scurrying back under the sofa.

"I didn't think she was actually going to *fire* it," Dorrie complained to Malcolm in a murmur.

Nicole wrapped the two parts of the statuette in Toomey's handkerchief. "That's all, Lieutenant."

"It took you eleven minutes this time instead of thirty," Toomey said, resetting the watch to read two o'clock. "I know, you were just pantomiming searching, that's all right. What about the lights?"

"I turned them off." She suited action to the word, and led the others back to the dining room window. "Then I left through the terrace gate—the ladder's on the other side of the wall, and the gate unlocks from the inside anyway."

As they all headed toward the gate, Malcolm slowed his steps and drew Simon back. "Have you seen *Naughty Marietta*?"

"What?"

"The old movie, *Naughty Marietta*—you've seen it, haven't you?"

"Years ago, on television."

"That's good enough. The Alhambra has been having a Jeanette MacDonald—Nelson Eddy film festival all month. That's the movie we went to see—*Naughty Marietta*." Malcolm hurried to catch up with the others.

Simon rolled his eyes. *Naughty Marietta!*

Outside the terrace wall, they saw the neighbor had dragged a lawn chair out of the garage and was sitting there waiting for the next act. Nicole wrestled the ladder back to its place against the garage wall and told the neighbor not to put it away as it would be needed again.

"Now give the broken statuette to Mr. Conner," Toomey instructed. "All right, everybody, that's what Ms. Lattimer did. Any comments?"

"Comments?" Lionel repeated. "Are we supposed to evaluate her performance?"

"I don't see why she had to ruin the desk," Gretchen said indignantly. "That's a Chippendale—Uncle Vincent paid six hundred thousand dollars for that desk."

"A bargain," Simon remarked.

"Yes, it was," Gretchen agreed. "Somebody offered him nine hundred thousand for it just last year."

"That much?" asked Malcolm. "I didn't know Chippendale prices were rising that fast."

"Could we *please* stop talking about furniture?" Toomey snarled. "We might as well go on. Murdochs—you're next."

The others watched as Simon boosted Dorrie up to the top of the wall. When she tossed the rope over for Simon, he gestured apologetically toward the ladder and said, "No moon that night." He climbed the wall.

Nicole snickered. "*I* saw it."

Toomey and the four others retraced their steps through the

terrace gate. Dorrie was rummaging through her backpack and pulled out a new can of Redi-Whip, which she handed to Simon.

"*You* brought the Redi-Whip?" Lionel exclaimed. "What for?"

Dorrie explained her intention to spray the alarm box, which they'd failed to locate. "I know, it's supposed to be shaving cream," she added, "but Simon uses an electric razor."

Nicole found this an interesting problem. "What about mousse?" she asked. "Hair-styling foam?"

Dorrie's hand went automatically to her blond curls. "I never use styling foam," she said absently. "It leaves a film on your hair."

"*Could* we get on with it, please?" Toomey growled.

They all moved around to the double doors leading into the library. "I think we used flashlights here," Simon said. "That's why I put the Redi-Whip down on the terrace—so I'd have a free hand."

"Aren't you forgetting something?" Toomey asked. "The table?"

"Oh, that's right." Simon struggled with the heavy wrought-iron table, shoving it up flush against the terrace wall.

"Excuse me, why did you do that?" Nicole asked. "Why not just go out the terrace gate the way I did?"

"That's what we did do, as it turned out," Simon explained. "But at the time I thought it wouldn't hurt if we had a quick escape route ready." He took a flashlight from Dorrie. "Well, is everyone ready for the big discovery?"

He opened the library doors, played his flashlight around the room, and "discovered" Sergeant Rizzuto slumped over the desk. Dorrie turned on the lights.

"Now I want you to take your time with this," Toomey cautioned. "Try to remember the exact *order* in which you did everything."

"I think one of the first things we did was sit down and talk it over," Dorrie said. At Toomey's gesture, she and Simon sat on the sofa. "Godfrey Daniel was here with us. Remember, Simon? He dug his claws into your pants leg."

"I remember," Simon said with a pained expression. "Do we have to repeat that part of it, Lieutenant?"

"Yep," Toomey said. "Where is he? Here, kitty!" A small

black-orange-white head lifted itself above the desk top in the general vicinity of Rizzuto's lap. "There you are, Godfrey!" Toomey carried the cat over to the sofa.

"Thank god," sighed the corpse. "He's been sharpenin' his claws on my knee for the last five minutes."

This time Godfrey preferred Dorrie's lap to Simon's. He lay on his back and allowed Dorrie to stroke his throat; a loud purring like rusty machinery being started up filled the room.

"What did you talk about?" Toomey asked sharply.

The Murdochs exchanged a glance. "About what we should do," Dorrie said. "Simon wanted to leave immediately—all this other stuff was my idea. Don't blame him."

"Didn't you speculate about the murder? Didn't you wonder who'd done it?"

"We may have," Dorrie said vaguely. "I don't really remember."

"Of course you remember," Toomey snapped. "Who?"

"Me," Lionel said with a comes-the-dawn look. "You thought it was me!"

"Lionel," Malcolm cautioned. "Don't volunteer."

Dorrie said, "Well, it seemed to me it had to be one of the three of us at Ellandy's, and it just didn't seem likely that, uh . . ."

"That Nicole had done it?" Lionel finished for her. "Thanks a heap, Dorrie!"

The only thing Dorrie could think to say in her defense was: "Well, Nicole suspected *me*!"

"Which one of us did *you* suspect, Lionel?" Nicole asked dryly.

Lionel started, then laughed shortly. *"Touché."*

"You are all making a mistake," Malcolm said firmly. "Stop this speculating. You can only harm each other."

"What possible difference could it make?" Simon asked. "Everybody suspects everybody else and nobody *knows* anything. I for one would be deeply grateful if the murderer would step forward immediately and save the rest of us from having to go through this nonsense all over again."

Lieutenant Toomey watched and listened, said nothing.

"It could make a great deal of difference," Malcolm said angrily. "Don't you see we've been set up? The only reason they're making us go through this charade is to get us to talk, to accuse each other. And you're all cooperating beautifully! Tonight is just a fishing expedition and you keep going for the bait! Do try to show some discretion, all of you! We don't have to—"

"Get to the point," Gretchen interrupted impatiently.

"I've already made my point," Malcolm snapped. "*Keep your mouths shut.*"

For once they all listened to him and a silence fell over the room, much to Lieutenant Toomey's disgust. Sergeant Rizzuto got up from the desk, stretched, and said, " 'Let's kill all the lawyers.' "

Malcolm whirled on him. "*What?* What did you say?"

Rizzuto shrugged. "It don't mean nothin', it's just a line from Shakespeare. *Henry VI.*"

Everyone in the room was staring at him.

"Part Two," the Sergeant finished lamely.

Toomey shook his head in disbelief. "Well, let's proceed, shall we? And this is no *charade*, believe me—I want you to be careful to repeat your actions exactly. What did you do first?"

"I took the file cabinet," said Dorrie.

"And I took the desk," Simon added. He held up his gloved hands. "No fingerprints."

Sergeant Rizzuto resumed his position at the desk, and the others watched with reactions ranging from amusement to annoyance as the two Murdochs proceeded to reduce the formerly spotless library to a shambles. This time Godfrey Daniel did not bat playfully at the sheets of paper Dorrie was tossing up into the air. Instead he perched on an arm of the sofa and watched with an expression of infinite boredom. Old stuff.

"Do you think you could dampen your enthusiasm just a trifle, Dorrie?" Gretchen asked through clenched teeth. "*I'm* the one who has to clean that up, remember!"

Dorrie made a what-can-I-do gesture and went on tossing papers.

Simon felt through Sergeant Rizzuto's pockets until he found the billfold planted there; then he slipped an inexpensive watch off the Sergeant's wrist. He paused a moment. "Dorrie, did I take the watch or did you?"

"I did, darling. You took the billfold."

"Act it out," Toomey commanded. They acted it out.

Gretchen said, "I could have you both arrested, you know. For theft."

"Gretchen, I just *knew* you'd think of that," Simon answered heavily. He and Dorrie gathered up the knick-knacks Toomey had told Mrs. Polk to make sure were placed about the room. Simon cocked an eyebrow toward Toomey. "I assume you want me to pantomime breaking the glass in the door?"

Toomey shook his head. "Do it," and before Gretchen could object: "Send us the bill."

With a put-upon expression, Simon dumped his loot on the sofa and went out on the terrace. He broke the glass from the outside. "Satisfied, Lieutenant?"

"Lights?" Toomey asked.

"On," both Murdochs said. With their booty, they led the way along the terrace and out through the gate. Next door, the neighbor's wife had joined him; they sat side by side in their lawnchairs, each holding a tall glass of something.

"Three-twenty," Toomey said, checking his murder watch. "A little less than an hour—the time's only approximate, of course. Are you sure you didn't forget anything?"

"Why didn't you take the painting?" Lionel wanted to know. "That Degas is worth a helluva lot more than all those little doodads you took."

"Too much to carry," Simon explained. "Besides, we didn't really want to steal from Uncle Vincent. Or from Uncle Vincent's estate, I suppose I should say."

"From *me*," said Gretchen.

"From you," Simon agreed. "Taking the Degas—well, that's far more serious than just picking up a few doodads, as Lionel calls them." He smiled sardonically. "There are limits to our criminality."

"I'm so glad," Gretchen said archly.

"You handled almost everything in that room," Nicole mused. "Didn't you wonder where the murder weapon was?"

"I didn't even think about it," Simon answered ruefully.

"I did," Dorrie said. "I just assumed the killer took it with him."

"*Him*," Lionel repeated ominously.

"Oh, Lionel, don't start," Dorrie fussed.

Lieutenant Toomey changed the setting on his murder watch. "It is now four in the morning. Mr. Conner, you're next."

Without a word, Malcolm moved the ladder to the terrace wall, climbed over, waited for the others to walk around and join him, crawled in through the dining room window, led the way to the library, replaced the two pieces of the broken statuette, turned out the lights, led the way back out, and returned the neighbor's ladder.

"Well, that was boring," Lionel said amiably.

"Why'd you take the statuette back?" Simon asked Malcolm. "Why not just get rid of it?"

"Because it is against the law to remove evidence from the scene of a crime," Malcolm said with irritation. "Or doesn't that mean anything to you?"

"My, my, aren't we touchy all of a sudden," Simon muttered, letting his own irritation show. "If you were all that concerned about legal procedure, you would have called Lieutenant Toomey here. Or somebody."

"He's right," Gretchen said. "We all meddled, one way or another. None of us is simon-pure."

"I do like your choice of words," Simon half-smiled.

"Share the guilt?" Malcolm asked Gretchen. "Make it easier for everybody to bear that way? Do I have to point out to all of you that I was trying to *restore* the scene as nearly as possible to what it was when the murderer left? I couldn't unfire the gun Nicole fired—but I could return the murder weapon and that's what I did and I'm not going to apologize for it!"

The other five suspects exchanged poker-faced looks and simultaneously broke into polite applause.

"*Et tu*, Nicole?" Malcolm said, hurt. She laughed and gave him a hug.

"You were getting a bit holier-than-thou, Malcolm," Lionel smiled.

"I do not understand how you can all take this so lightly!" Malcolm protested. "This is a *murder* investigation, can't you get that through your heads? You're all acting as if we're playing some sort of parlor game and you're giving it about as much thought as you would a game!" Lieutenant Toomey silently agreed.

"Well, excuse us all to pieces, brother dear," Dorrie huffed. "Only *you* know the proper way to behave—we should have known to take our cues from you."

"There—that's what I'm talking about," Malcolm retorted.

"We spend more time sniping at each other than thinking seriously about what happened here and who is responsible."

"Be serious, be responsible," Dorrie mimicked. "My god, how many times have I heard that!"

"Too bad you never listened," Malcolm snapped. "If you had, maybe you wouldn't be in the mess you're in now!"

"*I'm* in a mess?" Dorrie screamed. "What about you? Look where your *responsible* behavior has landed *you*! Don't you blame this on me, Malcolm Conner! You're in just as deeply as I am!"

"That's tellin' him, honey!" the neighbor's wife called out.

"Oh, good heavens!" Dorrie gasped, mortified. "Lieutenant Toomey, do we have to stand out here where everyone can hear?"

"No, I suppose not." He checked his watch. "It is now five ay em—"

"My turn?" asked Lionel. At Toomey's nod, he pulled a key from his pocket. "This time we go in through the front door."

Lieutenant Toomey thanked the neighbors for the use of their ladder and told them the police wouldn't be needing it any more. He suggested they go back to bed.

Through the door, back to the library. Godfrey Daniel lay stretched out on the desk, lazily poking a paw at Sergeant Rizzuto's outstretched arm, half-heartedly trying to get a game going.

"The first thing I did was to check to see if he was dead," Lionel said. He went to the desk and felt Rizzuto's pulse.

"Where was Godfrey?" Toomey asked.

"Uh, I don't remember. Not on the desk." He shooed the cat off. Then he hunkered down and picked up a sheet of paper from the floor. "I looked at every piece of paper I could find." Lionel was a sloppy pantomimist; he didn't pick up every paper on the floor and he barely glanced at those he did pick up. Toomey told him to slow down, the timing would be all off. Lionel said the timing was already off, but he made the effort to slow himself a little.

At last he finished. "Now comes the unpleasant part." Lionel went back to the desk and wrestled Rizzuto into an upright position in the wheelchair. "Uff. You weigh more than Uncle Vincent, Sergeant." Rizzuto didn't answer, busy playing dead.

Lionel wheeled him to the middle of the room. "I'm going

to dump you now," he warned Rizzuto. The Sergeant broke his fall with his arms and stretched out on the floor. Lionel took the automatic from the desk and thrust it under Rizzuto's stomach. Then he stood in the middle of the room and looked around. "Something else?"

"The blotter," the corpse prompted.

"Right." Lionel stepped over to the desk and held up the blotter. Rizzuto had taken a red felt-tip pen and written the word "blood" on it in large letters.

"Ugh," said Gretchen.

But Lionel wasn't looking at the blotter; he was staring at the folder that had been concealed underneath. Toomey watched him carefully, as did Rizzuto as well as he could from his place on the floor. Lionel picked up the folder. "It's Bernstein's report!"

"Thought you'd burned it?" Toomey asked innocently.

"I *know* I burned it," Lionel sighed resignedly. "What is this, Lieutenant, some kind of trick?"

"You admit burning it, then?"

"You just heard me admit it—hell, you already knew, or you wouldn't have put the damned thing there in the first place. I burned the report. All it did was cause trouble."

Dorrie said, "So why bother burning it? Everybody knew about it anyway. About, well, you and Nicole."

"Yeah, but nobody likes something like that lying around. I just thought it best to get rid of it. This has to be another copy."

"It's my copy," said Toomey. "Are you sure there wasn't another reason for burning it?"

"Of course there was another reason," Gretchen snarled. "He didn't want anyone knowing why he went to England!"

Lionel looked disoriented. "What do you know about—"

"England?" Dorrie interrupted. "You mean about four months ago? He went to visit a relative—wasn't that it, Lionel?"

"He went to visit *De Beers*," Gretchen said. "He went to apply for a, um, sightholdership, I suppose you'd call it—and he didn't want any of us to know!"

"Bernstein," Lionel guessed. "Bernstein gave you a copy of the report too?"

"What's this about De Beers?" Malcolm asked. "Is it true, Lionel?"

"Oh, hell, you might as well know. Yes, it's true. I didn't talk about it because I struck out. De Beers made it quite clear I didn't qualify for their little club."

"Not so little," Nicole murmured. "Didn't you even tell your partner? Dorrie, didn't you know?"

Dorrie shook her head. "Lionel, why did you try something like that behind my back?"

"It wasn't behind your back," Lionel protested. "I had this idea that if I succeeded in London, I could come back and say, 'Guess what! We're in!' Dumb, I know, but I wanted to surprise you."

"Oh," Dorrie said suspiciously, "you wanted to surprise me."

"Well, okay, I was hedging my bet as well. I didn't know how things would go in London—Dorrie, I don't understand what you're so irked about. Don't you see what a coup it'd be if we could get our rough stones straight from De Beers? We'd cut out all the middlemen!"

"Like Simon," Dorrie accused. "You were trying to take Simon's business away from him!"

"You've got it all wrong," Lionel sighed. "It was Simon's idea in the first place. We had it all worked out."

"Now *that* is a lie," Gretchen announced firmly. "Simon didn't know anything about it until I told him!"

Dorrie glanced suspiciously at her husband. "You knew? *She* told you?"

"Wait a minute, wait a minute!" Lionel objected. "There's a misunderstanding somewhere. Simon came to *me* with the plan and—"

"I'll say there's a misunderstanding," Simon interjected. "Lionel, what do you think you're doing? You know I didn't come to you with any 'plan' for dealing with De Beers. What's going on?"

Lionel looked thunderstruck. "Are you saying you did *not* suggest I apply to De Beers and then you would act as my agent and—"

"Stop!" cried Malcolm. "You're doing it again! Don't thrash this out in front of the *police*, for god's sake."

"That's exactly what I'm saying," Simon answered, ignoring Malcolm. "Your agent? Really, Lionel!"

Lionel took in all the curious and/or accusing faces looking at him and muttered, "I've got to sit down." He sat on the sofa.

On Godfrey Daniel.

Godfrey let out a yowl and wriggled loose. He leaped up on the desk, where he crouched hissing at his tormentor. The corpse sat up. "Ya know, I was wonderin' 'bout that cat," Rizzuto said. "He saw who killed his master. He ain't gonna be too friendly toward—"

"For Christ's sake, I just *sat* on him!" Lionel yelled.

"With Godfrey, you can't tell anyway," Dorrie volunteered. "I don't think he was especially fond of Uncle Vincent anyway."

"Sensible animal," Nicole murmured.

Lieutenant Toomey took charge. "Let's get back to this matter of De Beers. You lied about going to see them, Mr. Knox. And you destroyed the private investigator's report that would have given you away. And you seem to have lied about Mr. Murdoch's part in this—"

"*Seem* to have lied?" Simon asked indignantly. "He's trying to involve me in something I'm still not sure I understand."

Lionel sighed heavily. "Lieutenant, I told you yesterday I was embarrassed about my failure in London. We did talk about it, didn't we? Or are you going to say I'm lying about that too?"

"No, we talked about it."

"Okay. I knew then it would all come out eventually, but it didn't seem so important any more, in light of all the other things that have been happening. I don't know what Simon's game is—I can't explain that. But the dumb thing is, you're all looking at me as if I killed Uncle Vincent when all I did was burn the report. And I didn't burn it because of the De Beers business anyway! You're all off the track. Way off."

"Then why did you burn the report?" Toomey wanted to know.

"Oh, there was something else in there that could cause more bad feelings. Nothing really important."

"If it's not important, then you can tell us about it."

Lionel didn't want to say, but Toomey kept pressing him. "It was that part about Gretchen and Malcolm," Lionel said reluctantly. "I didn't see any reason for dredging that up."

Gretchen groaned. "Then you found out?"

Lionel shot her a look of annoyance. "Gretchen, I knew *at the time*."

Malcolm, for once, could think of nothing to say.

Toomey was lost. "*What* about Gretchen and Malcolm?"

Lionel waved a hand toward the file folder. "They had an affair. It's in that report."

Toomey flipped through the pages. "Not in my copy, it isn't."

Rizzuto made a rude noise. "Bernstein held out on us."

Simon's eyebrows had climbed up to his hairline. "Do I hear correctly? Malcolm and Gretchen? Oh, that's too delicious for words!"

"Knock it off, Simon," Gretchen growled.

"I didn't know a thing about it," Simon smiled broadly, clearly delighted with this further evidence of human folly. "Did you know, darling?"

"Yes," Dorrie said in a small voice.

"Let me get this straight," Toomey said to Lionel. "You burned Bernstein's report not because of the De Beers business, but because Mrs. Knox and Mr. Conner are having an affair?"

"*Had*," two voices corrected him.

"It's over now," Lionel agreed. "And yes, that's why I burned the folder."

Nicole laughed softly. "Galahad lives."

"I don't believe it," Gretchen stated flatly.

"And somehow, my dear estranged wife, *that* fails to surprise *me*," Lionel said. "Believe what you want. I don't care any more."

Estranged? thought Toomey. *When did that happen?*

"So what are you going to do, sit there and pout?" Gretchen screamed at Lionel. "You've been up to something and I want to know what it is!"

"I have *not* been up to something!" Lionel shouted. "I've told you everything and I've told you the truth!"

Dorrie covered both ears. "Oh, *do* stop yelling!" she yelled.

The library door opened. "Is everything all right?" Bjarne Pedersen asked with concern.

"No, everything is not all right!" Gretchen screamed. "Go away, Barney!"

But Lieutenant Toomey stopped him. "Ask Mrs. Polk to

make us some coffee, would you, Barney? I think we could all use a pick-me-up about now."

"Yes, sir, I'll go get her." Bjarne left.

"Coffee is *not* what I call a pick-me-up, Lieutenant," Simon objected.

"Nevertheless, it's what we're going to have," Toomey said. "Now I want you all to calm down—we're not going to solve anything by staging a shouting match. Sit down, everybody. Go on—sit."

Nicole and Malcolm sat on the sofa with Lionel; the others found chairs. Toomey checked his murder watch. The time schedule was shot to hell, but it was worth it if this new line panned out. He cleared his throat. "We have a glaring discrepancy here—Mr. Knox and Mr. Murdoch tell two different stories. Each one's saying the trip to London was the other's idea. Now, that's not the sort of thing that could result from a simple misunderstanding, so that means one of you is deliberately lying. The question is, which one?"

"Lionel," said Gretchen.

"Lionel," Simon agreed. "But I think Malcolm is right. This is not the time or the place to thrash this out."

"I think Simon is lying," Nicole said mildly, and shushed Dorrie when she started to protest. "Lionel wouldn't have any reason to lie about a thing like that."

"And what reason would *I* have, pray tell?" Simon asked, overly polite.

"Gee, I don't know, Simon. To avoid embarrassment? To disclaim any responsibility for Lionel's failure in London? You do tend to dissociate yourself from the rest of us whenever Ellandy's has trouble."

"That's not a very nice thing to say," Dorrie objected.

"It's not a very nice thing to *do*," Nicole pointed out.

Lionel spoke up. "Simon, you know damn well we had an agreement. You—"

"Then produce the contract," Simon demanded. "If we had a business agreement, there'd be a contract."

All eyes were on Lionel. "It was a verbal agreement," he sighed, defeated.

"He's lying," Gretchen said, meaning Lionel. "He killed Uncle Vincent."

"Whoa, that's a pretty big leap," Toomey cautioned. "You've

all lied to me at one time or another. Even those two." He nodded toward the servants, who were just then entering the library. Bjarne carried a tray with coffee pot and cups; Mrs. Polk had a platter of sandwiches.

"What happened?" Mrs. Polk demanded in her high voice, appalled at the condition the room was in. "How did all those papers get on the floor? There's no place to walk!"

"Just walk on the papers," Toomey told her. "Don't worry about it."

The housekeeper sniffed with disapproval but did as she was told. She hesitated, and then indicated to Bjarne that they should place their burdens on the desk.

"Everyone help himself," Gretchen announced, in no mood to play hostess.

"You stay," Toomey said to Bjarne and Mrs. Polk. "And thanks for the sandwiches, Mrs. Polk."

"Yeah, thanks," echoed Rizzuto, his mouth already full.

Lionel didn't want any coffee; he stood up and walked around nervously, his hands jammed in his jacket pockets, while the others crowded around the desk. Lionel's fingers started playing with something sharp and hard they found in his right-hand pocket; it was the phony diamond Dorrie had found in the vault earlier in the day. He took it out and looked at it under the end-table lamp. Good imitation.

"Don't sulk, Lionel," Gretchen said. "Have some coffee."

"I don't want any coffee," he answered testily. He tossed the fake diamond on the end table and sank back down on the sofa.

"Now, Mr. Knox," Toomey said, resuming where they'd left off, "did anyone else know of this ostensible agreement you and Mr. Murdoch had?"

"No, just the two of us."

"Could anyone have overheard you talking about it?"

Lionel thought back. "I'm pretty sure no one did."

Godfrey Daniel leaped up to the arm of the sofa, attracted by the bright shiny little thing that had suddenly appeared on the end table.

"Then it's just your word against his," Rizzuto said, stating the obvious.

"Simon would have told me," Dorrie said loyally.

"Thank you, darling." He blew her a kiss.

Godfrey's paw shot out and flicked the phony diamond off the table. He leaped to the floor in pursuit.

"Personally, I can't see why either one of you should lie," Malcolm offered. "What's to be gained? In Lionel's case, nothing more than passing the buck—involving Simon to share the blame for a business failure. In Simon's case, to let Lionel shoulder the blame alone. Ignoble motives in both cases, unworthy of either Simon or Lionel. But one version has to be true. My point is that it doesn't matter. Whichever is lying, that still tells us nothing of who killed Uncle Vincent. It's not germane—"

Dorrie laughed humorlessly. "Aren't you the one who keeps telling the rest of us to shut up?"

"I was simply trying to point out that we've gotten off the track."

Godfrey was scrabbling through the papers on the floor, making a lot of noise. "What *is* that cat looking for?" Toomey asked. "I'm not sure we're off the track at all. The motive for killing Uncle Vincent was money, in the form of the loan agreement or perhaps something else. Everything's connected."

"Oh, that's helpful," Nicole commented wearily.

"You never know," Rizzuto told her with an air of great profundity. Nicole sighed.

"Shall I get more coffee?" Mrs. Polk wanted to know.

Toomey told her no. "Somebody came in this room looking for something and ended up killing Uncle Vincent between ten-thirty and eleven o'clock. Mr. Knox, you have an alibi for that time, so you are not a suspect. Therefore you have nothing to lose by telling the truth. Do you wish to change your story?"

"Watch out for tricks," Malcolm warned.

"I am telling you the truth," Lionel said to Toomey. "My petitioning De Beers was something Simon and I worked out together, ahead of time. He did know about it—he suggested it."

"Not so," Simon denied. "We have talked about De Beers, of course, but I never suggested that Lionel—get away, cat!"

Godfrey Daniel was digging away with both paws at the papers around Simon's left foot. Bjarne Pedersen walked over to where Simon was standing and bent down. When he stood up, he was holding the fake diamond. "Did you drop this, Mr. Simon?"

"A diamond? No, I—wait a minute, let me see that." He held the stone next to a lamp. "Oh, that must be one of the imitation stones. But I don't carry them around with me."

Lionel glanced quickly at the end table where he'd put the stone and got a strange look on his face. "How did you know that was an imitation? What are you doing with fake diamonds?"

Simon was annoyed. "I frequently handle imitations. Customers sometimes order copies of real jewelry they own, for insurance purposes. Dorrie, you've made up copies yourself."

"Yes," she agreed, but the look on her face was the same as that on Lionel's.

Gretchen shot a look at Lionel. "Is that . . . ?"

He nodded. "Simon, that stone came from Ellandy's vault. Dorrie found it, mixed in with the real diamonds."

"What's this?" Toomey said.

"In our vault?" Nicole asked.

"I just found it today," Dorrie explained.

"What were you doing in Ellandy's vault?" Lionel demanded.

Simon wore an air of great patience at last wearing thin. "I've been in your vault on a number of occasions—you've taken me in there yourself to show me something or other. But I don't know how this imitation got mixed in with your stones. I haven't been in your vault for months."

"That's not true," Nicole said sharply. "You were in there the day after Uncle Vincent was murdered." All eyes were upon her. "Don't you remember?" she asked Lionel and Dorrie and Malcolm. "We were in Lionel's office and Simon dropped by to take Dorrie to lunch. She'd left some diamonds in *her* office and Simon offered to return them to the vault for her."

"That's right," Lionel said, his eyes wide. "I remember!"

"Good god," Malcolm muttered. "So do I."

Simon paled.

"Simon?" Dorrie cried fearfully.

"Mr. Simon?" Mrs. Polk asked Bjarne. He held up his hands I-don't-know.

"No alibi," Rizzuto reminded his superior.

Toomey didn't need reminding. "Mr. Murdoch—you told us you went straight home from the bar you all went to after that disastrous meeting Uncle Vincent called. Did anyone in the building see you come in? Did you speak to anyone?"

Simon's eyes darted around the room, assessing his chances.

He made his decision. "As a matter of fact, I didn't go straight home. I went to a movie."

"A movie!" The disbelief in Rizzuto's voice was obvious. "So why dint you tell us that before?"

"I was afraid it would make me appear insensitive—my going off to a movie like that while my wife was in at Ellandy's worrying herself sick over the fate of her business."

"Insensitive," Gretchen nodded.

"What movie did you go see?" Toomey asked.

Simon made an odd little throat-clearing sound. "*Naughty Marietta*. At the Alhambra."

Dorrie stared. "I'm married to a Jeanette MacDonald freak?"

Simon looked pained. "I happen to be an admirer of Nelson Eddy."

"*God*frey *Dani*el!" Toomey exploded, incredulous.

"Meow?" said Godfrey.

"I've never heard you mention Nelson Eddy in my *life*," Dorrie accused.

Toomey asked, "Did anyone you know see you at the movie?"

Simon did his throat-clearing bit again. "As a matter of fact, I didn't go alone. Malcolm was with me."

"No, I wasn't!" Malcolm shouted excitedly. "That's just a story we made up to alibi each other!"

Simon threw Malcolm a look of pure venom. "Oh, wonderful! *Terrific*. Good old reliable Malcolm!"

Toomey switched gears to throw Simon off track. "The day after Uncle Vincent died—did you substitute fake diamonds for real ones in the Ellandy vault?"

"Naw, he dint," Rizzuto interrupted, violating a basic rule of police procedure by answering for the suspect. "He wasn't takin' real diamonds out—he was puttin' 'em back."

Simon turned as white as Hamlet's father. "How did you . . . ?"

"*Putting them back?*" Toomey asked, not sure he'd heard right.

"How did you, how did you . . . ?" Simon was having trouble completing his sentence.

Rizzuto grinned. "Guessed right, huh?"

"My god, Rizzuto," Toomey said, awed. "You've solved the case!"

Rizzuto kept right on grinning. "Yeah."

Simon had recovered. "How did you come up with a fantastic notion like that?"

"What's going on?" Gretchen demanded.

"It's no good, Mr. Murdoch," Toomey said. "You've given yourself away. Just too many lies—they were bound to trip you up sooner or later. You're under arrest. Rizzuto, read him his rights."

The only sound in the room was Rizzuto's flat voice intoning the words of the Miranda Code.

"It was Mr. Simon," Bjarne nodded to Mrs. Polk. Dorrie wailed like a banshee and everyone started talking at once.

Over Simon's protests, Lieutenant Toomey pushed him down into a chair and drew up another one, sitting knee-to-knee. "This is what's going to happen," he explained in a reasonable voice. "Either I charge you with first-degree murder, or else you tell us what happened here and we try to work out a deal with the prosecutor's office. Either way, you're under arrest. So what's it going to be?"

"He has the right to consult with an attorney," Malcolm said hastily. "Lieutenant, you can't expect him to make a decision like that without having all his legal options explained to him. Simon, I advise you to say nothing at all until—"

"Malcolm," Simon said acidly, "*shut up.*"

"Your choice," Toomey went on. "First-degree murder means premeditated, and I don't think you planned to kill him, did you?" Toomey gestured toward Rizzuto with his head and circled one wrist with the fingers of the other hand. Rizzuto pulled out a pair of handcuffs and clamped them on Simon. Simon held his hands up in front of his face, staring at the cuffs, horrified; Dorrie wailed again. "First-degree carries a lot heavier penalty than the lesser charges, like manslaughter," Toomey said. "So what do I charge you with, Mr. Murdoch? Was it premeditated?"

"No, of course it wasn't," Simon answered waspishly, finally accepting the fact that they had him. "It was an accident. I had no intention of killing him or anyone else! I didn't mean to kill him even when I hit him!"

"Ugh," said Gretchen. "Tacky."

"Aw, Simon!" Dorrie was still wailing.

"So why did you hit him?" Toomey asked, knowing the answer but content to go through the motions now that he had his man. "Why?"

Dorrie wailed louder.

"Because he pulled a gun on me!" Simon protested. "You saw it! What was I supposed to do, stand there politely and let him shoot holes in me? I just grabbed the closest thing at hand—Dorrie, my love, *do* stop making that ungodly noise!" She stopped. "I saw him taking the gun out of the desk drawer so I just grabbed the statuette and hit him. That's all. There was nothing premeditated about *that*."

"How did you get in?"

"The same way as Nicole and Malcolm. Dining room window."

"Where was Uncle Vincent when you got there?"

"Not in the library, you can be sure. I thought he'd gone to bed—the library was dark, I had to turn on the lights. But he was still on the first floor somewhere. I don't know whether he saw the light under the door or if he was coming back for something he forgot or what—I don't think I made any noise. But he came in and found me looking through the file cabinet and . . . well."

"Simon killed Uncle Vincent," Nicole said as if trying to convince herself. "He really did!"

Gretchen suddenly laughed. "And Dorrie dragged him back here and made him go through all . . ." She trailed off when she saw Dorrie looking daggers at her.

Rizzuto picked up the questioning. "So whyja go back to the library in the first place?"

"To look for the promissory note, of course. Why else?"

Gretchen gave a satisfied little nod. "To protect Dorrie."

"No, to protect himself," Toomey said. "It had something to do with those fake diamonds. How would getting hold of the note help? You'd already substituted the fakes for the real thing, hadn't you?"

"Only two days earlier," Simon admitted. "I needed a lot of money in a hurry—"

"You stole from me!" Dorrie blazed suddenly. Everyone looked at her. "What kind of man would steal from his own wife? You knew Ellandy's was in trouble and still you went in and helped yourself to *my* diamonds just because *you* wanted . . .

whatever it was you wanted! *You* want, *you* need, it's always *you*!" Dorrie's voice was shrill and her face had turned red. "You low-down, sneaky, lying, underhanded—"

Immediately Malcolm and Lionel and Nicole jumped in and started the work of calming Dorrie down. They said *Now, Dorrie* and *Don't get excited* and *Take it easy* until she collapsed into a deflated silence. Lieutenant Toomey was astounded; it was the first time he'd witnessed one of Dorrie's flare-ups.

"Darling, listen to me," Simon said in his most persuasive tones. "I had every intention of returning the real stones within a week or two, believe me! I only borrowed them."

"Without asking," Lionel said disgustedly.

"I wouldn't *steal* from you, darling," Simon assured his wife. "Please believe that."

"But you changed your mind and put them back the next day after the murder," Toomey said. "Why?"

"I don't suppose you'd believe me if I said I had a change of heart?" Simon asked. "No, I didn't think so. It was Uncle Vincent's little bombshell that made me take them back. He announced he wasn't renewing Ellandy's loan, and Lionel immediately started talking about taking inventory. He and Dorrie and Nicole went in that night to get started—that was a very nerve-racking period for me, you can be sure. While they were checking the stones, I mean."

Lionel said, "You mean if we'd just stuck to it a little longer, we'd have found the phony diamonds?"

"Undoubtedly. I thought if I could get the promissory note and turn it over to you and Dorrie, you wouldn't need to go on with the inventory. Because once you found the fake stones, I'd be the first one you'd suspect. Lionel, you don't even allow your sales personnel into that vault. I'm the only outsider who's ever been in there."

"But you couldn't find the note," Toomey prompted.

"No. So the only thing to do was return the real stones and get the imitations out of the vault." Simon opened his right hand to reveal the fake diamond he'd been holding all this time. "I must have missed this one."

"Simon," Nicole said icily, "I'm glad they caught you! That was a terrible thing to do!"

"Oh, indeed? And have you told Malcolm how you got Dorrie and Lionel to make you a partner?" Simon asked bluntly.

"*I'll* tell him," Lionel said, and did.

Malcolm was horrified. Wound up, Lionel went on with the story of how the *fourth* partner had maneuvered *her* way in. Then they were all talking at once again, Lionel and Dorrie shouting at Gretchen even more than at Nicole, the two intruders. Mrs. Polk shouted at the others not to shout at Miss Gretchen. Bjarne looked embarrassed.

Toomey and Rizzuto exchanged a long-suffering look and waited them out. Toomey was surprised to learn Gretchen was now a partner of Ellandy Jewels; he'd suspected Nicole of pulling some sort of fast one to get herself a partnership, but he hadn't known Gretchen had weaseled her way in too. My, my, how things had changed. Eventually the furor died down. Malcolm was somehow reconciled to Nicole's duplicity; *in no position to preach*, Toomey thought. Malcolm and Nicole stood in the middle of the room hugging each other.

"Sweet," Simon remarked.

"One more thing," Toomey announced in an attention-demanding voice. "You said you planned to 'borrow' the diamonds for only a week or two," he reminded Simon, "and that sounds as if you needed money in a hurry. Had something happened?"

"The *Russians* happened," Simon answered. "When they—"

"Russians?" Gretchen interrupted. "How in the world can you blame this on the Russians?"

"Let me finish," Simon snapped. "Whenever the Soviets are losing revenue from their oil resources or whatever, they like to compensate by selling state-owned diamonds. If they do it often enough, they'll flood the market and the price of diamonds will drop to virtually nothing and even De Beers will be on welfare. But it hasn't happened so far, and I learned that this month the Soviets were going to release a large amount of rough. It looked like a good chance to make a killing." Simon blinked. "Unfortunate choice of words."

Toomey asked, "Couldn't you have converted some of your real estate holdings?"

"Not in time. I needed capital fast. I believe I told you once before, Lieutenant, that any merchant in the world would give his right arm for a steady source of diamonds that De Beers didn't control. So when Lionel failed in London, it looked as if the Russian diamonds were my best bet. Unfortunately, I wasn't able to follow through—thanks to Uncle Vincent."

"Aha!" Lionel pounced. "You *did* know about London ahead of time!"

"Yes, Lionel, we both know I knew about it ahead of time," Simon answered with exaggerated patience.

"So why did you lie?" Gretchen asked. "Why pretend not to know that Lionel had visited De Beers?"

Simon was silent a moment, trying to think of a convincing lie. He couldn't, so he told the truth. "That was a mistake, I see that now. I should have just said that you misunderstood me, Gretchen. But when you were telling me about Lionel and De Beers, at lunch yesterday—I didn't know yet that the police had set the time of death between ten-thirty and eleven. The last I'd heard they were still asking questions about when the fire went out and when rigor mortis set in and all that."

Gretchen frowned. "I don't get it."

"I do," Lionel said. "He means he didn't know three of us had an alibi."

"Simon!" Dorrie cried, shocked anew.

"Not you, darling," Simon said hastily. "Never you. Lionel was the one in hot water with Uncle Vincent, and it seemed logical that he'd be the one the police suspected." He glanced apologetically at the other man. "Nothing personal, Lionel."

Lionel's mouth dropped open. "*Nothing personal!*"

"Well, that should do it," Toomey said, standing up. "Unless . . . Rizzuto?" The Sergeant shook his head.

"Did you hear what he said?" Lionel asked Bjarne. "*Nothing personal!*" Bjarne clucked his tongue.

"Just a minute, Lieutenant," Malcolm said officiously. "Why are you bothering to charge him? It's clearly a case of self-defense. Simon, I'm not a criminal lawyer but I can recommend someone who—"

"Malcolm," Simon said tiredly, "I don't like you. I have never liked you. What's more, I can say with full confidence that I won't ever be proved wrong—I will never like you. Just don't talk to me. Ever. Again."

"You're upset," Malcolm said, and heard Gretchen snicker. "Lieutenant, the case won't even go to trial. You'll—"

"Oh, it'll go to trial, all right. You don't steal diamonds and kill a man and just walk away."

"Self-defense," Simon muttered.

"He put the diamonds back," Dorrie said, fully recovered from her snit. "What if we don't press charges?"

"We'll press charges," Lionel said firmly.

"Even if you don't," Toomey said, "stealing diamonds was the commission of a felony in connection with a homicide, and that means it's not up to you to decide whether to press charges or not. It's up to us. Pleading self-defense might work, though. But you're going to prison," he said to Simon. "We've got you on other counts. Felony theft, breaking and entering, interfering at the scene of a crime, withholding evidence, making false statements to the police, falsely incriminating an innocent person—"

"And runnin' a stop sign," Rizzuto added. Toomey just looked at him, not asking. "When I was tailin' him and Dorrie," Rizzuto explained, "when they threw that airline bag off the bridge? He ran a stop sign."

Toomey couldn't think of a thing to say to that. Instead, he told Simon again that he was going to prison. Then the Lieutenant laboriously squatted down and started stroking the cat. "Thanks for your help, Godfrey. I'm sorry we have to take your sparkly new toy away—how would you like to have a green latex froggie to play with instead?" Godfrey purred.

"Well," Gretchen said, staring at Simon. "I don't know what to say."

Nicole did. She put her arms around Malcolm's neck and announced, "I've made up my mind. I want to get married."

"What?"

"Married. You know—here comes the bride and I do and all the rest of it?"

Malcolm gave a small whoop of pleasure and scooped her up in a bear hug.

"I want to buy a house," Nicole said over his shoulder, "with huge grounds and a swimming pool. I want to have a child. Maybe we could get a dog. And a parrot."

Toomey laughed to himself as he stood back up. All along he'd thought Malcolm must have a wild streak that appealed to Nicole, when it turned out *she* had a conservative streak that appealed to *him*. Nicole had only tiptoed to the sound of a different drummer.

Sergeant Rizzuto nudged Simon to his feet. "Let's go."

The prisoner turned to face his wife. "Dorrie, my love, I don't suppose you'll be waiting for me when I get out?"

She looked uncomfortable. "I don't think so, darling. It could be such a *long* time. And when you get out, you'll, well, you'll be an *ex-con*, won't you? You understand."

Simon sighed like a martyr. "I do, unfortunately. A divorce, I suppose?"

"I think that's best, dear."

"I have to use the powder room," Nicole said to Malcolm. "I'll be right back." She left the library.

Quite a few changes in this tight little bunch, Toomey thought, watching her go. Nicole and Malcolm are getting married, he mused, Dorrie and Simon are getting divorced, and Gretchen and Lionel are separated. Nothing has ended the way it began. What happens next? Do the newlyweds live happily ever after? Does Simon return from prison a changed man? Do Ellandy's four partners learn to work together in spite of all that's happened? Will the lure of Gretchen's millions bring Lionel to attempt a reconciliation, or do Lionel and Dorrie get together? Tune in tomorrow.

Rizzuto took hold of Simon's arm and started steering him toward the door. Lionel suddenly jumped forward and grabbed Simon's other arm. "Let me help you, Sergeant," he leered.

"I don't need no help," Rizzuto said, surprised.

"Oh, but I insist! It's my pleasure!" Lionel gloated. "I can't tell you how *great* a pleasure it is! Nothing personal, Simon."

Rizzuto grinned at him and nodded. Simon gritted his teeth and accepted his fate. Toomey was following them out through the library door when he heard Mrs. Polk say to Gretchen, "If you think I'm going to pick up all that paper from the floor, you've got another think coming! *You* do it!" Toomey closed the door.

When the police had taken Simon away and Lionel had left, Dorrie and Malcolm drifted out to the front steps of Uncle Vincent's house, where they sat down to wait for Nicole.

"I'm getting married!" Malcolm exulted.

"Congratulations," Dorrie said desultorily. "I'm getting divorced."

"It's for the best, Dorrie," he said gently. "I know it hurts right now, but you're better off without him."

"I suppose," she sighed. "Why did this have to happen to

me? I followed all the rules! I was never afraid to explore my feelings or to seek in-self-knowledge. I committed myself to a structured, long-term personal relationship. I kept a positive attitude and sought out new areas of experience. So what went wrong?"

"I don't know."

"I do all the things I'm supposed to do. I play racquetball. I dress rich. I vote Republican. And *this* is my reward—a husband carted off to prison?"

Malcolm draped a comforting arm around her shoulders. "Come on, Sis, don't let it get you down."

"Oh, I won't. I'm just trying to *understand*."

"Speaking of racquetball, what about a game tomorrow?"

"Tomorrow?" Dorrie's eyebrows rose. "Isn't that rather soon after . . . ?"

"Ah, but who will know?"

"You're right," she giggled. "Who will know?"

Author's Note

The idea for this book arose from a time I was watching television all day every day for two straight weeks. The reason behind this marathon viewing is long and boring and you don't want to hear it. But I watched a *lot* of television.

One thing I watched was the weekday reruns of the old *Perry Mason* show. Of the ten episodes I saw, I think there was only one in which somebody did *not* say, "But he was already dead when I got there!"—or some slight variation thereof. It got so I was waiting for the line every day.

Then it occurred to me it might be fun to write an old-fashioned mystery story with clues all over the place and red herrings galore, and with the kind of plot that keeps complicating itself for no reason other than to keep the reader guessing. And of course the characters must be the sort of people who would never dream of calling the police when they find a dead body.

Therefore I want to dedicate this book to the makers of *Perry Mason* and to those responsible for all the other old mystery series in which *story* was more important than car chases, shoot-outs, and fistfights. In their comfortable, traditional way, the old shows were fun.

ABOUT THE AUTHOR

BARBARA PAUL is the author of *Kill Fee, The Renewable Virgin, The Fourth Wall, Liars and Tyrants and People Who Turn Blue, First Gravedigger, Your Eyelids Are Growing Heavy,* and *A Cadenza for Caruso*.